LADY PRESIDENT

LINDA OWEN

This is a work of fiction. The events and characters described herein are imaginary and are not intended to refer to specific places or living persons. The author has full ownership. It may not be reproduced, transmitted, or stored in whole or in part, without the express written consent of the author, except in the case of brief quotations embodied in critical articles and reviews.

LADY PRESIDENT

All Rights Reserved.

Copyright © 2013 Linda Owen

PRINTED IN THE UNITED STATES OF AMERICA

ISBN: 978-1-63192-291-6

"For I know the plans I have for you, declares the Lord, plans for welfare and not for evil, to give you a future and a hope"

(Jeremiah 29:11).

ACKNOWLEDGMENTS

I would like to express my gratitude to the many people who helped me with this novel, especially those who provided support, read it, offered comments, and assisted in the editing and proofreading.

I will always be grateful for the help of my friend David Holmes, who once worked in the White House. His advice and guidance, as well as his meticulous fact checking, made this book possible.

Above all, I want to thank my husband Ervin, who supported and encouraged me in spite of all the time it took me away from him. I have been blessed.

Chapter 1

～

As Air Force One cruised through the clouds, President Stephanie Franklin entered her airborne office and slid behind her desk. Looking down, she blinked and looked again, closer, shocked to see another letter in that familiar childlike scrawl. She pulled in a ragged breath and opened the unsealed envelope. It was another threat on her life.

She assured herself that the Secret Service would protect her; but her heart still skipped a beat as she stared down at the scribbled words spewing venom and hate. If this letter was like the others, there would be no fingerprints and the paper would be untraceable, but she quickly stuffed it into a plastic sleeve and pushed the intercom button.

"Adam, please come to my office."

After her press secretary replied he was on his way, Stephanie moved to a window seat and gazed out at the familiar terrain below. She guessed that they would land at Andrews Air Force Base in about twenty minutes. She was exhausted. Just minutes ago, she had considered taking a quick nap—that was before she saw the letter.

She read it again. The door opened and Adam Thorsten entered, flashing a contagious smile. Today, as she had done for over a decade, Stephanie instinctively smiled back. Relief coursed through her. He always knew what to say to lift her spirits.

As he sat next to her, his grin faded. He searched her face with lucid, penetrating eyes.

She took a deep breath and prepared for bad news.

"Did you see this?" He held up a newspaper and pointed at the headline above the fold.

"Oh, no! Sibaba has a bomb?" A wave of alarm swallowed her. This day was getting worse by the minute.

Adam read from the article aloud. "The African nation of Wakembezi refuses to comment on the rumor that it is building a nuclear bomb. However, President Bantu Sibaba recently stated in a television speech that he intends to push his growing nation onto the world stage by making it nuclear-ready."

Stephanie felt a knot growing in her stomach. "It's true, you know. My guess is he already has the bomb. This isn't good—he's a madman."

Stephanie studied the presidential seal on the back wall. She had been president of the United States for twenty-seven months with no international incidents. She had been lucky. Now she had to live up to her campaign promises.

"I've prayed this wouldn't happen."

Adam leaned towards her. "Your voters will expect you to control him."

She shook back her blonde hair. "You remember what he's like. He's the one who wants control."

Adam fell silent, waiting for her to speak again.

"I promised there wouldn't be a war while I was in office."

"That's still possible. You stopped Sibaba from ethnic cleansing. If anyone can handle him, you can."

"That was a long time ago."

"But Americans won't care about that. You won the Nobel Peace Prize, so they'll expect another miracle." He placed the newspaper on her lap. "What are you going to do?"

Stephanie pursed her lips. "I don't know. I suppose the press will want a statement when we land."

He nodded.

For a moment silence filled the room, with Stephanie lost in memories of the years when she lived among the African tribes. She wondered if Sibaba had changed. She remembered him as a volatile dictator. Somewhere in the back of her mind, she heard a whisper of caution. What could she say that wouldn't offend him? She needed to think this through carefully.

Pushing herself back to the present, she decided to change the topic. She handed Adam the letter. "I received another threat."

His eyebrows clinched as he read. "It looks like the same handwriting as the others. Why did you open it? It could have had anthrax."

She had not thought of that. "Everything I get on my desk is already checked. I just assumed—"

"Well, maybe this one wasn't. I'll tell Dalton Mercer as soon as we land. He'll want to question everyone onboard." His eyes fell again to the letter. "What is this, the third one?"

"I think it's the fourth. I usually don't see them. My staff sends them directly to Home Security." She handed him the envelope. "There's no stamp."

Adam bit his lip. "How'd this get on your desk?"

"Now that's a good question."

Chapter 2

∼

Dalton Mercer tried to shake the gnawing feeling that something bad was about to happen.

The security chief shaded his eyes and stared up at Air Force One as it circled above Andrews Air Force Base. Soon the shiny silver bird would taxi down the runway and come to roost at Hanger 19, but only after Dalton gave them clearance.

"The pilot is squawking about the delay," said the radio operator in the tower.

"Does he know about the gasoline spill?"

"Yes, sir."

Dalton's jaw tightened. "Tell him to keep his shirt on."

Dalton didn't like delays either. What he hated most was a last-minute glitch in his meticulous safety measures. Thirty minutes ago the Secret Service had been ready for the plane to touch down on the east landing strip. After a damaged hose leaked 5,000 gallons of gas on the taxiway, the president's arrival had been switched to the west runway. That meant scoping out the new area and transporting the press from one end of the base to the other.

A bus barreled towards him. The driver braked to a stop and stepped off, followed by dozens of men and women in heavy jackets.

There are more people than usual, Dalton thought.

It was a chilly, wet morning at the beginning of spring, not the kind of day most people would pick to spend hours outside. Still, hundreds of curious bystanders and reporters had not hesitated to climb onto crowded shuttle buses, and shiver in the cold for over an hour to witness President Franklin's landing. Now they had been relocated and crammed behind a velvet rope that would separate the VIP section from the president. It stretched for twenty-five yards, so spectators arranged themselves in small clumps that thinned out and extended to the stainless steel posts that anchored the cord.

Dalton's eagle-like gray eyes stared at the soldiers standing like bookends at each end. It occurred to him that someone in the center could slip under the rope.

Hearing voices, he swung around. A uniformed police officer, leaning against his cruiser, talked with a National Guard captain in the jeep parked beside him. When they spotted Dalton watching them, the cop strolled over.

"You're head of security?" he asked, flashing his badge. When Dalton answered with a quick nod, he continued from behind tinted sunglasses, "I wanted to offer you any help you might need. My chief sent me."

The shoulder patch on his blue jacket said *Temple Hills PD*. Dalton had once played golf with the chief of police of the nearby suburb.

"Great. Give him my thanks." Quickly Dalton turned again to scrutinize the growing group in the roped-off area. He pointed a thin finger. "Go stand over there—in front of the crowd. Make sure everyone stays behind the rope."

As the patrolman galloped over to his assigned spot, Dalton stepped over to the jeep driven by the captain. "Are your teams patrolling the perimeter fence?"

"Yes, sir. Dogs too."

"Have they reported in?"

"Yes, sir." He gazed intently at Dalton. "What's so different about today? What's going on?"

"Just a feeling in my gut. Nothing more." As he tilted his head to gaze up at the president's Boeing 747, uncomfortable thoughts again peppered his mind. He couldn't tell the soldier that President

Franklin had received threatening letters—enough to worry the Secret Service.

The captain stood adamant, his arms folded. "We've got seven layers of security, including a double barbed-wire fence and monitored cameras. Nobody's breaching this base."

Dalton knew that. He wished he felt reassured. "Go ahead and tell the tower to bring in Air Force One."

"Yes, sir." The soldier stepped out of the jeep and began relaying Dalton's orders via walkie-talkie.

Dalton hurried toward the tarmac as Air Force One made its descent. He had never been absent from his post when a president stepped off the aircraft. He didn't intend the annoyance of last minute changes to alter his perfect record.

* * *

Reporter Cheri Eastley arrived out of breath, late, and angry that her car broke down on the very day she would get to question President Franklin. After trudging half a mile in tight shoes, she had flashed her press ID at the gate, only to find out she had missed the two buses that shuttled journalists to the press conference. She had hitched a ride with a Marine and now, ten minutes late, she was relieved to see that Air Force One was still in the air. She dashed toward the roped-off section reserved for reporters.

As she approached, Cheri noticed Beth Overton, the newly hired photographer at *Scoop*. She was gaunt with a childlike face and red hair in loose waves down her back. She stood there frozen, scanning the crowd, looking lost and confused like someone in a foreign country. When she noticed Cheri, the tension in her face softened.

Without even a greeting, Cheri grabbed Beth's arm and dragged her through the bystanders. The overwhelmed intern followed obligingly, gripping a camera close to her chest.

"From now on, claim your place as soon as you arrive," Cheri said, heading to the area closest to the president's waiting helicopter. A wide-eyed Beth nodded, obviously thankful to have someone as her mentor.

They pushed and pressed a path through clusters of people. An elderly man grumbled obscenities after Cheri stepped on his foot. She smirked and continued to tug at her photographer's sleeve. As they closed in on a spot against the rope barrier, Cheri found two teenage males, both over six-feet tall, watching for the president's arrival.

"You guys are tall enough to see anywhere." Cheri reprimanded through gritted teeth. "Move."

One boy sneered. "My dad is the base commander."

Cheri refused to back down, especially to an obnoxious eleventh grader. "The press has priority in this section." Although not altogether true, her clear and vigorous command caused the teens to retreat as if she were their principal.

The instant they shuffled away, Cheri claimed a prime view of the tarmac. She found herself sandwiched between Beth and a burly man with a remote television camera. In front of her, on the opposite side of the rope, a tall police officer patrolled back and forth, until finally he planted himself in front of her.

Cheri tapped his back. "We can't see."

He mumbled a polite apology without looking at her. His eyes remained transfixed on the aircraft as he strolled off. His fingers trailed along the rope until he finally anchored himself a few yards away.

From behind Cheri came a baritone voice. "Hello, hot-shot reporter."

Cheri turned to see a laughing, bald man in his mid-thirties. "Manny!"

He gave her a friendly hug. She felt a momentary warmth creep through her. She adored Manny, perhaps even loved him. For a minute she was actually happy.

"Beth, I want you to meet Manny Blake." She winked at him. "He thinks he's a real legit reporter because he works for the *Post*."

He chuckled. White teeth gleamed in his smile. Before he could utter his usual barb, Air Force One landed and taxied towards them.

Cheri turned Beth around by her shoulders. "When the president steps off the plane, get a shot of her ducking the press."

Beth screwed on a telescopic lens and aimed it at the airplane. "Why would they rope off this area if we can't see her?"

A scowl flickered on Cheri's face. "I've been covering our Lady President for over a year. She changes her mind all the time. If she doesn't want questions about Sibaba, she'll avoid talking to us today. That's her MO." Her gaze settled on Manny. "How many press conferences do you think she's cancelled?"

He shrugged. "Too many."

"She figures if she's elusive, we can't find anything bad to write about her."

"When did that ever stop you?" Manny teased.

Cheri smiled, her reply equally as taunting. "When did you ever beat me to a story?"

"That depends if you're talking about your fictional tales or factual news."

Cheri's eyes narrowed in protest. "That's not fair, Manny."

He gave her hand an affectionate squeeze. "Easy. This time I think you're right. President Franklin is afraid of the press."

"How did she get to be president, anyway?" Cheri grumbled.

Beth replied, frostily, "Forty-eight million women voted for her. And I was one of them."

With Cheri temporarily stunned by Beth's backlash, Manny continued his playful assault. "Whoa. A Lady Franklin supporter, huh?"

"Well, we all make mistakes, Beth," Cheri chimed in.

"I don't think it was a mistake. Don't you care about keeping America out of a war?"

Before Cheri could respond with dignity, President Franklin stepped to the door of the aircraft. Hearing the bystanders respond with a mixed crescendo of cheers and jeers, the three press representatives returned to business.

Manny moved away from the women to hassle another reporter. Cheri saved his spot, expecting him to return as soon as he realized the police officer obstructed his vision.

Her attention shifted to President Franklin and three Secret Service agents as they descended the steps of Air Force One. Midway to the pavement, she delayed, and turned to say something to her press secretary. Adam Thorsten squeezed by her and the protective detail, so he could precede them off the steps. The president remained there, poised, smiling and waving to the crowd.

"I told you! She's sending Thorsten to talk to us *again*," Cheri snarled. "Why didn't I hire a lip reader?"

"We all make mistakes, Cheri," Beth retaliated with a sly smile.

"Sure, we all make mistakes," Cheri scoffed. "That is, all but her ladyship here. She can't make a mistake if she spends the rest of her term never making a decision!"

Cheri wasn't sure that Beth had heard her, but she was pleased to see the new photographer energetically snapping one picture after another.

Chapter 3

Stephanie tired of waving. From the portable stairs of the airplane, she stared out at the crowd standing behind the velvet rope.

After Adam strolled to the press section, she stepped onto the tarmac and made an effort to match Dalton's gait on the way to the helicopter. Seven Secret Service agents flanked them, their trained eyes darting back and forth between the president and the crowd.

"I planned to talk with reporters myself," she said to the security chief. "Are you sure this is necessary?"

"Yes." Dalton's face was more serious than Stephanie had ever seen it.

At that moment, a shot rang out.

Surprised, Stephanie turned toward the media section to see if Adam was unharmed. Less than a second later a bullet chipped the concrete near her feet and a horrifying realization hit her: *He's shooting at me!*

In the time it took for her protectors to press her to the pavement, Stephanie saw the shooter was a Temple Hills police officer. He pointed his Glock 22 at her and fired again.

The crowd disbanded quickly, countless voices cursing and screaming as they fled for their lives. They dashed a few yards and fell to the concrete. Their cries grew louder as they packed together, cemented by fear.

Timothy Burnside covered Stephanie with his heavy body; the other agents circled her like a football team going into a huddle.

With drawn weapons, they scanned the crowd for the menace with a gun.

Stephanie tried to raise her head, but Burnside pushed her face down again against the tarmac. It was cold and rough against her cheek. In that one second of sight, she had seen Agent David Goldman sprawled on the concrete with a bullet in his left shoulder, a bullet intended for her.

As she lay still, smelling garlic on Burnside's breath, she heard more shots fired. A bullet flew near them and hit the pavement a few feet away. She held her breath and the rest was a blur.

* * *

It was over in a matter of seconds. When the agents saw the crowd dispersing, and the assassin clearly visible, they began to return fire. Even Goldman, blood dripping down his limp arm, squatted with his pistol braced on his knee, and began shooting at the man in the police jacket.

"Don't shoot into the crowd!" Dalton shouted, too late.

A lot can happen in a split second. With a burst of bravery, a spectator later identified as Manny Blake dove under the rope and tackled the shooter at the waist. A teenager beside him reached over the cord, attempting to seize the man's shooting arm. Like a well-trained soldier on a battlefield, the assassin toppled Manny with an elbow blow to the chin, and then whirled and fired two bullets into the young hero.

The president's protective detail shot the assassin in four places, including the neck, where he bled profusely. At the same moment, Manny recovered, sprung to his feet behind the assassin, and attempted to tackle him again. There was no turning back the shells, and Manny was also hit by the fusillade of bullets.

Dalton sucked in a big breath. As he rushed towards the downed shooter, he wondered what he would tell the president. There was no way to justify this body count.

He and two agents ducked under the rope to examine the bodies for life. The dead hero and the assassin lay side by side, arms looped as if they had been friends. Blood covered the concrete and soaked their clothing.

"Do you think this guy is really a police officer?" Agent Karen Kelsey asked.

Dalton removed the shooter's sunglasses and compared his ID. "This isn't Officer Browne," he said with a flat, empty gaze.

The female agent leaned closer. "There is a resemblance, though."

The shooter had hidden his eyes beneath dark glasses. "He shouldn't have made it through security," Dalton hissed. He crouched to pick up the gun, and finding it was police issue, bagged it. He pulled back the officer's jacket, revealing a bullet hole, surrounded by caked, dried blood.

A realization rippled across Karen's face. "Looks like the real Officer Browne is dead."

"Yeah." Dalton stood, pondering the situation. "This guy was on a suicide mission. He had to know there was no way he'd get off this base." He scanned the crowd, and spotting the National Guard captain, waved him over. "Please show Agent Kelsey the police car this guy rode up in. Check it for evidence."

They dashed through a pack of curious bystanders. As the crowd parted, Dalton spotted Cheri navigating her way towards him.

His eyes narrowed. He knew Cheri as a tenacious reporter who worked for a sleazy tabloid. By his past dealings with her, he guessed she had already written a sensationalized story in her head, even before she checked the facts. Now she was coming to see what she could learn about the shooter.

Dalton cringed. This was no time for an interview.

Ignoring the TV cameras, Dalton stooped down to dig through the pockets of the dead. He identified the brave citizen as a reporter for the *Post*, and the teenager as a military dependent. The assassin had no identification on him.

For a second Dalton stared again at the victims. He would never find the words to describe their courage. It was impossible to comprehend, really, even though he had witnessed it. He had never thought anyone outside the Secret Service would die for the president. This was a remarkable act of heroism and self-sacrifice.

"Do you know who the shooter was?" Cheri shouted. She scurried towards him, her small tape recorder in an outstretched hand.

Dalton shook his head, refusing to say anything, and turned back towards the plane. Before he could retreat, Cheri reached him.

"Come on, Dalton—"

He observed the curiosity on her face replaced by stunned horror. She had spotted Manny lying in a puddle of blood. She rushed to the body, mouth agape, and sank down next to him. She screamed a long, piercing wail, her eyes lifted to the heavens.

Dalton hurried to move her before she defiled the crime scene. She was limp as he lifted her up, her feet sluggish.

The *Scoop* photographer ran to embrace her. Cheri screamed and cursed as she led her away.

* * *

When bullets stopped flying, Agent Burnside helped Stephanie to her feet.

Adam rushed toward them, fear carved into his face. He gripped her shoulders. "Are you okay, Steph?"

She nodded, dazed, speaking as through in a trance. "He tried to kill me—My God!"

"Let's get her out of here. Now!" one agent shouted.

Adam took Stephanie's elbow and propelled her towards the helicopter, but they discovered the propellers were no longer whirling.

"Not there," Burnside said. "She could be shot down. This way." He led the president and her staff into a nearby aluminum building.

As they scurried along an unlit hallway and into an office at the end of the corridor, Stephanie moved like someone in a fog. Dazed, she thought she heard someone radio for an ambulance.

After a few minutes, she sat in a chair next to Adam. She took a deep breath to collect herself, and then gazed up at the somber faces of her protectors.

"Is everyone all right?" she whispered, finding her throat had tightened up.

"Goldman was hit," Burnside replied. "He's on the way to the hospital."

"I'm so sorry." Stephanie choked back the tears.

Another agent offered good news. "We got the shooter."

Stephanie sat trance-like. "He was a policeman."

"I doubt that." Burnside was still talking as he disappeared into the hall. "Whoever he was, he deserved what he got. I'll go see what I can find out."

For a time everyone was silent. Stephanie could hear the vibration of the window unit that heated the office. A flash of memory swept over her. "I saw other bodies on the ground."

The agents stared back at her, but said nothing.

Alarm bounded through her. "Did someone in the crowd get killed?" Her eyes floated from face to face, finally landing on a gray-haired agent who stared wide-eyed, his own coloring completely gone. "Tell me," she demanded of Agent Stanley.

"Accidents happen," he replied. His tone was adamant, but his eyes spoke regret. "You had to be saved, Madam President."

Accident. Stephanie knew what that meant. Someone else had died in her place. All that came out was a low moan.

"Somebody get the president a drink of water," Adam said, burying her small hand in his two larger ones.

"No—No," Stephanie protested. "I'm okay, really." She breathed heavily. "Someone please phone my mother and my aunt before they hear about this on the news. Tell them I'm safe. And find my husband."

Chapter 4

Agent Nat Bobbitt followed the president's husband off the elevator at the Valencia Plaza Hotel. Today Tony Franklin wore one of his best disguises. After borrowing a pair of dirty jeans from the gardener and stuffing one of Stephanie's blonde wigs under a baseball cap, he had entered the delivery door near the kitchen. He carried an oversized box, which had once packaged a RCA television. By lifting the box high against his chest and pulling the cap down on his forehead, Tony managed to camouflage his face. Anyone seeing him enter the hotel would think he was simply delivering a television set.

Tony moseyed down the hall with Bobbitt matching his gait. They passed two maids pushing a towel cart toward the elevator, but neither looked directly at them. As the men reached the suite, Bobbitt chuckled heartily, with a sting of admiration. "You could get past anybody. I bet you could even fool your wife!"

Tony tossed the box against the wall. "People in these places don't pay attention to workers." He opened the door to survey the spacious room. Its luxurious soft silk drapes and matching white and pink velvet sofas did not seem to interest him. He crossed the room and inspected the only thing that mattered: the mattress of a king-size bed.

Bobbitt shut the door. Following protocol, he peeked under the bed and then inspected the bathroom. "I see lunch has already been delivered," he said, indicating two covered trays on a silver cart. "Anything else, sir?"

"Did you give Macy the room number?"

"Yes."

"Good. I don't want her talking to anyone at the desk."

Bobbitt knew the game plan and so did his partner Josh Stein. They had shadowed Tony long enough to know the rules. If you were his bodyguards, he expected your complicity during his adulterous trysts. You were to be secretive and careful. You were to ignore all communications via earpieces and radios. Since the Secret Service could easily find your location by honing in on your cell phone, you were to shut it off.

Most of all you were to be nonjudgmental about Franklin's extracurricular activities.

Bobbitt stood at attention, watching Tony remove his hat and wig.

"You got a wife, Bobbitt?"

"Yes. Ten years."

"You got a girlfriend?"

Bobbitt hesitated, surprised by the question. Tony had never asked him anything about his personal life. "Actually I do, Mr. Franklin."

Tony chuckled. "I knew it. Birds of a feather, you know."

The door opened. Macy Youngblood entered, wearing a large floppy hat and sunglasses.

Stein, who had escorted her upstairs, waited patiently in the hall.

Bobbitt delayed his retreat. He watched Macy toss her disguise on a chair and glide, arms outstretched, towards her lover. She had a slow, sultry walk that could bring any man to his knees. Sucking in a lecherous breath, Bobbitt shut the door behind him.

"We really pulled it off," Bobbitt cheered, slapping Stein's hand with a high five.

"I never doubted it, did you?"

Bobbitt scratched his dark cheek. "Most Americans know Franklin on sight." Besides being the president's husband, he was a well-known actor. "Remember the TV show *McMaster for Hire*?"

Stein nodded. "Yeah, he was pretty good in that."

"Franklin told me he learned a few tricks about disguises from the show's makeup artists."

Bored, Stein looked around. "We forgot to bring some chairs out here."

"It's too late," Bobbitt snickered. "Franklin is all over her by now." He pressed his ear tightly against the door. "I don't hear anything. She's usually so vocal." Smiling, he snapped his head back to find his partner dialing his cell phone. The smile disappeared. "Hey, what're you doing?"

"I thought I'd tell the desk we need chairs."

Bobbitt snatched the phone and shut it off. "You know what Franklin said."

"Come on, when has anyone tried to track him through our phones?"

Bobbitt had no rebuttal.

"Anyway, the desk knows we're guarding someone up here."

Bobbitt leaned his back against the wall. Earlier that morning they had convinced a wide-eyed hotel manager that a pop star had checked in for rest and relaxation. Anonymity was necessary and so was a large suite on an unoccupied wing.

He chuckled at the memory of the manager hovering with expectancy near the service elevator, hoping to get a look at the celebrity who paid such an extravagant sum to guarantee his privacy. While Bobbitt stepped onto the elevator with Franklin, Stein had kept the man at a distance.

"Maybe a maid will come back," Bobbitt suggested. "Then we can get chairs out of another room." As soon as he said it, he remembered Franklin had bought out the entire wing.

Stein unwrapped a stick of gum and tossed it into his mouth. He studied his watch. "I'll bet you a fiver he's out of there in twenty minutes." He accentuated his challenge by slapping a five-dollar bill on top of a hall table.

Bobbitt shook his head and extracted a bill from his wallet. "No, the president is out of town, and they've ordered lunch in. It'll be at least two o'clock."

After a few minutes of silence, Stein put his earpiece back in his ear, despite Bobbitt's protests. "I don't like being cut off from the others," he complained. "I don't care what Franklin said."

He listened intently, pressing his earpiece deeper into the ear cavity. His face paled. "Something's happened. It sounds like the president had problems at the airbase."

Bobbitt replaced the earpiece wired to the microphone running up his sleeve. The chatter reported President Franklin's safe return to the White House.

The elevator opened and Dalton Mercer hurried down the hall. Startled at the sudden arrival of their superior, a wide-eyed Stein snatched his money off the table. Bobbitt, looking equally as guilty, stuffed his wallet back into his pocket.

"Where is he?" Dalton demanded.

Bobbitt and Stein exchanged confused glances.

Their befuddled silence agitated Dalton. "Haven't you guys told Mr. Franklin yet? The press could be here any minute."

Bobbitt swallowed hard.

Dalton reached for the doorknob, but Bobbitt blocked his entrance. "You can't go in there, sir. You know how Franklin is—and he's with a woman. He said he'd can whoever interrupts them."

With an impatient grunt, Dalton pushed him aside. "He can't fire me. If we don't get him out of there now, stuff is going to hit the fan and your asses with it."

He knocked loudly and tried the locked door. He knocked again.

Chapter 5

~

Unaware of Dalton's arrival, Tony and Macy were lost in a hot embrace. Tony loved her soft skin. He ran his thin fingers slowly down her back. He wanted her more every minute.

Macy pushed away. "Tell me you love me this time," she whispered, her eyes pleading.

He put his finger beneath her chin and lifted it. "Sure, you know that." He spoke without thinking. It was a lie, one that had always flowed easily off his tongue. He had told so many women the words they longed to hear, with the skilled voice of an actor.

Tony hated it when women pushed for a commitment. He felt uncomfortable with emotional ties—he had told Macy that months ago. What did she expect from him next?

He stared into her dark eyes. Truly, he loved many things about this Kentucky beauty. He pushed her long, raven hair away from her face. He studied the flawless complexion that made her look younger than her thirty-two years and the long legs that had walked the runway in the Miss America Pageant. She was beautiful. She was smart. She was fun, and being with her made Tony feel ten years younger.

Unexpectedly he realized he was *actually* in love with her.

Before he could speak, Dalton knocked on the door. The two lovers stared at each other, as if awakened from a dream. With the second knock, the moment was lost, and thoughts of passion subsided like the last breeze after a tornado.

With a sigh of disappointment, Macy muttered something not quite audible and slipped beneath the sheets.

The knocking persisted.

Tony cursed and bounded to the door like a warrior ready to do battle. "Bobbitt, I told you to *never*—" Locking eyes with Dalton, he froze, his intended rant forgotten.

Dalton entered talking. "This is an emergency, sir. Someone just shot at the president." He flicked a reproving glance at his agents who trailed behind. "What's wrong with your radios? I've been calling you back to the White House. We couldn't reach you on your cell phones either."

Stein turned his phone back on. "I'm sorry, sir," he stammered, looking like a child caught cutting school.

Tony's brows met as he sank down on the bed. "Is Stephanie hurt?"

"No, sir. But you could be in danger too. We need to get you home. *Now*."

His head in his hands, Tony remained on the edge of the bed, numbed by the news. He looked up in time to see Dalton glance awkwardly at Macy, who still sat up against the headboard, covered with the sheet.

"My apologies Miss Youngblood." Dalton was polite but obviously uncomfortable. He quickly returned to the problem at hand. "Mr. Franklin, we've got to rush. Your calendar has you scheduled for lunch in this hotel. Anyone who can read will find you. We expect reporters to swarm downstairs any minute."

Tony blurted out an obscenity and reached for his worker's disguise. "Stein, you and Dalton go downstairs. Tell any press you see that I canceled lunch to be with my wife. Bobbitt and I will go out the back."

He tugged on his jeans. When he gazed in the mirror to straighten the wig, he noticed Macy's unhappy reflection in the beveled glass. "I'll be outside in a moment," he told Dalton.

The agents disappeared into the corridor, Bobbitt and Stein trailing behind Dalton like sheep.

"Honey, I've got to go. I want you to stay here for at least an hour. Eat the crab salad. Take a long bath—or a nap. But don't leave here. Stay out of sight."

Her lips formed a pout. "You want me to come back to the office?"

Tony shook his head and returned to the bed. He wanted nothing more than to take her in his arms and show her how deeply he loved her. Instead, he kissed her very, very gently.

"I love you, Macy."

She embraced him tightly. "Of course you do, silly boy. I wouldn't be here otherwise."

They kissed again, the spark of passion still obvious to both of them.

Again, as earlier, a knock on the door interrupted them.

Tony stood, hesitating only for a second. "I've really got to go, honey. You understand the seriousness of this, don't you? I'm sorry. I'll make it up to you."

Macy called after him as he crossed to the door. "Call me later?"

He nodded and quickly made his exit.

* * *

The room was quiet. Alone, Macy continued sitting in the bed, pondering all that had happened. While the bodyguards were in the room, she had said nothing, taking it all in. She had been irked by their interruption and puzzled by Tony's behavior. It was obvious he had more anxiety about the reporters than about Dalton finding them together. Tony also seemed truly alarmed about his wife's near death. Surprising, since he had told Macy repeatedly that he did not love Stephanie.

For the first time, Macy's gaze switched to the beautiful room, its plush taupe carpet, silver embossed wallpaper, and oversized sofas. Along the wall, near the French windows that led to a balcony, was a cart with the lunch Tony had ordered.

She glided across the room to examine the contents of the meal. When she lifted the lid, her eyes widened. There, on silver trays were all of her favorites: crab salad, finger sandwiches, caviar, and an assortment of fruit.

He did this for me, she thought with delight. The hotel. The food. The admission of love. *It's only a matter of time before he leaves Stephanie for me.*

She picked up a small plate, heaped crab salad on a crescent, sprinkled some grapes on the side, and relaxed cross-legged on the bed. Placing the plate beside her, she fluffed the pillows, leaned back against them, and turned on the TV.

Every station reported the assassination attempt. On Channel 14, Macy settled on an on-the-spot report from a trailer park on the outskirts of Baltimore. Standing in front of the assassin's trailer, while police searched his belongings, a reporter identified the shooter as Herbert Victor, a farm worker from Iowa. He had lived in the park for several weeks.

"At this time there is no information to clarify why he would want to kill the president," the reporter said. "What we do know is this: Victor killed patrolman Frank Browne of the Temple Hills Police Department and used his badge, uniform, and patrol car to get on Andrews Air Force Base."

Finishing the sandwich, Macy turned her interest to a champagne bottle standing at attention in an ice bucket next to the bed. She poured herself a glass of champagne and washed down the remaining crumbs.

Too bad she couldn't share this with Tony. After three weeks of telling him that she was tired of meeting in borrowed cars and empty government offices, he'd finally decided to spend money on her at a chic hotel. *He does love me*, she assured herself. Good food and plush surroundings would just have to replace his lovemaking this time.

Chewing a grape, Macy directed her concentration back to the television. The same reporter was now interviewing the manager of the trailer park. The elderly man with a stomach that rolled like a pumpkin over his belt said that he'd had a number of complaints from Victor's neighbors about him. With the microphone thrust close to his mouth, he began to recount a series of complaints about the dead man. He droned on and on.

Bored, Macy threw her long legs over the side of the bed and headed for the bathroom. She turned on the shower and waited for the warm water. The heavy spray drowned out the TV, so she glanced back at the screen to see if she had missed anything interesting. What she saw was a montage of pictures of the president. Stephanie leaving Air Force One… Stephanie ducking bullets… Stephanie being escorted into the airport offices. There was also video of the panic-stricken crowds at the airfield and Dalton checking the body of the dead assassin.

Her interest renewed, Macy snatched the complimentary robe from its hook and wrapped it around her. Returning to the room, she plopped again in front of the set.

A reporter interviewed Stephanie's physician, Debra Pierce, a middle-aged woman with dark skin, meticulously neat, who carried herself with confidence. She reported, "President Franklin had a complete checkup at Bethesda Naval Hospital. She is completely unharmed, not even bruised from her fall to the pavement."

Macy stared at the TV without blinking. "Just my luck," she muttered.

At that moment, Macy first pondered murder.

Chapter 6

∼

The secretaries parted, allowing a path for Stephanie to enter the Oval Office. Dawn spoke first, her eyes curious. "Thank God you're okay. How do you feel, Madam President?"

Stephanie feared a meltdown. She pasted on a smile and sauntered into the office. "I'm fine."

Nancy pushed her dark-rimmed glasses up higher. "Have you eaten? I can get you a sandwich."

"No, thank you." An hour earlier Stephanie had been famished. Now her stomach was doing flip-flops. She struggled to breathe normally, determined to appear unfazed by the shooting.

Dawn followed her. "What can I do?"

Stephanie forced herself to think of other things. "Please see if you can find my husband. He hasn't been answering his cell."

"Yes, ma'am." Nancy returned to her desk, lifting the phone before she sat.

After shutting the door, Stephanie buzzed her chief of staff. Going to the large bay window, she admired the first colorful blooms of spring until Roberta Casey knocked.

When she entered, she wasn't smiling. That wasn't so unusual. Roberta was somber by nature, scholarly-looking, with a tilted nose that lent her an elegant, vaguely aristocratic air. She stared at Stephanie. "I'm surprised to see you here. Don't you want to take some time off?"

Stephanie remained standing. "Oh, no. That way the assassin wins. I don't want the newspapers portraying me as incompetent. Do you think a male president would go hide in his quarters?"

Roberta didn't reply, but instead changed the subject. "We need to talk about something else." Her tone was more serious than usual. "Please sit down."

Baffled, Stephanie stared hard into those dark, solemn eyes and retreated behind the desk.

Before Roberta could utter a word, Adam Thorsten poked his head in. Roberta waved him inside. "I asked Adam to join us. Since he lived in Africa at the same time you did, I knew you'd value his input."

A jumble of questions swirled in Stephanie's head, but in her present state, she had trouble sorting them. She watched Adam slide into a nearby chair.

"What have you decided about Sibaba?" he asked.

For the second time that morning, a tidal wave of anxiety washed over her. She pursed her lips. "I don't know. I want to pray about it before I do anything."

"Americans want to know if he really has a bomb," Roberta said.

Stephanie smoothed out the wrinkles in her skirt. For the first time she noticed the green linen was covered in dirt smudges from her fall.

"Don't you think you should talk to him?" Roberta asked.

"I'm not up to it today. I'm still a little shaky."

The chief of staff continued, unabated. "I suggest a simple press release for now. Just assure our citizens they're safe."

Adam stood to leave. "I'll take care of it."

"Wait. Reassure the people I'll keep my promise," Stephanie said. "We wouldn't go to war."

Roberta stirred, crossing and uncrossing her legs. "Don't mention that in the release." Her eyes shifted from Adam back to

Stephanie. "It's unfortunate you ever said that. It's a promise you might not be able to keep." She paused, scratching her chin. "Of course presidents break campaign promises all the time."

Adam drew in a deep breath that released the rigid set to his shoulders. "Luckily you only said it in that one interview."

Stephanie arched an eyebrow. "But I promised. I don't care what other presidents have done."

Chapter 7

~

Vice President Kenneth Chang came from the West Wing to speak with reporters. An amiable-looking man in his fifties, stocky and muscular, he walked slowly, surrounded by his usual security, who dictated his stride. Trailing a few feet behind were a covey of White House staff, including York Benson, Stephanie's assistant, whom she had sent to be her eyes during the press conference.

As York quickened his step, narrowing the distance between them, Chang glanced out of the corner of his eye at the diminutive man. There was nothing imposing about him, but what he lacked in stature he made up for with a tenacity that had earned him respect around Washington. He was fiercely loyal to the president and that often intimidated Chang. As a politician, he was used to people watching him, but he didn't like the idea that York might be spying on him for the president.

"Were you at Andrews when the shooting happened?" he asked York.

The aide nodded. "Pretty scary. Bullets were flying everywhere."

"What did you see?"

His face crumbled into a sheepish grin. "Not much. I hit the concrete and didn't look up until it was over."

They strolled together in silence. The agent at Chang's side slowed, looked back towards the White House, and fell behind.

Chang turned to see Dalton racing across the thick green lawn in an attempt to join the phalanx of agents. The unbuttoned jacket of his suit ballooned behind him, exposing the revolver he carried in a holster strapped to his left shoulder. As he closed in on the group, matching the vice president's steps, the security chief slowed his pace and buttoned his coat. By the time Chang spoke into the long-necked microphone on the north lawn, Dalton stood at attention behind him.

"I've seen President Franklin," the vice president told anxious reporters. "We had a brief visit."

He had learned long ago the traits of a successful politician. At the top of his list was a passion for his country and its virtues. That meant loyalty to his party and the reigning monarch of politics, in this case President Franklin. Even after an election, the campaign always continued, for there was always a future election. His image mattered. Chang never forgot that the public responded well to the politician with a caring nature.

"I'm happy to report that she's doing well."

The media shouted dozens of questions simultaneously.

Swiftly, with a smooth transition that evidenced a polished politician, Chang began his prepared statement. "The president is grieved about the two men who died trying to save her life. This administration considers them American heroes. Their sacrifice is as significant as any hero of war. They will be decorated by the president like soldiers."

"Has the president talked to their families?" someone asked.

"Actually, she telephoned them a few minutes ago. President Franklin was moved to tears by their sacrifice."

The questions began again. "When can we see President Franklin?" asked a reporter with NBC.

"Soon," Chang said. "The president will meet with the Joint Chiefs of Staff tomorrow as scheduled. They plan to discuss the implications of Wakembezi having a nuclear bomb." He smiled graciously at the reporter. "But today she asks for some time alone with her husband. I think we all can understand that."

There were more questions. One man's obtrusive voice resonated above the others. "What would you have done if the president was killed?"

Chang frowned, his dark Chinese eyes becoming two dark slits. "What would I have done?" he repeated, stunned. "I would have done what I'm elected to do—I've sworn to serve my country. I'm the vice president." His last sentence was a declaration, a self-affirmation, spoken with confidence.

As Chang continued to answer questions, a profound thought hit him: *If things had gone differently, I'd be president right now.*

Chapter 8

Because the White House allowed no parking, Senator Philip Lowe trudged several blocks on a prosthetic leg to see Stephanie. Wearing an overcoat to repel the stubborn D.C. chill, he made his way towards Pennsylvania Avenue, his cane clicking sharply on the pavement. As he stepped from the curb, his companion, Willy Wurtzel, reached out with iron fingers to steady him. Lowe grunted and jerked his elbow free. "I'm not an invalid, Willy."

"Sorry, sir."

"I lost my leg in the Korean War. I learned decades ago to manage just fine."

They walked in silence as they approached the White House. At the northwest gate outside the West Wing, a Secret Service agent sat inside a guardhouse behind bulletproof glass and spoke to him though a speaker.

He had a polite smile. "May I help you?"

"Yes." Lowe replied, "I'm here to see President Franklin."

"Do you have an appointment?"

Lowe's eyes narrowed into a scowl. "I don't need an appointment. I'm one of the leaders of the president's party."

"Who are you?"

"Senator Philip Lowe."

"People are supposed to submit their request weeks in advance. Security checks are done before you are allowed on the grounds."

Lowe's impatience flared. "I've been inside dozens of times. Don't you have my clearance on file?"

The agent turned his attention to his computer screen.

Willy interceded. "This man is the Minority Leader of the Senate. How can you possibly turn him away?"

The sentry drilled him with a stare. "It's nothing personal, sir. I've turned away Mickey Rooney and Shaquille O'Neal. They didn't have an appointment either."

"They weren't President Franklin's political advisor. I am."

"I'm sorry, sir. The president is in seclusion."

The rejection wasn't a surprise. This was not the first time Lowe had been given a cold shoulder. Once he had joined a White House tour and attempted to slip away unnoticed. Two agents had halted him before he made it to the staircase. Another time he had changed the date on an old, handwritten invitation from Stephanie. That day, following protocol, the sentry had called the president for clearance. Stephanie had refused to see him.

A sullen moment passed. Slowly an idea formed in his mind. Kenneth Chang owed him. He would go to Chang's office. After visiting with the pleasant but corpulent secretary, he would slip away to the Oval Office on the same floor. Maybe Stephanie would be there.

"Vice President Chang will see me," he said, his tone relentless.

The guard's irritated stare became somehow appraising, as if he sought to read Lowe's mind. "You need to call him. He'll send someone to get you."

It was a test. Fuming, Lowe fumbled in his overcoat for his cell phone. As he dialed, his mind raced. *What if Ken isn't in his office? What if he's in a meeting? What if he says he'll call me back tomorrow? What will I do then?*

The friendly voice of Chang's secretary answered.

"Angie, I need to get through the gate. Please tell this guard to let us in."

"The vice president is at a press conference right now," said Angie. "Are you trying to join him?"

That called for a lie. "Yes. I'm at the northwest gate."

"I'll send a member of our staff to escort you."

In a few minutes Angie's assistant Claude made his appearance. The gate opened and Lowe and Willy entered a cage-like area with fence on all four sides.

"It's like being in prison," Willy mumbled as a guard locked the gate behind him."

"They can trap someone— like a terrorist— in here," Claude explained through the bars.

In front of them now was another guardhouse. Lowe slid his driver's license photo into the ejected tray, and a guard compared it to his social security number and past information.

Willy followed his example. Since they had been cleared on an earlier visit, the gate was unlocked. After a further hand scan with metal detectors, they were released to their sandy-haired escort.

Grumbling about the long delay, Lowe limped away in long strides, at first leaving Claude behind. Reaching the steps, he slowed and climbed with difficulty, even with his cane, up the steps and into the West Wing. "Have you seen the president upstairs?" he asked Claude.

"No, but I heard she was in the Oval Office."

"Good. I want to see her as soon as possible."

Claude's head snapped around. "I understood you had an appointment with Vice President Chang."

The senator flashed their companion a high-wattage smile. "While he's at the press conference, I thought I'd check on the president—to see how she's holding up after what happened."

They walked in silence until Claude's cell rang. He frowned as he listened to the caller. "That was Angie. She said the vice president will be further delayed. He's agreed to an interview for *NBC's Dateline.*" He flipped the phone shut and they moved on.

Inside everyone talked about the assassination attempt. Much of the staff was confused and distracted. Although Lowe's trek through the halls was an arduous task physically, he found no one blocking his journey along familiar corridors. That surprised him at first, until he reminded himself that his was a familiar face to the entire staff. After President Franklin's inauguration, he had been a regular guest in her office and at her dinner parties.

Then, without warning, Stephanie had decided to wean herself of his influence. What irked him the most was her lack of gratitude. When he thought of the two years he had dedicated to getting her elected, and another two years guiding her decisions from behind the scenes, he wanted to hurt her, to wrap his chubby fingers around her neck and squeeze the life out of her. For weeks, his anger had played havoc with his blood pressure. He would take his heart medication, lay down in a quiet room, and plot his revenge.

His lips twisted into a smug smile. At last he was going to have the face-to-face encounter he deserved! He would tell Stephanie what a silly girl she was. Imagine thinking she could govern a nation without any expertise! He would remind her that he was a leader in the Senate and she did not want him as an enemy. Most of all, he would remind her that he had created her—at least the image, the facade that the American people saw.

"Did you ever see the movie *My Fair Lady*?" he asked as they neared the elevator.

Willy answered. "Sure. Years ago. This guy takes a flower girl and turns her into a lady."

"I did that for Stephanie Franklin."

"How's that?" their guide asked. "The Taylors are a wealthy family. She was a debutante and all that."

"Yeah, but she was no politician. She didn't even know what a filibuster was until I got hold of her." Lowe stopped to rest his aching leg a moment. "Do you think she's beautiful?"

The men nodded.

"I spent a fortune. I brought in hairstylists and designers. I taught her what to say. What Stephanie Franklin is she *became*."

Once inside the elevator, it was a fast trip to the brightly lit corridor on the next floor. As the three men neared the Oval Office, they found themselves blocked by a stern-faced agent guarding the door. "I'm sorry," he said politely, "but the president is not accepting visitors."

Lowe jabbed his finger at him. "Do you know who I am?"

The remark was unmistakably more of a threat than a question, but the guard refused to be intimidated. "Yes, sir. You're Senator Lowe." He emphasized each word, giving his voice a polite but commanding tone. "You're not on the list, sir."

The senator gave him a furious stare, but he still would not yield.

At that moment Lowe felt a strong hand grip his shoulder. He turned to face Dalton Mercer, who had just returned from the press conference.

"Dalton!" he thundered, somewhat relieved. "Tell this imbecile to let me see the president!"

Dalton shook his head. "You'll have to leave."

Lowe ignored him. "I'm the guest of the vice president."

"Okay, but you're not seeing President Franklin."

The senator's dark pupils shot daggers at him. "I'm on the black list, aren't I?"

"You'll have to leave," he repeated, his tone icy.

Lowe leaned with difficulty against Willy and lifted his cane in protest. "You tell her she's making a mistake. She'll be sorry if she doesn't see me soon!"

Turning his cane into an axle, he maneuvered himself in a half circle and headed back the way they had come. "She's still playing games, Willy," he grumbled. "Come on. Help me back to the limo." Willy obliged, saying nothing.

As they entered the elevator, Lowe turned back to see the befuddled stare of their hoodwinked escort. Before the doors closed, Dalton joined them.

"I can find my way out," Lowe snarled.

"I know. But I'm going to make sure you don't take any detours." Dalton said nothing else, only followed his charges off the elevator and watched them until the gates locked behind them.

As Lowe stepped away, he heard Dalton raving at the guards for allowing them on the grounds. He also demanded they flag Lowe's name on the computer.

"I might as well throw in the towel," Lowe said. "I won't get inside again, unless Stephanie realizes she needs me."

As they slowly tramped back towards Pennsylvania Avenue, Lowe continued fuming. He felt humiliated. Thoughts of revenge bounced around in his brain. *Stephanie won't get away with this.*

Turning his head, he spotted Vice President Chang heading to the limo parked at the curb. "Hey, Ken. Got a minute?"

The vice president joined them. "Where are you parked?"

"The lot on Nineteenth Street."

"I'll get my driver to take you to your car," he offered, signaling for help. Two agents large enough to play defense for the Redskins lifted the old man off the curb and whisked him towards Chang's state car.

Willy opened the back door and waited.

"Did you see President Franklin?" Lowe asked.

"Yes. She's okay." Chang eyed him inquisitively. "What's wrong?"

"No one in this place will give me the time of day."

Chang glanced at his watch comically. "It's 5:45."

The joke fell flat. Lowe tried to suppress his anger. He shrugged and stepped into the car.

"I have time for you." The vice president offered a gracious smile. "How about a drink at my home?"

The senator's face brightened. It looked like the trip hadn't been a waste after all.

Chapter 9

～

After he ordered Lowe to leave, Dalton strolled to the Oval Office. As he swung open the door to the secretarial area, he spotted Tony Franklin rushing towards the president's office with a bouquet of yellow roses.

With Bobbitt in tow, Tony darted past Dawn's and Nancy's desks without giving either secretary a glance. As he disappeared inside, Bobbitt slowed his pace, and like a trout off the hook, plopped into a cushioned chair next to Dawn.

The phones rang persistently. Nancy scribbled a message from a caller.

Dawn stood next to her desk, phone in hand. "The president is in a meeting at the moment." Her voice was cordial. "I assure you she is perfectly all right. May I tell her of your concern?" Another line rang. She ignored it and waved a hand of recognition to Dalton as he rushed by.

A few feet from the opened door, Dalton glanced at his watch. It had been nearly three hours since the shots were fired. One hour for Dalton to find Tony's liaison hideaway. A second hour for Tony to sneak out of the hotel and change into the charcoal dress suit he now wore. The yellow roses were evidence that his car had driven to the nearest florist. As for the remaining time, Dalton guessed Tony used it to concoct a story that would explain his absence.

By the time Dalton entered the office and shut the door, Tony had his arms around Stephanie and they were kissing. The president obviously needed the embrace; she clung to her husband even after the kiss, as if attempting to cement their two bodies together.

As Dalton scrutinized the scene, he noticed tears in Tony's eyes. *The louse has never stopped acting,* Dalton thought. What he saw reminded him of an episode from Tony's soap opera days. There Tony was, the deceptive husband (every soap opera needs one!) bearing flowers as a sign of his love and loyalty.

Somewhat uncomfortable with what should be a private moment, he moved to where Adam and Roberta sat in leather chairs near the president's desk. Pouring himself a cup of coffee, Dalton stood with his back to Tony, loathing him, as he began his well-rehearsed dialogue. "Darling, are you all right?" His voice was full of fear. "What a horrible thing to happen."

"Yes—Yes, it was," she said softly.

Dalton glanced over his shoulder at the president. She struggled to remain stoic, but her husband's touch caused imprisoned emotions to surface. She choked on her words. "I really needed you."

"I'm here," he said, thrusting the roses into her hands.

Stephanie smiled, but it was obvious Tony expected a more animated response. "This is my favorite flower," she told the others, flaunting the roses as evidence of Tony's love. After Stephanie stuffed the roses into a vase, she asked the question that had obviously haunted her for hours: "Where have you been, Tony?"

Tony turned an awkward moment into a performance. "I can't believe it happened—but we were driving to Maryland—I wanted to talk to a producer about a movie deal. We had a flat. When Bobbitt went to get out the spare tire, it was flat too. We left the car at a station for repairs, so no one was there to answer the car phone. It was after lunch before the flats were fixed—"

Dalton snapped around, his face as expressionless as a poker player. In that instant, as his eyes locked with Tony's, Dalton knew that Stein was busy finding a producer and having a flat fixed somewhere in Maryland.

The story was ridiculous, of course. It made a mockery of security protocol. Would the president choose to overlook that agents wore radios for instant communication? Or that the Secret Service would have sent another limo?

Tony shifted gears, not allowing time for Stephanie to ask those questions. "Who was that lunatic shooting at you?"

"The FBI is working on it," Dalton answered. "Right now, from his fingerprints we know he's an Iowa farmer. He killed a cop and stuffed him in the trunk of the patrol car. He used the police ID and cruiser to get on the base. We're trying to tie him to those crank letters—"

Tony raised an eyebrow. "You're getting threatening letters?" It was the first honest reaction Dalton had seen.

Stephanie leaned back against the edge of her desk. "It's rather ironic, isn't it? I ran on a platform to end world violence, but I can't even feel safe in America."

Tony did not seem to be listening. He directed his attention to Dalton. "Could there be a conspiracy? Are we seriously in danger?"

Dalton stepped onto the rug, closing the distance between them. "We do not know if the shooter acted alone. Until then, we can best protect you and the president if you both limit your travel to and from the White House."

Troubled lines surfaced on Tony's brow. "We have to stay inside like prisoners?"

Dalton nodded.

"For how long? I'm going to Cancun next week. I have a role in a movie. If I'm not there, the director will replace me!"

Tony's selfishness was exasperating. Dalton had less respect for him every day. Whenever he observed Tony's self-involved nature, Dalton's reaction was usually mild annoyance mixed with amusement. But today the president had nearly died. Dalton was tempted to ruin Tony's cinematic profile by breaking his nose.

Take a breath. He counted to five, delaying his reply, determined to control his temper.

It was Stephanie, the wife, who responded to the question, rather than Stephanie, the president. She hugged Tony around the waist. "I thought we might take advantage of this, Tony, and spend some alone-time together." She gave him a devoted smile. "Let's have a romantic dinner tonight, just the two of us."

"Oh, sure. That'll be great." Tony's tone was more submissive than ecstatic. "But I have to be on location," he complained again, his attention focused only on Dalton.

Their eyes locked in combat. "We'll know more by then," Dalton answered.

Tony must have seen something in Dalton's eyes that he interpreted as warning lights. He transformed himself into the husband everyone expected him to be. With sudden enthusiasm, spurred on by afterthought, he pulled Stephanie closer, whispering something in her ear that only she could hear. Stephanie flushed, and smiled away the embarrassment.

"I'll see you upstairs," she said. "But first I have to finish up some business."

The statement, laced with cordiality, was still an obvious dismissal. Dalton quickly made his way for the outer office, with Tony close behind. *The actor still knows an exit line when he hears it,* Dalton mused.

The two men walked together in silence through the doorway of the Oval Office and past the secretaries' desks to a remote corridor.

"How long have you known about Macy and me?" Tony asked in a whisper.

"I didn't know. Not until today."

Offering an outstretched hand, Tony thanked Dalton for his discretion.

"I didn't do it for you," Dalton replied, ignoring Tony's hand. "I took an oath to protect our president. To me, that doesn't mean just physical protection."

There was a frosty silence.

His message was clear. Tony retreated toward the presidential quarters like someone navigating a minefield.

* * *

In a matter of minutes, Stephanie settled into an established routine, in an attempt to salvage what was left of her day. She picked up her personal schedule, printed on green stationery and embossed in gold with the presidential seal. She found it hard to concentrate. In spite of her good intentions, the assassination attempt had left her more frazzled than she wanted to admit. Now the energy she had mustered after the shots had waned, zapped by a myriad of emotions.

Dawn joined them, pen and pad in hand, and sat with Roberta, Adam, and York. The four faced the president's desk in chairs arranged in a hospitable semicircle.

Stephanie spoke to her private secretary. "Cancel the planned interviews for the Supreme Court candidates. Give them my apologies." She heard her voice quivering but was unable to control it.

Dawn scribbled something, but said nothing.

Roberta changed the subject. "Did you see the letter I left on your desk this morning? Dalton wanted you to read it."

That explained how it got on the airplane.

Stephanie frowned. "Why would he want me to read trash like that?"

"He hoped you'd recognize the writer. Do you have it with you?"

Stephanie pulled the letter out of her briefcase. The razor-edged words had cut deep into her soul. Refusing to look at it again, she handed it to Adam.

"Wasn't the guy who wrote it killed today?" he asked.

"Dalton isn't sure about that." Roberta's sharp eyes fastened on Stephanie. "Whoever wrote this said some things here that indicate he was around during the presidential campaign. In one place he mentions wanting to kill you during the Philadelphia debate. He says he was ten feet from you and could have done it easily."

Roberta swerved her gaze to Adam. "Dalton says you were in Philadelphia too. He believes one of you might know the assassin. He wanted you both to see if something clicks."

Nerves prickled on the back of Stephanie's neck. In a stunned tone she said, "I don't recall anyone. Do you, Adam?"

Adam's eyes fell again on the abusive scribble. "You never did anything in your life to make someone hate you this much."

"See if this helps." Dawn read a report from handwriting experts. "They say it's a male. He loathes women. He's introverted and suspicious by nature. A loner—"

"And he wants me dead." Stephanie breathed in a laugh as she poured bottled water into a paper cup.

Adam frowned. "How can you make light of this?"

"What else can I do? Besides, I'm the most protected leader in the world. The Secret Service proved that today."

She glanced at the time. Tony waited upstairs.

"I'll look at the letter again tomorrow. Maybe I'll remember something then." Stephanie slipped from behind the desk. "I'm going to my quarters now."

"Please don't leave yet," York said, holding out a paper in his hand.

Stephanie eyed him curiously. "What have you got for me?"

"A message from Senator Lowe."

She groaned. "Throw it away."

York hesitated, causing Stephanie second thoughts. "What is it, York? Does he say anything that he hasn't said over and over?"

York shook his head.

"Let me guess. He's asking to see me. He's telling me for the hundredth time that I need his help to run this country."

York waved the letter like a fan. "He's concerned about the bomb scare, like everyone else, Madam President."

A tidal wave of anxiety washed over Stephanie. "Are you worried about Sibaba having the bomb?"

"I think everyone is, Madam President."

She skimmed Lowe's message and pitched it on the desktop.

"There's absolutely nothing Lowe can do to help President Franklin with this," Adam said. "I know more than he does. He didn't live ten years in Wakembezi like I did."

York's eyes flashed at him, but he said nothing.

Roberta cleared her throat. "Let's talk about Sibaba before you go."

Stephanie wasn't sure why she felt so drained, but she did. "Not today. Tomorrow. Everything can wait."

Chapter 10

∼

The bedroom was dark. The only light came from a small lamp in the adjoining room, its rays reflecting off a mirror and bouncing onto the darkness near the foot of the bed.

At one a.m. Stephanie stirred under the sheets. She reached out for Tony, and finding him gone, decided in drowsy thoughts that he must be in the bathroom.

She heard whispers. At first, they seemed part of a dream, far off in a well; but as she awakened, she realized that she heard Tony's voice.

Forcing her eyes open, she surveyed the dark room. The bathroom door was open. Near the windows, by the green velvet chairs, a silver cart held the remains of a romantic dinner. On it were a pile of dirty dishes, extinguished candles, and an empty wine bottle. Near the wheels of the cart were her bra and panties, discarded like the other items in the cart, as if they too no longer served a purpose.

She smiled and sat up in bed. Memories of a night of lovemaking danced though her still foggy brain.

The whispering continued. Wondering if they had visitors, Stephanie pulled herself out of bed and snatched up her robe. As she tied the sash around her waist, she admired Tony's beautiful yellow roses, now housed in a crystal vase on an antique table. She smiled. She felt euphoric, happier than she had been in a long time.

The trauma of yesterday's shooting behind her, still smiling, she headed towards the sitting room. Through the opened doorway, she could see Tony's reflection in the antique mirror on the opposite wall. He was on his cell phone.

"You know that's not possible," he whispered. "I'll figure something out."

Stephanie sensed something ominous in Tony's tone. She stopped, sinking her bare feet into the carpet.

"I think about you all the time," Tony said. "There's never been another woman like you—"

Stephanie stood frozen, numbed by the shock, tears swelling in her eyes.

"Listen, honey, I've got to go," he said. "I'll call you in the morning."

Stephanie wiped her eyes with the palm of her hand and raced back to bed. When Tony returned, she lay on her side, facing the opposite wall. He crawled into the bed next to her, and soon he snored lightly. Stephanie continued to stare at the wall until she could no longer stand to be in the same bed with an adulterous husband. She crept from under the sheets and planted herself in a chair by the window.

Staring at the outline of Tony's body in the darkness, she wondered if he had ever loved her. In retrospect, it occurred to her that perhaps she had married Tony too quickly. Their courtship, swept up into the whirlwind of the presidential campaign, had lasted six short months.

Stephanie had not yet captured her party's nomination when she first met him. After that day, it had been a steady climb to the presidency. Without question, Tony had boosted her chances of winning.

Thinking back, Stephanie remembered the day she first saw him. By then she had declared her candidacy and was on the media circuit. At 4:30 in the afternoon, exhausted from three previous interviews, she had entered the New York studio where ABC filmed Tony's talk show.

She had asked for a cup of coffee, but after two sips, with no time for the caffeine to kick in, she had been hustled into the makeup room. There she had seen Tony sitting in a chair, telling a joke to the hairstylist, when the director summoned him to a quick conference. Glimpsing her on his journey to the door, Tony had spouted a quick hello and dashed out of the room.

Fifteen minutes later Philip Lowe arrived. He and Stephanie stood behind the camera watching the sound crew running wires along the floor. "What do you think of Tony Franklin?" Philip asked matter-of-factly.

"He's taller than I thought. He's always seated when you see him on TV." What she didn't say was she had always been attracted to tall men.

"They tell me he's got good ratings. Women like him," Philip said with a grin. He beckoned Tony over while the crew finished checking the lighting.

The first time their eyes met, Stephanie felt warmth dancing through her. She had never experienced such chemistry, even with her husband Howard.

"Treat my girl right, Tony," Philip said. "She's going to be the next president."

"You're too pretty to be a president," Tony retorted with a fetching grin, his blue eyes moving over her body. Stephanie blushed; but she found herself attracted to a man for the first time in years. She stared at him, a tanned, curly-haired matinee idol, and felt like a tongue-tied adolescent.

Tony grabbed her hand and led her to the set, where two chairs had been shoved like bookends on either side of a glass-top table. He pointed to one of the chairs and glanced quickly at cue cards, as the director began to count down the seconds.

When they came on the air, Tony interviewed her about her dead husband, about her peace platform, and finally about her relationship with the dictator of Wakembezi. Then, glancing at notes on a card, he switched the conversation to her childhood.

"I'm told you nearly died at the Columbian embassy when it was attacked by rebels."

"My father was an ambassador there. He and lots of people died at the hands of terrorists. My mother hid me. We were the only two to survive the massacre."

"Did that experience influence your strong stand against violence?"

Stephanie hadn't considered that. "I was only three, so I don't remember it. I didn't understand how horrid war is until my husband's Air Force jet was shot down. I never had Howard's body to bury. That left me with a hatred of war. I want to shield the women of America from experiencing the pain I felt."

The conversation took a surprising turn.

"You're really pretty," Tony said. "I think I'm in love."

Stephanie smiled. He was flirting with her.

"There's just one thing I have to know," he said, leaning close to her. "I hear you stopped Sibaba from wiping out an entire African tribe. How'd you do that?" His eyes took on a playful intensity.

Stephanie paused. It was too long a story to tell today. "I prayed a lot, and I told him how I felt. Most people are afraid to talk to him. But he listens."

Tony flashed a wicked smile. "Did you sleep with him?"

"Certainly not!" Stephanie answered, astonished. "I can't believe you'd ask me that!"

"I only asked because I want to know about the moral fiber of my future wife," Tony teased.

It had all been a joke. Stephanie felt like a straight man in a comedy team whose partner had changed the script. She stared, wondering what to say.

"It seems to me that you'd have a better chance to win the election if you were married," Tony continued.

"There have been presidents without spouses—"

"Do you have a boyfriend?" he interrupted.

"No," she replied, dropping her eyes.

"Well, maybe that's for the best," Tony teased. "It's ludicrous to call your husband a first lady."

Caught unawares, Stephanie laughed.

"What does a first lady do, anyway?" Tony asked next, keeping up the comic pace.

"She has speaking engagements, and she's the hostess at White House functions." Stephanie found herself hypnotized by Tony's warm blue eyes.

"Do the first ladies have their own staff?"

"Yes," Stephanie answered, still puzzled at Tony's departure from the preplanned questions.

"They live in the White House, have lots of servants, and get to sleep with the president. Is that right?"

Stephanie nodded.

Without warning, Tony knelt at her feet. "Sounds good to me," he said with a boyish grin. "I'm applying for the position!"

Stephanie found herself laughing with the audience. Tony was amusing as well as good looking, so she had been flattered when he stopped her at the exit and asked her to dinner.

She had enjoyed being with him. She had also liked being on the arm of a celebrity—although he kept reminding her she was a celebrity herself. In no time, he had won her heart by devoting himself to her campaign. He helped raise two million dollars by recruiting television and movie stars to perform at benefits.

While *The Tony Show* went into summer reruns, Tony had pursued her on the campaign trail, showing up for her speeches and flying with her from city to city. In less than one month Stephanie's approval rating in the polls doubled, and Tony had a supporting role in a TV movie.

After Stephanie and Tony appeared together at the Emmy Awards, the supermarket tabloids labeled them as sweethearts. Paparazzi followed them everywhere. Somehow reading that they were in love had made Stephanie believe they were.

Everyone had said they were the perfect couple: the newspapers, her campaign staff, and Philip Lowe—

Stephanie cringed. *Philip Lowe.* Why hadn't she thought of that before? Philip Lowe had introduced them. He had suggested the marriage take place before the election. He had insisted on live media coverage of the wedding, so that the whole nation felt invited to the ceremony.

She wondered if Philip had planned from the very beginning for Tony to marry her. What if the two of them had schemed to get her elected, and love had nothing to do with it? The thought made her feel angry and violated. If her suspicions were true, what would the matchmaker Lowe have offered Tony as a dowry?

The answer came to her immediately. Philip had the money, power, and friends to do just about anything. If he could manipulate an election, he could easily arrange for Tony's acting jobs. Maybe Philip had been responsible for the string of TV movies and the motion picture soon to be filmed in Cancun.

Stephanie sat curled up in the velvet chair, wondering what was fact and what was fiction. One thing was certain: Tony had a mistress. Stephanie was too angry and upset to sleep.

Chapter 11

After the sun came up, Kenneth Chang and Philip Lowe ate their breakfast on a deck outside Lowe's Virginia home. Across the table from the elderly senator, eating a cantaloupe, Chang evidenced little appetite, even though he rose two hours earlier than usual, thanks to Lowe's telephone call.

"How old are you, Ken?" Lowe asked, talking while he chewed.

"Fifty-two."

"You're a fine specimen of good health. You're stocky, without fat—"

"I watch what I eat." Chang's eyes hunted out his Secret Service detail, now stationed in the circular driveway. They were close enough to see, but not near enough to hear. "If I didn't know you better, I'd think you're coming on to me."

Lowe laughed out his words. "Heavens no. I'm trying to say that you look presidential."

The vice president smiled. Lowe had hold of his Achilles' heel.

"You know a candidate's appearance sways a lot of voters."

Chang nodded.

"I also like your quiet demeanor. Some may mistake your silence as a sign of shyness, but I know you're a deep thinker. A president needs to have moments of thoughtful contemplation."

That was true. Chang prided himself in examining both sides of an issue, thus avoiding snap decisions. He was pleased Lowe understood that, but this was not one of those moments. Something about this secret meeting disturbed him.

Lowe pointed at the sun peeking her pink eyes over the horizon. "Nearly every spring morning I sit out here and listen to the birds singing," he said, finishing off his pancakes.

"The view is spectacular," Chang said kindly, wondering why Lowe had summoned him so early. It was a typical spring morning—too chilly for his liking. He would have preferred eating across the table from his wife and children.

Lowe pointed with his fork to an oriole singing in a nearby tree. Chang looked for the bird, for hers was a familiar song; but he could not spot her amid the thick foliage. He pushed the empty cantaloupe shell away and waited.

At last, Lowe spoke his mind. "You're going to have to run against Stephanie," he said, now chewing on a piece of sausage.

Chang disagreed. "The time's not right yet."

"She's got no sense for the job, Ken. None!"

"But she'd have to do something really stupid for the American people to turn on her. I've told you all along—she's no idiot."

"She's going to ruin this country."

Chang ignored the exaggeration fueled by anger. He stabbed his fork into a piece of sausage. "I assume she still won't see you."

His answer was a string of expletives.

Silence settled on them. Chang measured his words. "We need to talk about what you did the other day. You lied about our meeting."

"I had to get inside the White House somehow."

"Don't do that again. I don't like being implicated in a lie."

"I thought we did each other favors."

Chang clamped his mouth shut and feigned a smile.

Willy arrived with a fresh carafe of coffee. He hovered beside Chang to refill his cup, and stood at attention until Lowe waved him away.

"I know you have an appointment with Stephanie on Friday," Lowe said.

"Is that why I'm here? If you wanted me to put in a good word for you, you could have called me."

"I don't say anything of importance on the telephone," Lowe snorted. "You never know who is eavesdropping."

Chang nodded thoughtfully. "Okay, but I'm becoming paranoid about our secret meetings. I worry that the president might hear—"

Lowe wasn't listening. "I'm going to destroy her," he snarled. "She'll be on her knees begging for my help, and she won't get it!" His eyes revealed unabashed hatred in their smoky depths.

Worry tugged at Chang's brow. "What are you going to do?"

Ignoring the question, Lowe asked one of his own. "You still want to be president, don't you?"

"You promised me I would be."

"You will. *At any cost.*"

Chang's dark eyes narrowed into another frown. "What are you going to do?" he asked again.

Lowe patted the vice president's wrist with a pudgy hand. "Nothing I do will hurt you, Ken. Trust me."

Chang wasn't sure he believed him.

Chapter 12

At seven o'clock the sun slid through an opening in the drapes, its rays resting on the back of the velvet chair where Stephanie had spent the night.

Tony stirred, rubbed his neck, and turned over in bed. The first thing he saw when he opened his eyes was Stephanie, secluded on the other side of the room.

He yawned. "How long have you been up?"

"Most of the night."

Drowsily he sat up and reached for his robe. "Another night burning the midnight oil, huh?"

She stood by the bed, glaring down at him. "I'd like to claw your face."

He rubbed his eyes. "What is it, Steph?" He reached out for her but she eluded him.

"How quickly you forget," she fumed, her words sarcastic.

Tony stared at her with eyes still not quite awake. "What do you mean?"

"We had a special time last night. It was so special you forgot it this morning!" She retreated into the bathroom and slammed the door behind her.

Tony bounced off the bed and bounded to the bathroom. "Hey, what's going on?"

There was no reply.

He wiggled the locked doorknob. "Stephanie?"

He heard her raised voice clearly through the door. "I know."

"What do you know? Come out here and talk to me!"

At first Stephanie didn't respond. Slowly the door opened a crack, just enough for Tony to see the tears streaking her cheeks. "Why did you marry me?"

"The question surprised him. "I love you."

"No. You did it to give your career a boost."

"You've got it wrong—"

"You hadn't starred in a TV drama for years. Now you're working in films again."

"That has nothing to do with us."

"You married me because Lowe wanted you to. Love had nothing to do with it." Her voice cracked. "I know that you forced yourself to make love to me last night. Now you can't wait to go join your whore this morning!"

The door slammed shut again.

Tony's brows knitted in a pattern of alarm. "Stephanie! Come out of there."

"I can't stand to look at you!"

He could hear her crying.

He leaned against the doorframe and tried to decide what to say. *So she knew about the affair. It didn't matter how she found out or who told her; all that mattered now was what to do about it.* "Come out here," he demanded again.

She kept weeping. She let out a mournful wail to God. She cried so loud and long that Tony tired of her hysterics. He dressed himself and went to have his coffee in his office.

Chapter 13

After an hour's drive from D.C., the president's car pulled off the highway and onto the mile-long asphalt road that led to the Taylor mansion. It had rained the night before in Maryland, and low clouds still lingered over the one-hundred-and-fifty-acre apple orchard that lined the drive. Ahead, on the ridge, towered the three-story family homestead, its shuttered windows opened as if to offer sanctuary.

Tony had broken her heart. After a dismal morning trying to maintain a presidential facade, Stephanie found herself yearning for her family. All she had left in the world was her eighty-year-old aunt and her ailing mother. Today she desperately needed to be with someone who loved her.

She stepped from the car and gazed up at the home where she spent most of her childhood. Memories of better times catapulted through her mind. Smiling, Stephanie climbed the steps where two Secret Service agents had already stationed themselves. One of them, David Goldman, stood as erect as the tall white columns on the porch, a sling on his arm the only evidence of yesterday's shooting.

Stephanie stopped to thank him. "Why aren't you on sick leave?"

He smiled. "It's just my arm. I had worse wounds in the Iraq war."

Dalton interrupted by joining them on the steps. "Goldman just wants to show off his badge of courage," he chuckled.

He opened the door for Stephanie, but she delayed to shake Goldman's good hand. "I can't thank you enough."

"I'd do it again, ma'am."

Looking into his earnest eyes, Stephanie knew it was true. Frankly, she didn't understand the kind of loyalty that would motivate a man to die for someone else. During her first encounter with Dalton, he had told her the Secret Service would willingly give their lives to protect her. However, she had never thought about it again until the bullets stopped flying.

Stephanie's gaze glided from face to face. "I want to thank all of you for my life."

They smiled back.

Before stepping inside, Stephanie suggested that Goldman join her, so he followed her over the threshold.

In the entry they were greeted by a cheerful maid, who rushed off to announce the president's arrival. Stephanie and Goldman stood briefly in the entrance that led to the hand-carved banister of the curved staircase.

Stephanie's gaze wandered over the pale marble floor of the lower hall to the delicately hued mural that stretched across the hallway just above the stairs. She smiled, her mind rippling with memories of happier days. It was on that landing she had received her first kiss from a freckle-faced boy whose name she'd now forgotten. In the adjoining dining room, Stephanie spied the rectangular table that she had climbed on to swing on the chandelier. The result was an embarrassed nine-year-old and a light fixture torn from the ceiling.

It was good to be home.

She turned her attention to a woman with grizzled gray hair who hurried towards them. It was Allison, the housekeeper, who had long ago made herself indispensable to the Taylor household.

"I'm glad you're okay," Allison said, throwing formality aside to give Stephanie a maternal hug. Then she gave Goldman and his sling a quizzical stare.

"This is David Goldman. He took a bullet for me yesterday."

Allison's eyes widened. "All of us in this house are grateful," she said, offering him her hand. "I want you to taste my cherry pie. Come to the kitchen with me."

"I'm going upstairs to see Mother," Stephanie called after them, heading towards the stairs. "Please tell Aunt Catherine I'm here."

Without slowing her pace, as she began to climb the stairs, Stephanie's eyes scanned the portraits of her renowned ancestors. Here was the Taylor clan, their history proudly displayed by paintings that lined the wall to the top of the staircase: Horse breeder Andrew Taylor and his wife and twelve children; merchant Jeffrey Taylor with his twin sons and three daughters; Senator Charles Taylor and his four sons. There were wedding photographs and paintings of stern-faced men in military attire. Debutante pictures. Graduation pictures. Babies in their christening gowns. Babies on their mother's knee. Babies. Babies. *It all ends here with me*, Stephanie thought sadly. *I'm the last of the Taylor*s.

Near the landing, she stopped to look into the deep-set eyes of her mother's father, and somehow felt disapproval in his stare. "Where are the children?" he seemed to ask.

Stephanie trudged upward. There, at the top of the stairs, in a gold ornate frame, was a photograph of her mother and father at President Kennedy's inaugural ball. They had posed in the midst of a dance step, like an Arthur Murray dance duo, her mother's violet gown swaying above her ankle as she arched her back and pointed a dainty toe.

At the top of the upper balustrade was a picture of Stephanie being sworn in as president. That was all. For the first time Stephanie realized there was no portrait of her as a baby. She made up her mind to ask Aunt Catherine about that later.

The hallway was dark except for light coming from a window at the end of the corridor. Stephanie approached the door to her mother's room, opening it slowly to peek inside. A nurse sat reading.

In the hospital bed, buried beneath white sheets, was the skeleton-like form of Stephanie's mother.

Seeing the president, the nurse popped up, as if at attention.

Stephanie tiptoed into the room. "Hello, Helen. It's been a while, hasn't it?"

Helen smiled, visibly happy that the president remembered her name.

Stephanie peered down at her mother, pale and lifeless, her long gray hair matted flat against the pillow. She slept with her mouth partly open, snoring rhythmically. It was hard to believe that this was the same beautiful and stately woman in the portrait on the stairs.

"Has anything changed?" Stephanie asked.

The nurse shook her head.

Stephanie leaned closer. "Mama? It's me."

Amanda Taylor opened her lids and stared at Stephanie with glazed eyes.

"It's Stephanie, Mama."

The gaze was without recognition.

Stephanie stared back, not knowing what to say.

Amanda began to talk in a young voice. Her eyes focused on an invisible past that no one else could see. "I'm Amanda," she said, as a child introducing herself to a stranger. "My daddy is a toymaker. He gave me my favorite doll."

Bewildered, Stephanie pressed for recognition. "It's Stephanie, Mama! Remember?"

"No-o-o-o," she moaned, her head shaking with agitation.

Intervening, the nurse patted Amanda's shoulder. "That's all right, sweetie. You rest now."

Amanda continued her ramblings, her voice reaching a shrill. "Where's my doll-baby?"

Fighting tears, Stephanie stepped to the window and looked down at the lawn. After a few moments of silence, she asked, "Is she always like this, Helen?"

"Not always. She has some good days."

Amanda continued to digress, conversing with some phantom from the past. "My baby—Samantha. I lost Samantha."

Helen checked her pulse. "She's been talking a lot about that doll today. It must have been important to her at one time."

"I don't know. I was never very close to Mother. I don't know why— I wanted to be." Her voice cracked. "I really needed to talk to her today."

"Won't I do?" The cheery voice belonged to Aunt Catherine, who stood in the doorway, leaning on her cane. "Come on, I want a hug."

* * *

After lunch, they sat alone in the study, side by side in wing-backed chairs near the fireplace. Stephanie had waited anxiously for a time when they could talk, isolated away from the servants and Secret Service. Now that the moment was here, she wondered what Catherine could say to allay her tortured soul.

"I don't know why I came here today," Stephanie muttered. "I don't know what I expected from Mother."

As always, Aunt Catherine was perceptive. "I suspect you needed to get away from being president."

Stephanie forced a weak smile. "Being nearly killed is enough to rattle anyone."

Catherine sipped her coffee. "Are you going to be okay?"

"Sure."

"I warned you when you decided to run," she said softly. "Politics isn't the glamorous, exciting life you thought, is it?"

"I wanted to be president. I thought I could make a difference."

"I told you that you were in over your head."

"Please, Auntie—"

"I watched your grandfather's political career for twenty years. I saw him age into an old man at fifty. He died of a heart attack at fifty-eight. I don't want that for you."

They stared together at the portrait of Ian Taylor on the wall above the fireplace.

"Do you remember my father? He was a good man," Catherine said.

"Yes. I was young, but I remember going to his second inauguration."

"He had dreams and principles too. Being the governor of New York wasn't good for his blood pressure. Then that dreadful presidential campaign did him in." Catherine paused, watching Stephanie nonchalantly as she sipped her coffee. "Do you hear what I'm saying, child?"

"I'm fine." It was a reply more of denial than assurance.

"No—No you're not! You can't deceive me, Stephanie. I raised you. I've been more of a mother to you than anyone else has."

"I know." Stephanie touched her aunt's hand. "I love you very much."

"It wasn't your mother's choice to live in a psychiatric facility. She loved you, Stephanie. She just wasn't capable of taking care of you after the carnage in Columbia."

"I know."

Catherine's eyes drilled into her. "What's wrong, Stephanie? It's only one o'clock in the afternoon and you look haggard. You've lost weight—"

"Only a little." Another weak denial.

"Are you sleeping well?"

"I sleep but I get up tired."

"You have a stressful job. I guess this thing with Sibaba doesn't help."

Stephanie nodded. "I talked to him early this morning. He says he has just as much right to the bomb as the other countries that have it."

"That doesn't sound promising."

"I'll talk to him again. Maybe we'll have a summit with other world leaders."

"I know you must be worrying about this. Are you sure you can handle the stress?"

"Yes."

"You should see Doctor Pierce."

"That's what Adam thinks."

"Adam?"

"My Press Secretary. You met him during the campaign. He handles my publicity."

Catherine's raised brows registered her concern. "Oh, yes, the writer you met in Africa. Quite handsome, as I recall." She stared into the fireplace thoughtfully. "Are you aware, my dear, that you have been here an hour and not mentioned your husband once?"

Stephanie's voice dropped. "Well, no—I guess I haven't."

There was a strained silence.

"It's time you tell me everything."

Talking about it was hard. She inhaled a deep breath. "Tony's cheating on me." Having said that, the rest was easy.

Chapter 14

Tony sat in his office waiting for Macy and brooding about his shaky marriage. For hours he had worked crossword puzzles and listened to TV news, waiting for the nearby offices to empty of employees. He wanted to tell Macy about Stephanie's suspicions.

Finally she entered the room and latched the door. As she sashayed over to him, her hips swaying like a pendulum, his blood pumped, faster, hotter. Her body called to his, her sensuous aroma attacking every nerve ending. All thoughts of Stephanie's morning tantrum vanished.

He leaped from behind the desk and pulled Macy to him, taking her mouth with his. Their kisses had never before been so intense, possibly because Tony thought this might be the last time they were together.

"I love you, Macy," he breathed deeply, pinning her against the desk.

"Sure. That's why you keep hiding me away in offices and hotel rooms." Her sarcasm bit at him.

"I'm not kidding, Macy. I do love you."

She studied him with eyes shaded by thick lashes. "How much do you love me?"

It was obvious she had her own agenda. "You really know how to spoil the mood."

"How much do you love me?" she asked again. Her eyes pierced him.

"Come on, honey. You know I signed a prenuptial agreement."

"We never talk about it. Can't we talk about it?"

Tony answered with a begrudging nod.

"Don't pretend you haven't thought about Stephanie dying. We came so close to being together. If she'd just been killed at the air base—"

Tony's mind registered alarm. "What are you saying?"

"Tell me you've never thought about it."

"I guess I did—on that day—but—"

Macy cuddled up to him. "Let's do it."

"Sure. Where? On the desk? The carpet? In the closet?" he teased.

Tony's attempt to derail the conversation had failed. Macy was not amused. She exploded, hitting his chest. "Stop it. If you can't take me seriously, we're done."

She pulled from his embrace, but he pursued her, seizing her arm in a tight grip. "Don't do this," he pleaded, rattled by her display of rejection. Cradling her face in his hands, he tried to force another kiss. "I tell you I love you."

She turned her head to avoid his lips. Her voice, hard and demanding, allowed no dissent. "Prove it."

"My God, Macy, you're frightening me."

"You keep telling me you'll do anything for me."

A sinking feeling hit his stomach. "Are you talking about murder?"

She answered with a raised eyebrow.

"I can't. Don't do this to me."

Macy freed herself and retreated to the door. "I'll turn in my notice tomorrow."

Before he could react, she had her hand on the latch. Tony loped after her again and stopped her from turning the knob.

"Let me go, Tony!"

Defeated by her icy gaze, Tony released her. They stood for a moment, staring at each other, a battle waged in silence. He sank on the sofa, his face buried in his hands. "I'm no murderer, Macy."

When she didn't reply, he looked up to see a slight smile curling her lips.

She thinks her plan is working, Tony thought, determined to hold out. This was insane. Somehow, he would find a way to talk her out of killing Stephanie.

Like a tiger sensing her prey's weakened condition, Macy pounced on him, putting her arms around his neck. "We'll call it an accident."

He shook his head in denial.

"I'm talking about a little accident. A fall down the stairs or in the shower. No one will suspect." Her hands stroked his face and neck.

Tony fought to stay focused. "There'll be an investigation. She's the president!" Fear closed his throat. He decided not to tell Macy about Stephanie's suspicions, afraid she would want the murder done at once.

"We'll plan it carefully," she said, nibbling on his ear.

Her kisses moved across his neck, then his cheek, as she sought his lips. He uttered a low groan and turned his head to welcome her mouth. One passionate kiss and lust replaced reason. Breathless, as the passion escalated, he heard surprising words bubbling forth from some cranny in his brain. "There's all that money I'll inherit."

She smiled, satisfied. "Yes, Tony. You'll have all that money—and me."

* * *

After leaving Macy, Tony returned to the president's quarters for a change of clothes. The first thing he saw was his yellow roses crammed into a garbage can. Through the open door to the bedroom, he spied a mountain of clothing on the bed—slacks, shirts, ties. *His clothes.*

A maid hurriedly stuffed his toiletries into a suitcase. Stephanie entered from the dressing area, toting several of Tony's suits. She tossed them on top of his designer shirts as if they were nothing but trash.

Tony entered like a bear protecting his lair. "What's all this?"

For a second Stephanie's eyes met his, but she turned away. "We're moving you to the Lincoln Bedroom."

Tony stared at her, stunned by what was happening.

The maid continued packing. She glanced up awkwardly at Tony, her light brown eyes sympathetic but not supportive.

"Stella, I need a moment alone with my wife."

Closing the suitcase, she exited into the sitting room, shutting the door behind her.

Tony let out a barely audible gasp. "Can't we talk about it?"

"I must be the laughing stock of the White House." Stephanie sat dejectedly on the end of the bed. When she finally raised her face to glare at him, anger spewed from her eyes. "Did everyone know but me?"

"There's nothing for them to know. You're imaging things," Tony began, attempting to sit next to her. Instantly, Stephanie was on her feet, darting away from him as if he had leprosy. He continued to sit, gazing up at a beautiful face streaked with tears.

He eyed her critically. "You care too much about what everyone thinks, Steph. Why not care what I think for once?"

"What do you mean?"

"Everything we've done together since the day we married, we've done with the American people—or with Adam or York or Philip. We do nothing together that your staff hasn't planned."

He rose from the bed and stalked towards her. "I feel like a hired escort who should be grateful that I'm allowed to appear with you in public!"

With arms folded, Stephanie did not retreat. "So it's my fault you're seeing another woman? That's a lame excuse." The hysteria in her voice climbed, and her rebuttal became brutal. "While I was nearly killed—whisked to and from the hospital—you were too busy to rush to my side. I know you were with her."

Stephanie paused for him to say something, but he sat with his lips pinched together. She raved on. "You show up two and a half hours later with roses, saying you love me. You think that makes things okay, do you?"

He needed to placate her. His voice softened. "I do love you. I just need someone to pay attention to me, Steph. You're interested in everything but me. You're so busy being president, you're not much of a wife."

The truth jolted her. Silence hung between them like a fogbank.

"If you divorce me, you'll get nothing," she reminded him.

A shadow of worry clawed at his mind. "I don't want to divorce you, Steph."

"Doesn't your whore expect you to leave me?"

His jaw dropped. He had never heard her use language like that until today. He tried to recover, but she bolstered her attack. "It's her or me. You can't have us both."

Panicked, he lied. "I broke it off, Steph. I was foolish, I know. But I ended it after you were nearly killed. I realized how much it would hurt to lose you."

"Liar! I heard you on the phone with her." She strode to the door, yanking it open. "I want you out of here! I can't stand to look at you!"

Tony's eyes fell on an astonished Stella standing a few feet away. He ignored her and pressed his shoulder against the door, attempting to shut it. "Come on, baby. Let's try to work it out," he pleaded, touching Stephanie's cheek.

"No! No! Just go!" Stephanie escaped into the sitting room. "Stella, please finish up in there."

Stella scooted past Tony, her face flushed with embarrassment. Tony eyed the girl for a moment, thinking; then he pursued Stephanie into the adjoining area. He would make one last attempt; he would attack her weak spot. "If you move me out, people will talk about it. You want that in the newspapers?"

"How do you think we're going to keep your infidelity a secret?" Stephanie snarled. "If you can't keep your pants zipped, how do you expect people not to notice?"

Tony swallowed, silenced by her ferocious response.

"If I weren't president, I'd divorce you in a second."

If you weren't president, we wouldn't be married, he thought.

She softened her savage tone. "You're right; I don't want the media to find out. We'll say you snore. You moved to the other bedroom so I can get my rest."

He bit his lip. At least that excuse made him sound like a good citizen, concerned about the state of the nation.

At that moment the telephone rang in the bedroom. By the time Stephanie stepped over the threshold, Stella had answered it.

"It's your aunt," she said, handing Stephanie the receiver.

"Hello." Stephanie gasped, and strained to hear what Aunt Catherine said. "I'll be right there," she said at last, her voice weak. Putting the receiver in its cradle, she raised troubled eyes to Tony.

"My mother is dead."

Chapter 15

Three days later five limousines left the Taylor mansion and inched their way down a dogwood-lined route to the tract designated as the family graveyard. Making the trip with the president's Secret Service were Aunt Catherine's servants and a handful of friends whom Stephanie had invited to the house for breakfast that morning. They included her personal staff from the White House, her physician Debra Pierce, several politicians who had known her mother, and the surviving members of a bridge club that Amanda had joined at her church.

The bright morning sun splattered its rays across the windshield of the president's escort limo, obscuring the road ahead. Blinded by the glare, Dalton ordered the driver to stop. He exited the car for a moment, glancing up the road and back at the other limos transporting the mourners. Then he sent several agents ahead on foot.

From the ridge, he viewed the ribbon of highway that sliced through Taylor land on the way to Finksburg. There, only a few hundred yards beyond a cast-iron fence, he spied cars, trucks and vans lining both sides of Highway 91. Through breaks in the trees, he could see people sitting on their hoods and in chairs in the beds of their trucks. They drank warm coffee and chatted as if they were waiting for a football game.

Burnside joined him. "Looks like a circus," he grunted, peering through his binoculars.

Seizing the glasses, Dalton took a closer look. Along the shoulder of the road, he spotted three television vans, probably ready to interrupt programming for a live telecast. By now someone had noticed the caravan of limos on the ridge. Camera operators hugged the fence like hunters on the first day of doe season. With today's technology and zoom lenses, it would be impossible to keep the media from witnessing the graveside funeral.

Dalton breathed heavily. Not until his eyes assured him of the presence of state troopers did the tension in his neck disappear. *Okay*, he told himself, *the governor made good on his promise. We can protect the president.*

"Not a practical place to put a cemetery," Burnside said.

"It was here long before the state decided to put a road through the property." Dalton began his hike back to the limo. With Burnside matching his hurried stride, he continued talking. "I understand there are Taylors buried here who fought in the Civil War. That's how the family was able to keep the state from bulldozing the graves."

"You're telling me Taylor burials can never be private?"

Nodding, Dalton returned the binoculars and the two men climbed back into the lead limo.

* * *

As the caravan inched down the strip of road, coiling past lush green acreage, a jackrabbit dashed across the road behind the first limo. The second car, following Dalton and the security entourage, slowed slightly, allowing the animal to escape its wheels. From inside the president's limo, as they drove down the ridge to the cemetery, Tony perceived the expectant throng through peepholes in the thicket of trees. To an actor who craved publicity, there was nothing more marvelous than a crowd. This one was like any audience waiting for a show to begin. At a funeral they expected drama and pathos, and they would get it.

As the car pulled through the iron gate, Tony turned his attention to the main players in the drama: Stephanie and her aunt, sad and silent, holding hands. Today he had been on his best behavior. He sat across from them, determined to play the part of the devoted spouse and to grieve when they stepped into the spotlight. First, because Stephanie had asked him to do it, knowing that the press would note his absence. Secondly, because her request indicated to him, in spite of their separate living quarters, that there was a chance for reconciliation.

Tony had decided that reconciliation was what he wanted—not because he loved Stephanie, but because of the stipulations in the prenuptial agreement. Divorced, he had nothing; married, he was still in the public eye and would receive a monthly income from Stephanie.

The other alternative was to kill Stephanie and thus inherit a million dollars from her life insurance and whatever millions were in her trust fund.

The money was tempting. Still, Macy's murder plan was insane. *Deep down she's not really serious,* Tony told himself. *She's just a woman in love who doesn't want to share her man.* In time he expected her to settle into the role of mistress and accept that he had to stay married.

Somehow he would have to get Macy to understand that he had been raised with Hollywood morals. Never in his life had he considered bedding only one woman. He had never given that kind of commitment to anyone in his entire life, not even to President Stephanie. He had been infatuated with her; that was true. She was beautiful and genteel. How many men had the chance to be the spouse of the most important woman in the world? How many men stepped into the international spotlight every day?

At this stage in his life, as he approached fifty-four, Tony did not want to give that up. He loved Macy desperately, and his lust for her gnawed at him every minute of every day. Even if he had loved Stephanie, he still would not have been faithful.

That's just the way it has to be, Tony decided, leaning forward to peer again at the mob on the highway.

* * *

Inside the third limo, Adam was unusually quiet. Wishing he were with Stephanie, he had unwillingly traveled the route to the cemetery with the other members of her staff.

"Did you know Amanda Taylor?" Roberta asked from the seat facing him.

He nodded. "I usually saw her when I visited the estate."

Curiosity flooded her eyes. "I forget sometimes how long you've known the president. Was her mother anything like her?"

"No." Adam knew he sounded curt, but his feelings for Stephanie's mother were deeply personal.

Looking out the limo window, he let his mind drift back to the day he met Amanda Taylor. He and Stephanie had just returned from Africa. Even then, Amanda lived in a world clouded over by madness. Still, she had made him feel he was not the sort of man she had in mind for Stephanie, and she had done it rationally.

"What is your heritage?" she had asked. "Does your family have money?"

"No. But we weren't poor. My folks were schoolteachers," he had said, uncomfortable with the scrutiny.

"Stephanie is a lady, an heiress. She was born and raised to follow in the footsteps of Taylors who have the money and influence to change the world," Amanda had said. "Her great-aunt was the national president of the Red Cross, so Stephanie's humanitarian efforts in Africa were acceptable. But now that she's home, she will resume the lifestyle of a Taylor."

She paused, waiting for her point to sink in. He had no idea what to say.

"The Taylors are the Rockefellers and Kennedys of the twenty-first century. Stephanie needs to find a husband in our social circles," she added with all the sensitivity of a blunt axe.

It had been a snobbish thing to say. However, Adam knew how important Stephanie's family was to her. That night Amanda Taylor had doused Adam's plans of proposing to Stephanie as they strolled in the moonlight after dinner. Instead, he had resolved to be her friend as long as she wanted. She had no idea how much he loved her.

* * *

As the limousines made their way slowly through the arched entrance, its iron sign rusty and worn, Catherine sat clasping her niece's hand. Weakened by the events of the last few days, Stephanie pressed her head against her aunt's shoulder and wept. Catherine sighed, eager to get the funeral over.

The first three cars passed a six-foot hunk of granite with TAYLOR engraved on it, and parked in a scrap of shade beneath a clump of oak trees. The remainder of the caravan continued along the horseshoe drive and stopped on a small knoll between the graves and the highway.

The president's escort team hustled out of their cars and circled her limo. Catherine accepted an agent's hand and stepped out first. Spotting the throng assembled on the highway, she frowned. "We can't even mourn in peace," she grumbled, steadying herself on her cane and taking Stephanie's right arm.

Stephanie wiped her eyes with her free hand. "I'm sorry. The press follows me everywhere."

Stephanie and Catherine strolled towards the funeral canopy where the minister waited by the newly dug grave. Several agents walked ahead of them, with Tony behind them. They walked quietly, two by two, as dictated by the narrow asphalt path. Behind them, from the third and fourth limos, filed Dr. Pierce, Roberta and Adam, and other members of the White House staff.

Catherine turned as a white Mercedes screeched to a halt. A silver-haired man in his eighties hurried over a path of acorns and twigs to join them. It was Raymond Hargrove, their family's lawyer for nearly forty years.

"Late as usual," Catherine said, more of a declaration than a criticism.

He smiled and patted her hand. "It's a beautiful day for a funeral."

She nodded. It was true. Everywhere lilies pushed their green berets through the earth. Apple blossoms clung to tree branches that reached for an azure sky.

Leaning heavily on her cane, she strolled slowly, trying to disguise the limp caused by painful knees. Hargrove moved on ahead with the insistence of agents. With his swift gait, he soon arrived under the canopy and sat with the other guests.

Looking back again, Catherine's gaze settled on the Chang family as they spilled out of the last limo. The vice president, his wife Lily, and even the two sons, were all dressed in expensive-looking, tasteful dark suits. The eldest, a teenager, tugged at his younger brother's sleeve, just in time to stop the boy from stuffing a lizard into his pocket. Their four-year-old sister, decked out in a navy and white-striped dress, clung tightly to her mother's hand as the family approached the gravesite.

They didn't know Amanda, Catherine thought. She supposed they had come out of respect for Stephanie. Few of the people here today actually knew her sister-in-law. They couldn't possibly understand the loss she and Stephanie felt. They hadn't known Amanda when she was the most popular girl in New Haven. They hadn't known the happy Amanda who loved to host parties and play with her children. They hadn't known her before the massacre at the embassy.

For Catherine, the loss of Amanda Harper Taylor was truly a loss. She had been like a sister when they were schoolgirls, and she became family with her marriage to Catherine's brother. Because Amanda's mind had never been the same after the tragedy in Colombia, Catherine felt that she had lost her twice.

Breathing heavily, Catherine paused to rest.

As the group detoured from the path into the dirt and twigs, flagged on by Dalton, Tony moved off the asphalt and planted himself next to Catherine. "Can I help you?" he asked, flashing his most charming smile.

Catherine shook her head. "I'll be okay in a minute. Go on ahead." Her eyes followed him as he hiked on. "Why is he here?" she asked Stephanie, every word heavy with contempt.

"I had to bring him. You know that," Stephanie whispered. "There's no reason for the world to know we're having problems."

The remark forced Catherine's gray eyes back to the highway where the press perched like vultures awaiting their prey. "It's unfortunate that our cemetery faces the main road," she said. "They're making a carnival of this. It was the same when your grandfather died. They actually sneaked cameras into the church during the service."

As the two women continued to stand immobile on the path, Stephanie's eyes scanned the tombstones around her. "I haven't been here since I was a girl," she muttered. "Where are my grandparents' graves?"

Catherine pointed with her cane to Stephanie's right, about six feet away. The plot had newly cut grass around the headstones of Ian Taylor and his wife Hattie (who according to the inscription had died ten years before him of some puzzling blood disease). A few feet beyond, in a plot shaded by a loblolly pine, were Catherine's older brother and uncles, their red granite tombstones prominent against a backdrop of older stones, now faded gray after decades of harsh Maryland winters.

"You really ought to come out here sometime and explore your ancestry," Catherine said, beginning to tread again in the direction of the funeral canopy.

Stephanie slipped in beside her, her eyes searching the graves. "There's a small headstone next to Dad's. It has the name *Samantha* on it. Who was she?"

Her aunt shot her a curious glance. "You don't know? Oh, child, we have a lot to talk about when we get home."

Chapter 16

Stephanie and Catherine isolated themselves in the study while their guests munched on a buffet in the dining room. The table offered an elaborate assortment of glistening hors d'oeuvres, finger foods, sliced baked ham, and pastries. A number of mourners milled about, but most lined up to the table, all looking hungry, and all talking in low, earnest voices, drowned out by classical music.

From where they sat, several paces beyond the archway that divided the rooms, Stephanie watched Roberta and Dr. Pierce fill their plates. Her mother's nurse Helen trailed behind them, nibbling on a carrot stick as she waited patiently for the line to inch forward.

"Is Helen staying on?" Stephanie asked her aunt.

"No. She works for an agency. They'll place her somewhere else."

"You won't need her?"

Catherine chuckled. "I'm old. I have arthritis. But I'm not at death's door."

Stephanie squeezed her hand. "Not for a long time, I hope."

Catherine turned her head, her eagle-like eyes focusing on someone else in the adjoining room. Gray brows swept down over her eyes, screwed together in thought.

Stephanie followed her aunt's gaze to Tony. After fetching a plate for Raymond Hargrove, Tony hovered, asking the elderly lawyer questions. When Hargrove turned away to greet the vice president and his wife, Tony sprinted towards the study.

"Hargrove is ready to read the will," he announced.

Aunt Catherine eyed him scathingly. "He's waited forty years. He can wait a few more minutes."

Tony shrugged and lifted his glass as if to toast the matron. He drifted away into the crowd.

"His eyeballs have dollar signs in them," she said.

"The money is mine, Auntie. You and Mother saw to that with the prenup."

"He'll ride the carousel as long as he can, dear."

Stephanie swallowed, her cheeks turning red. "I shouldn't have told you about our problems."

"It doesn't matter. Amanda and I never cared for him anyway."

After a moment of silence, anxious to change the subject, Stephanie asked the question foremost on her mind. "When are you going to tell me about Samantha?"

"She was your sister—actually your twin."

Stephanie froze in surprise. "Twin!"

Catherine grasped Stephanie's hand with arthritic fingers. "I never realized you didn't know. It's been so long ago. Samantha died with your father in Colombia. You don't remember?"

As she shook her head, regret filled her heart. "I remember nothing, not even Father."

"It was a terrible thing for a child to see. You were three or four years old." Aunt Catherine paused to consider her clouded memories.

Seeing the nurse's return to the buffet table, Stephanie recalled her final visit with her mother. "When I was here the other day, Mother mentioned Samantha's name. I thought she was talking about a lost doll."

"It haunted her, leaving Samantha to die. She had no choice, of course. She was lucky to save you. Still the guilt gnawed at her mind."

Gloom settled over them in the silence.

In the next room, the housekeeper arrived with a tray of sandwiches for the buffet table. Catherine tapped her walking stick on the floor, a signal that Allison obviously recognized. In seconds, she stood beside the matron's chair.

"Go into the attic and hunt through the old black trunk," Catherine said. "See if you can find a pink picture album."

Allison nodded and vanished into the crowd.

"It's been such a long time ago, Stephanie. But I kept the newspaper clippings in the album. Maybe they can tell you what I can't remember." For a moment Catherine's gray eyes seemed to disappear into a dark well. Then her irises lit up. "I remember that all of you were in the embassy and there was a party going on. When terrorists attacked the house and burned it, Amanda hid with you outside in the greenhouse. Samantha was inside with the nurse."

"Why wasn't I told any of this?"

"Your mother saw all those psychiatrists for years, you know, and still she couldn't talk about it. They said she forced herself not to remember Samantha. It was something like amnesia. She never mentioned your twin to anyone, so after a while I forgot too."

Reality bit at Stephanie. "She always got worse when I was around."

"Yes," Catherine agreed. "You were identical, so you were a reminder of Samantha."

"I've wondered why there are no pictures of me as a baby on the stairway."

"There were only pictures of the two of you. Amanda put them away." Catherine sighed. "I'm sorry, dear. We'll hang them up now as soon as Allison finds them."

Raymond Hargrove entered with Tony at his heels. "Excuse me," Hargrove said with an apologetic grin. "Before I go, I'd like to speak to President Franklin about the will. Or would another day be more convenient?"

"I have a very full schedule. Let's talk now." Stephanie attempted to stand. She felt strangely dizzy and nausea swept through her. The room looked unsymmetrical and jagged. She felt her entire weight pressing behind her eyes.

Unaware, Hargrove shifted his gaze from Stephanie to Catherine. "It's quite simple really. Why don't you ladies show me out?" He offered Catherine his arm and the two strolled towards the foyer.

Only Tony noticed Stephanie stumbling forward, awkwardly grasping an end table for balance. As he reached out to steady her, Stephanie's vision returned.

Tony looked closer. "Are you okay, Steph?"

"I just twisted my ankle," she lied, and together they followed the elderly pair through the crowded room to the front door.

I'm okay, Stephanie assured herself. *No one but the biblical Job has endured the kind of week I've had. Nearly killed. Betrayed by my husband. Snubbed by Sibaba. Loss of my mother.* Now, in addition to that, she had just found out about a dead twin sister. Everything piling up all at once had hit her like a sledgehammer.

Halting by the stairs in the entryway, Stephanie returned her attention to Hargrove, as he explained her mother's bequest. "The will is simple. There's no reason to have a formal reading, unless you request it."

Allison came dashing down the staircase, waving a picture album. Halfway down the steps, she stopped, realizing her intrusion.

The lawyer continued. "Unfortunately Amanda never updated her will, so most of those mentioned in it are now deceased." He pulled the document from a coat pocket and pushed his spectacles higher on his nose. "Since Stephanie and Samantha were to share all monetary remains, that means you inherit twenty-seven million dollars in stocks and assets, Madam President. As you know, Amanda owned the family toy factories, and the twins were to have that too, so of course that is Stephanie's now as well."

Tony leaned forward, pressing against Stephanie's shoulder. "You had a sister?"

Stephanie replied only with a nod. She shifted her attention to Hargrove, who was still talking. "Since Ian and his brothers are all dead, and now Amanda, you own the house and lands, Catherine."

Stuffing the document back into his pocket, Hargrove turned again towards the door. "I'll let you know when everything is probated. There will be a short delay while I certify the deaths of the other heirs."

Without warning, a wave of dizziness hit Stephanie again, this time bringing her to her knees on the marble floor. In an instant, Allison bounded from the staircase to catch Stephanie's head in her lap. Before Stephanie blacked out, she heard someone shouting for Doctor Pierce.

When she woke, a minute later, she felt a wet cloth on her forehead. Someone had stretched her out on a sofa in the living room. Doctor Pierce had a grip on her wrist, timing her pulse.

Dazed, Stephanie stared up at concerned faces. Tony pushed through the crowd, looking truly worried, like a devoted spouse. Behind him Aunt Catherine, distressed but still standing, supported herself with her cane and Hargrove's elbow.

"I've been worried about something like this," Aunt Catherine said, her voice barely audible.

"That's silly. I'm fine," Stephanie responded, sitting up.

The doctor's eyes pierced Stephanie like an x-ray. "Are you still faint?"

"I'm better now." However, it was another lie. Stephanie touched her stomach, afraid she might vomit.

"Nauseated?"

"My stomach is a little upset—but it's just nerves." Stephanie looked up again at the distressed faces. "Look folks, I've just come from my mother's funeral!"

"I want to give you a checkup tomorrow," Dr. Pierce said. "You cancel everything until we get some tests done. Don't eat breakfast, so I can do a blood panel."

"Maybe you're pregnant," Lily Chang chirped.

The remark stunned Stephanie, as did the transformation she witnessed in the people surrounding her. Frowns disappeared, swapped for grins. Stephanie scanned the faces, astonished that the mention of a baby could turn passive women into a vigorous tribe of chattering and giggling females.

Stephanie contemplated the possibility. "At my age—I can't be pregnant. Can I?"

"Women in their forties have babies all the time," Lily insisted.

Stephanie's gaze rested on Tony. They exchanged uncomfortable stares, a single idea forming in both of their minds. What would they do if Lily Chang was right? Could Stephanie forgive Tony's scandalous behavior? Could they start over for the child?

Dr. Pierce waved her arms to hush the crowd. "Hey!" she shouted. "Let's let a doctor diagnose this! Everybody move back!"

In a matter of minutes, the Secret Service emptied the house of its guests. The doctor tucked Stephanie into the bed in her old room, with Karen Kelsey camped outside the door. Other Secret Service agents scattered out on both floors. Stein and Bobbitt escorted Tony back to his new quarters in the White House.

As Stephanie lay in bed trying to sleep, she pondered the pleasing possibility of motherhood. To bring a child into the world would be a wonderful thing, even if she did not remain married to Tony.

Thinking back, Stephanie had to admit something had always been missing in her life. None of her achievements and successes ever filled the hole inside. She regretted not having a baby with Howard—his sudden death had cheated her of a chance at maternity during her prime childbearing years. Was it a parental need that had gnawed at her all these years? Or was it the twin she missed, the other half of the egg that had split and shared her mother's womb for nine months? Had she been missing Samantha all these years?

Just before she dozed off, Stephanie began to have mixed emotions about the next day's medical tests. No matter what, she sensed that her life would never be the same. More than anything, she wished that she could get control of her life. Thoughts of the fate of Job plagued her once again. *What next, God?* she wondered. *Job lost his health, his wealth, and his children.*

Chapter 17

Nat Bobbitt joined up with Tony outside his temporary quarters, and they strolled together to his office in the East Wing. Tony hadn't been there for days.

On the way, they detoured down the corridor that led to the secretarial pool.

During the year he'd guarded Tony, Bobbitt had learned to sense Tony's thoughts. Right now, the First Gentlemen's concentration was lascivious. Bobbitt knew this, without a doubt, because Tony had a cocky swagger when he was on the prowl—and today he had begun to strut as soon as they exited the elevator.

Bobbitt guessed that Tony planned to whisk Macy away from her desk. How would he get her discreetly into his office? Bobbitt was eager to see how Tony managed it.

"I suggest you meet her in the elevator, sir."

Tony shot him a surprised look. "Am I that obvious?"

Bobbitt grinned.

Tony's eyes became little slits. "Am I a source of amusement to you?"

The bodyguard squared his shoulders. "No, sir. You're an inspiration."

Tony smiled and they continued their journey.

Bobbitt counted the times he had helped Tony with his clandestine liaisons. He concluded that Tony's affair with the White House secretary had started three months earlier. In spite of Bobbitt's denial, sometimes their rendezvous were a source of entertainment.

Once he and Stein stood outside a stalled elevator at the Library of Congress and prohibited puzzled workers from fixing it. Another time, Tony banished the agents from his limousine in freezing, snowy weather. Then he and Macy had made vigorous love to the cadence of rock music on a blaring stereo.

Now Tony slowed as they approached the secretarial pool. He hesitated, visibly unsure of his plan; but still he ambled towards Macy's desk, not looking at her. Somehow, he managed to get her attention, communicating with a wink. Bobbitt held his breath, sure his companion had made a risky mistake, but Tony moved on, nonchalantly speaking one by one to the entire secretarial pool. He inquired if the new secretary liked her job. He asked another about her son who was in the hospital. He asked if anyone had heard the morning's weather forecast. He did his best to relate to each of them, although Bobbitt doubted that Tony remembered their names.

"How is the president doing?" one of them asked.

"She's back to work as usual. The country is in good hands."

He didn't want to think about Stephanie, so he moved on until he reached Macy's desk. "How are you doing today, Miss Youngblood?"

She seemed to enjoy the charade. "I'm fine, sir."

"I received a letter from a woman inviting me to speak at a graduation ceremony. She claims she was a friend of yours in high school."

"What's her name?"

He put on a baffled face. "I can't remember. Later on today, when you finish what you're working on, come to my office. I'll show you what she wrote."

Her eyes twinkled. "Yes, sir."

That's transparent, Bobbitt thought. *Do they think no one saw through that?*

They left the secretaries and ambled down the quiet hallway to Tony's office.

"Come have some coffee with me while I wait for her," Tony said. It was more of an offer than an order.

Inside they sat in silence, sipping the steaming brew, each pondering his private thoughts. At last Tony shared his. "Has your wife ever figured out you were cheating?"

"If she suspects, she's never said anything."

"Stephanie knows about my affair with Macy. Well, she may not know who the woman is, but she knows I'm fooling around."

"Just deny it."

He shook his head. "She heard us on the telephone."

Bobbitt sucked in air. "What're you going to do?"

"I don't know."

"Is Macy worried about her job?"

"She doesn't know about Stephanie's suspicions yet. I'm going to tell her today. She has a right to know, don't you think?"

Bobbitt sipped from his cup. "Why ruin a good thing? You said yourself the president doesn't know it's Macy." He planned his words carefully. "If you tell Macy, she's going to freak out. She'll probably break it off to save her job."

Tony rubbed his chin, thinking. "I'm in love with her, man. I hadn't planned for that. I've never had feelings like this for a woman before."

Bobbitt wondered what he would do in similar circumstances. He ran his finger around the rim of the cup. "Will you get a divorce?"

Tony shrugged. "I'm trying to figure out how to keep Macy and Stephanie too. I'm not ready to end my marriage."

Chapter 18

◈

The moment Adam saw Stephanie sitting alone in the dark chapel he knew something was wrong. This was her sanctuary, a place where she and God met and discussed the state of the world every morning before she made her trek to the Oval Office. However, today, unlike most days, the chandelier's bulbs were not burning, and no one had lit the candles.

Until Stephanie Franklin entered the White House, no chapel existed. Following in the footsteps of Harry Truman who added a bowling alley and Franklin D. Roosevelt who added a heated pool, Stephanie had transformed one of the offices in the West Wing into a small but serene place of worship. Paid for by private funds, it had oak paneling and four short pews with crosses carved in the sides. The seats had been arranged in two rows on either side of red carpeting. The handcrafted altar was complemented by a large Bible and a two-foot gold cross. Although there were no windows, Stephanie's designer had created a façade of stained glass images and nailed to the walls two multi-colored depictions of the nativity and Christ carrying his cross.

To the president's critics, Stephanie had said, "I will not apologize for my faith." She had compared herself with Roosevelt who had needed the heated pool for his polio. Just as Roosevelt's physical body had needed the exercise, Stephanie felt a place of worship would strengthen her spiritually. She also made it known to all her staff that they were free to pray there too; in fact, two White House interns had been married there the previous year, and an evangelist had a short ceremony in the chapel on the National Day of Prayer.

After going by the Oval Office and finding it empty, Adam had tracked Stephanie to the chapel. He spotted her on a front pew, her shoulders heaving involuntarily. He knew she was crying. The scene dispatched a red flag of alarm in his heart and he hurried inside.

As he approached her, she turned away and blew her nose into a tissue.

"What's happened?" he asked.

She looked up at him with water-filled eyes. "My life is a mess."

Adam hurled himself on the pew and pulled her close. She clung to him, crying softly, neither of them speaking.

This was one of those moments when Adam felt the most awkward—holding her in his arms as a friend and wishing she was his wife. Several times he had resolved to tell her how he felt, but circumstances always prevented it. She had been in love with Howard's memory or in love with Tony.

He continued to love her silently and worry about her excessively, to the point that he could not have a serious relationship with any other woman. No matter who he dated, she wasn't Stephanie. No one was like Stephanie.

"What's the matter?" he asked.

"Tony's cheating on me."

His eyes narrowed. He had been hearing rumors for months.

"I love someone who doesn't love me back. I should hate him." She paused to wipe her eyes with another tissue. "I've been sitting here trying to decide what to do. I feel like such a failure."

"Tony is the one who failed you." Adam couldn't keep the bitterness from flooding his voice. "I never trusted him."

"Why didn't you tell me?"

"You loved him. I wanted you to be happy."

"If he divorces me, it'll probably ruin my chances for a second term."

He rubbed her tears from her cheek. "Divorce won't bother most Americans, Steph. We may have to defuse a scandal, but voters will take your side. You're the victim. If the tabloids get hold of Tony's tainted White House affair—"

Stephanie sat straight up, as if jolted by electricity. "She's here? Right here in the White House? Tell me who she is!"

Adam had blurted his last words without thinking. Looking at the agony in her eyes, he regretted adding to her pain. He shook his head. "Don't pursue it, Steph. It'll only hurt you more."

She stood up, trembling with anger. "Do you want me to find out from some rag sheet like this?" She tossed an issue of *Scoop* on his lap. "Cheri Eastley makes it sound like we had the shootout at the OK Corral at Andrews Air Force Base. She infers I told the Secret Service to fire into the crowd."

"You can't stop irresponsible journalism, Steph."

"But what if someone tells her about Tony's affair?"

That was an unsettling thought.

"If it happens, we'll handle it."

Without another word, Stephanie stalked up the aisle and down the hall to the Oval Office. Adam scurried close behind, trying to catch up.

She sank dejectedly into a cushioned settee. "If I divorce Tony, all I'll have left is this job. I don't want to lose it too!"

Adam's tongue longed to say, *divorce him and marry me*! But he couldn't. Stephanie wanted so desperately to be reelected. Instead, he continued to be the proverbial best friend and asked, "Do you still love him, Steph? Do you want him back?"

They sat in silence for several minutes. Adam took her soft hand and squeezed it between his two burly palms. "You're going to be all right, Steph. You have strong principles and a good heart. The voters will see that in spite of everything."

Stephanie stared intently at him. "I have to know who she is."

"I'm not sure you do. Just hang back and wait. He'll tire of her."

Her eyes widened with a sudden realization: "Does the whole staff know?"

Adam mashed his lips together.

Stephanie bolted to her desk and rang for Dawn. Within seconds, the secretary arrived, a pen and pad in hand.

Stephanie's voice quivered. "Who is my husband sleeping with?"

Dawn's dark face crinkled with surprise. Then she told Stephanie about Macy.

Chapter 19

After five days sleeping in the Lincoln Bedroom, Tony opened the door to the president's quarters without knocking. He lumbered through the rooms until he found Stephanie eating lunch in the dining area. She glanced up at him and back down at her plate. She reached for a crescent roll and buttered it without acknowledging his presence.

He gave her a quizzical look. "I thought you had to fast for another blood test today."

"I changed it to tomorrow. I can't remember being this hungry."

"You keep putting it off. What are you afraid of—that you're pregnant with my baby?"

She didn't answer.

He studied her as she chewed. "Do you think you're pregnant?"

"I don't know. How do you feel about it?"

"Every man wants a son, Steph."

Her silence augmented the restraint between them.

Tony reminded her that he was leaving for Cancun on a morning flight.

"Tell me again how long you'll be filming there."

"Several months."

She nodded and swallowed slowly. When she spoke, her voice was business-like, as though she were negotiating with a foreign ambassador. "You have three choices, Tony. First, you can take Macy with you to Cancun."

His eyes fluttered in surprise.

"Yes, I know who she is." Stephanie stared at him with icy eyes. "I want you to get her out of your system. I hope you'll come back to me."

Interested, Tony pulled up a chair and straddled it. She was more determined than he had ever seen her. "Okay, I'm listening."

"Your second choice is to divorce me and end up with no money."

"You're sounding more and more like a president every day," he teased.

"Or there's a third choice," she continued, unabated. "You can continue to see Macy discreetly and be my husband in name only. I'll support you until I'm out of office."

Tony rubbed his chin. "What are you going to do about Macy?"

"I don't want to see her again. If she keeps her mouth shut, I'll send her file to a senator's office. We'll call it a promotion."

"You're being really great about this, Steph."

"No, I'm not. I don't have any other choice. You have several."

Tony leaned forward to make eye contact. "I won't divorce you."

"Thanks. And what do you want to do about Macy?"

"I'll take her with me."

Not looking at him, she took a bite of tenderloin. "Keep your security team quiet. I don't want it in the newspapers."

When she did not look up, Tony stood and left the room. He perceived that he had wounded her again. However, his regrets quickly disappeared, replaced by one joyful thought. Tomorrow he would spend all night with Macy, and in the morning they would be waking up together for the very first time.

Chapter 20

The newsroom was so quiet Cheri Eastley could hear Beth filing her nails. Cheri sat with her feet propped up on her desk, reading the latest *Scoop* edition. On the front page, a banner headline announced the newest in fabricated news.

"Lady Stephanie Guilt-Ridden!

Neglected Mother Dies Begging for Love."

Below the headline was a large photograph of Stephanie, tears streaming down her face, as she clung to her aunt at the funeral.

Hearing the heavy steps of Ed Braum, the two women focused their attention on *Scoop*'s corpulent managing editor. He smiled down at them. "Nice story. Good pictures too. Nothing like a tearful president to sell papers."

"She really was crying," Beth said. "But I doctored it so we could see the tears. It was a snap with Photoshop." She returned her nail file to her purse.

Cheri's ringing cell phone interrupted them. She gripped it in her pudgy hand.

"I have another tip for you," a familiar voice whispered. "President Franklin is pregnant."

"Thanks for telling me. I'll need the name of the doctor. Was it Dr. Pierce?" Cheri began taking notes. "Look, don't you think it's time we meet?" The other end of the line went dead. "Hello?"

"What's up?" Ed asked.

"I've got another hot one on the president. It's an exclusive." She began typing.

Ed leaned over her shoulder to read the copy. "The president is pregnant?" Excited, he sent Beth to find a picture of President Franklin with her husband. "Be sure they look like they're celebrating," he added, as Beth scampered away.

Ed continued to read the computer screen. "Who's your source, Cheri? Any idea?"

"It's a man. Probably an aide or butler. Who cares? The stories have been good ones." She stopped typing, staring at the screen, pondering aloud. "I wish I could tie this baby to an affair or a scandal."

Ed's eyes narrowed into two dark slits. "Management doesn't want a lawsuit with the president, Cheri."

"*Scoop* has lawsuits all the time. We're a scandal sheet; that's what we are, Ed."

"You're concentrating on President Franklin too much lately. Why not dig something up on a Hollywood celebrity for a change?"

Cheri flashed him a scornful glance and kept typing. "Because right now I've got a source in the White House. If Woodward and Bernstein had ignored Deep Throat, there would have been no Watergate."

She continued to pound the keyboard, pausing only once to brush the hair away from her face and to sneak a sideways glance at Ed. Finally he wandered away.

By the time she finished her article, Beth returned with a photograph. "Look at this."

A photographer had captured a happy First Couple at a New Year's breakfast. Stephanie and Tony had posed for the camera, linking arms, toasting with orange juice in long stem glasses. They smiled, gazing into each other's eyes, as if celebrating good news.

"Good choice," Cheri said. "In black and white, it'll look like champagne."

Beth sighed. "Oh, then this one won't work. A pregnant woman can't drink."

"Precisely. I'll say she's having a hard time giving up the booze."

Chapter 21

Senator Lowe and his driver sat in the limo and waited. Willy had selected the roadside park on a remote farm road in Virginia as the perfect spot for a clandestine meeting. It was way after midnight and they had sat for nearly an hour, waiting for Willy's friend to show up.

Every now and then Willy would get out of the limo and stare down the farm road. He reminded Lowe of a caged tiger at the zoo, the way he paced, back and forth in agitation.

In time he returned to the belly of the limo and sat beside his employer. "He's never this late," he said, looking at his watch.

"You're sure you can trust this guy?"

"Yeah. I knew him in prison. He knows how to keep his mouth shut."

Lowe snipped off the end of a cigar with a silver cigar cutter and stuck the rolled tobacco in his mouth.

Willy fumbled into his pants to find the lighter Lowe had given him at Christmas. "If you've got second thoughts about this, we can get the gun somewhere else," he said, holding out an offered light. "Don't you have a cousin who manufactures firearms?"

Lowe thrust the end of his cigar into the flame. "Yeah, I thought about that. But I don't want the gun traced back to me," he said between puffs.

Willy nodded.

"And I don't want any more mistakes, like last time. That kid you hired for the hit wasn't experienced enough to do the job."

"He was smart enough to get onto the base."

Lowe stilled Willy with a raised hand. He was not interested in excuses. "I want someone who can hit what he's aiming at. I want a professional."

"That'll cost big bucks."

"I'll go as high as twenty thousand. Do you know someone who'll kill a woman?"

Willy shrugged his big shoulders. "I know guys who'd kill their own mother for money like that."

"Would you?"

"Nah, but killing a woman ain't a problem."

With that, Willy stepped outside and paced the asphalt. Lowe's eyes followed him, until he disappeared beyond the beam of the headlights and into the darkness.

Lowe closed his aging eyes and leaned back against the headrest, letting his mind work. He congratulated himself for finding the ideal minion. He had sized Willy up the moment he saw him.

On that winter afternoon, Lowe had arrived in Harrisburg, Pennsylvania, for a joint meeting with the State Board of Corrections and ten local churches. He had toured the nation for weeks, drumming up support for the Prisoner's Rehabilitation Act, which was then still in Congress. That day, in a passionate speech, he had demanded that all states systematically review barriers to ex-cons finding housing and jobs. Declaring that good citizens hire parolees and help them to change their lives, Lowe proudly vowed to hire an ex-con himself.

Present at the gathering were three men wearing orange prison attire. One by one, they shared their mistakes and their hopes for the future. When it was Willy's turn, he reported that many of his friends had returned to prison in just a few months—due in large part to a lack of interest by the public and limited resources for parolees.

"When cons are released, they aren't given enough money to help find housing until they can get a job," Willy said. "You get

$200 gate money. How do they expect you to stay away from former friends? You'll need someone's help to survive."

Lowe took a good look at him. A fresh scar showed red against the leathery skin of his face, starting just to the left of his eyebrow. He looked as if he'd had a rough time in prison.

A woman on the board asked what Willy would do if he found himself without help.

"Anything."

"Would you break the law?"

"I'll do what I have to do."

The words bounced around in Lowe's brain. After the program, all three inmates approached Lowe for the job, but he had already made up his mind. He had come there hunting for someone like Willard G. Wurtzel.

Fortunately, the law permitted expungement of records for nonviolent criminal offenses. Although Willy had committed manslaughter, Lowe levied his senatorial influence on the committee. Soon Willy was released and his crime erased. That way he could enter the White House with Lowe.

Willy's gratitude had molded him into the perfect lackey. He was already a killer. Now he was Lowe's killer.

Headlight beams cut through the darkness, bringing Lowe back to the present. A sedan, white, needing a wash, sped off the road. It passed the limo and came to a screeching halt several yards away. A bearded man wearing a wrinkled work shirt jumped out and shuffled to the back of his car. He popped the trunk and waited, hands on hips.

As Willy lumbered towards the sedan, his friend looked past him, trying to identify the purchaser of the weapon. Lowe smiled, knowing his anonymity was protected by the darkness and the glare from bright headlights. He watched the two men speak briefly, and exchange the envelope of money for a rifle.

Sale completed, Willy ambled back to the limo, holding the rifle in outstretched hands as if he had an offering to the god of war. He delayed by the opened car door until the sedan disappeared.

"He wants another thousand for a silencer," Willy said, depositing the weapon at Lowe's feet. "He got greedy when he saw the limo."

"Who does he think I am?"

"I told him you were in the mob."

Lowe laughed. "That'll tighten his lip."

"I told him I need the silencer by the end of this month."

"Was he curious what you want it for?"

Willy's lips curled upwards, becoming an ugly smirk. "I told him I was going hunting."

Chapter 22

～

Air Force One flew through a cloudless sky towards Washington, D.C.

Three weeks after her mother's funeral, Stephanie had boarded the presidential aircraft to view damage from an earthquake that had separated the Alaskan pipeline in a dozen locations. What she had seen was a thick, black muck that splashed the landscape. In several areas, the oil spilled back into the earth, into the massive gashes the quake left behind. Elsewhere the oil poured like black tar into the rivers that flowed through the national wildlife preserves and into the Arctic Ocean. Oil coated highways and homes and clung like gooey paste to the wings of thousands of water birds.

Stephanie heard a knock. The door opened and Adam entered with a stack of news reports from the communications room. He smiled at her.

Sometimes, like today, she wondered if the warmth in his blue eyes was actually love. Instantly embarrassed by such foolish thoughts, she pushed them away, attributing them only to the stark loneliness of her bedroom. Adam was simply a gentle, caring man, and there was no reason to believe his feelings went deeper than that.

"I'd never seen an oil spill before. That was quite a shock." He placed the papers on her desk.

"I love our country, Adam."

"I know."

"I want to do a good job. I've worried about Sibaba destroying our nation with bombs. I never expected destruction like this."

She didn't feel like talking, so said nothing else.

His eyes swept over her with a slow, unhurried regard. "Did you get the blood test done yet?"

"Yes. I saw Dr. Pierce after Tony left."

"You seem worried about something. Is it Tony?"

She shook her head.

Silence again.

She felt his eyes piercing her like laser beams. He stood close, waiting, but Stephanie still struggled with matters she was not yet willing to articulate. When she offered no response, he retreated to leave her alone with her thoughts. *Experience has taught him patience*, Stephanie thought. *He knows I always tell him everything when I'm ready.*

She moved to a window seat and peered down through the thin, evaporating clouds. A lake, a small pool from the air, reminded her of an oasis in the Kalahari Desert where she once spent the night when she was in the Peace Corps.

Comforting thoughts of Africa crept into her brain and crowded out the uncertainties that overwhelmed her. She welcomed the sweet, sentimental memories.

"Think of Africa," she told herself. Closing her eyes, she let her mind travel back in time. She counted the years. Had it really been a decade since she received the Nobel Peace Prize for helping the Kennel tribe? That had been a challenging time. Through it all, Adam had been at her side. Stephanie smiled, remembering that day at the oasis when she met the man who was to become her closest and most trusted friend.

Before that day, Stephanie and her Peace Corps companions had traveled in a jeep across Africa for three days in the bush. They had come, each for their own individual reasons, to serve humanity on a continent that was plagued with civil wars and famine.

Although Stephanie had come for these reasons, she had also traveled there in search of an inner peace. She desperately needed to deal with her first husband's death. Why had Howard's jet been shot down when he was only delivering food and medicine? She had never understood why he died, when only three days later the Fifty-Day War ended in a truce.

Married only sixteen months, Stephanie had become a widow at age twenty-six. Without a husband, children, or much to believe in except the love of God, she had joined the Peace Corps. She requested to go to Africa and then spent several months learning the languages. It hadn't worried her that she was journeying into the hot pocket of the world, where South African nations constantly warred with each other. Sibaba's army had conquered one country after another and absorbed them into his new nation of Wakembezi.

As soon as she arrived in Angola, Stephanie and the other volunteers ventured from village to village. After weeks of taking medicines and supplies to remote tribes, the group detoured towards the former nation of Malawi, where they heard a nearly wiped-out tribe had relocated. Not finding them, they drove onward, tracking the nomadic tribe for two days through the huge sand basins of the Kalahari. There they finally reached a thin tributary of the Orange River.

When they arrived at the oasis, thirsty and sunburned, Adam sat under a palm tree with his face buried in a copy of the *New York Times*. He looked up at the jeep, but his oversized hat cast a shadow over his face. Only when she approached the palms did Stephanie get a good look at him. He stood politely and removed his hat, revealing a tanned face and sandy blond hair. He was tall, handsome and athletic-looking, and Stephanie instantly liked his smile.

Stephanie's driver recognized Adam as a former war correspondent for NBC. "I'm freelancing now," Adam said, shaking hands with the Peace Corps team. "I stayed on after the Fifty Day War ended. I couldn't make myself leave."

"You like it here that much?" the driver asked.

"Sure. But I want to be the one to break the story when things bust loose here. Africa has a modern-day Stalin. He plans to conquer the whole continent."

He quickly turned his attentions to Stephanie. His first words, abrupt, had surprised her. "I'm sorry about your husband."

"Do you know me?" she asked.

"It's my job to know things. You're Ambassador Taylor's daughter, aren't you?"

She nodded, perplexed.

He grinned sheepishly. "What's a nice girl like you doing in a place like this?" It was a trite thing to say, but his droll delivery made her laugh. It was the first time she could remember laughing since Howard died.

Stephanie enjoyed Adam's company, so she spent much of her free time with him. One day, taking a break for sightseeing, they climbed up a mountain to view the waters of Victoria Falls tumbling over 360 feet to the river below. The view was breathtaking. When she saw the green fronds and abundant wildlife parading along the banks of the Zambezi River, Stephanie knew that she had found the right spot.

"This is where I can say farewell to Howard," she said, choking on her words.

Adam put his arm around her and said nothing.

After a few minutes, she articulated her thoughts. "I love the people here, but I came to Africa on a pilgrimage. This is where Howard died. There was no body for me to bury, so I've been hunting for a beautiful place where I could say goodbye."

Adam had been supportive. He retreated several hundred yards down the rocky path, leaving her alone with her memories and her tears.

After that day, Stephanie began to see him as an older brother. He teased her about her New England accent and she laughed at his futile attempts to speak Swahili. In the evenings, Adam would write about the plight of the African tribes for a wire service. In the mornings, she would teach English to people in a nearby camp.

Adam was a realist; she was an idealist who believed love could bring all peoples together. Yet they became inseparable. Stephanie tagged along to translate for him whenever he interviewed someone. He went with her while she taught adults with sunken eyes how to boil water and mix it with powdered milk. He snapped photographs of her holding children with swollen bellies in her lap while they were inoculated. He wrote about it; he wrote about her and her missionary-like heart.

After ten years on the African continent, they returned to the States, still inseparable. Before the presidential campaign, Stephanie lived on the family estate in Maryland with her mother and Aunt Catherine. Adam lived in an apartment in D.C., writing his bestseller entitled simply *Stephanie*, an account of Stephanie's relationship with the African people. They dined together twice a week. When President Bantu Sibaba began his conquest of north central Africa, Stephanie and Adam traveled the talk show circuit together, plugging his book.

Once Aunt Catherine asked Stephanie why she and Adam had not fallen in love. All Stephanie could say was, "We were in love with Africa and its people."

Now she pondered the question again.

* * *

The plane hit an air pocket. Stephanie opened her eyes, surprised she had dozed off. She had dreamed she was scooping broth into the empty bowls of hungry Africa children. Adam had approached her from behind, pressed his body against her, and kissed the back of her neck. She had melted, yearning for more. As the kisses continued, she had turned her face to welcome his lips—but then remembered Tony and her wedding vows. She jerked back at the last second, forcing herself awake.

Where did those romantic feelings come from? She shook the fog out of her brain and stared out the window at the landscape below. The plane veered slightly to the northeast. It crossed over West Virginia where a mesh of national forests ignored state boundaries, their green canopy of branches reaching out and wrapping themselves around the edges of the Appalachian Mountains.

Still groggy, she reached for a cup of water. As she sipped, she eyed a photograph of her inauguration. It had sat in its golden frame on her desk for two years, among the clutter, with Stephanie rarely noticing it. Today was different.

She stroked the frame. This was the moment in history when she had taken the weight of the world on her shoulders. She had her hand on a Bible while the chief justice of the Supreme Court administered the oath of office.

She gazed at the cheery faces in the picture. To Stephanie's immediate left were Tony, his white teeth set in a high-wattage smile, and Aunt Catherine, who hunched on her cane. Behind her were Ken Chang and his wife Lily. Standing at the back with the others, eyeglasses catching the camera's flash, was a self-satisfied Philip Lowe.

As Stephanie stared at his face, conflicting emotions flooded her mind. Lowe was a schemer and manipulator. She didn't trust him anymore, but he had deserved to be there that day. He had truly been her mentor, and Stephanie had wanted him on the platform to witness her oath of office. In the silent moments, when her thoughts abounded, she recognized that she would never have been elected without him.

She remembered now the day he had approached her about being a candidate. She had attended the party primary in New York, more curious than serious about the election process. The delegates squabbled incessantly, with little progress in sight, so Stephanie took an early lunch break at a coffee shop around the corner.

She had only a few bites of sandwich left when Philip appeared at her table and introduced himself.

"I know who you are," she said, smiling. "I've seen you on TV."

He chuckled. "I've seen you on TV too—a lot lately. May I join you?" Not waiting for an answer, he flagged the waiter and ordered a cup of tea with a sandwich. "I heard your friend's book is a bestseller."

She smiled. "I'm proud of him."

"I've read it. You're quite a woman."

She blushed, wondering if he had made a pass.

Abruptly he switched the topic of conversation. "Have you always been interested in politics?"

"Yes—well, not like you, Senator. My father was an ambassador. My grandfather was mayor of New York."

"Ian Taylor was a good man. I threw my hat in the ring the same time he did. I nearly won the nomination, but he swung all the conservatives."

She squinted at him. "I'd forgotten he was a presidential candidate."

"Too bad he lost. He cared about this country with a passion I rarely see anymore." Lowe kept talking while she chewed her sandwich. "We need someone like him to take the White House back," he said. "Who do you like?"

She mentioned the governor from South Carolina.

"He can't win. We don't have anyone who can win," he said candidly. "We need someone the American people admire. A fresh face in politics—someone like you, Stephanie."

She nearly choked as she swallowed. "I'm flattered but—"

"Don't say no. I'm going to help you," he said. "I'll meet with all the Republican senators and representatives, and Republican governors too. I'll make you the presidential candidate."

Her heart beat faster. "Why me?"

"You care about justice and the down-trodden. Think what you can do for the people of our nation, Stephanie."

"I have no experience."

"Neither did President Eisenhower."

"But he was a war hero."

"To the American people you're a hero." He took a deep breath. "This is what I'm thinking: You're part of a political dynasty— and the Taylor name still means a lot to voters. Also, you won the Nobel Prize. People admire what you did in Africa. With Sibaba causing havoc right now, international relations with Wakembezi is a hot political topic."

"How can you possibly think I'm ready to be president?"

"You're not. No one is prepared. However, you can win the election because, as I said, I'm going to help you. And I'll assist you when you're in office too."

The excitement made her light-headed. "Have you thought this through?"

"Yes. I'm not an impulsive man." He took a sip from his water glass. "You'll run with Kenneth Chang. He's the best man for vice president."

She hesitated, but could think of no one else to suggest for the job. Her thoughts soared upward, as she asked for God's guidance.

"I know Ken will do a good job, Stephanie." Unaware of her prayers, Lowe had become impatient for her answer. "Look, I know what I'm doing. I've been in politics for thirty-five years."

"You should be on the ticket. Not me."

He shook his head. "Americans don't vote for old men. Ken Chang is a nice-looking guy in his fifties. Plus he's had two terms in the senate."

"Let me pray about it."

"No, Stephanie, the iron is hot. We've missed two primaries. We need to jump on this quick before your chance of winning goes down the tube." He took off his gold-rimmed glasses and polished the lenses with a rayon handkerchief he kept in his pocket. "Ken is your prefect running mate. You can't win without him."

She believed him. Immediately she realized she wanted to be the president. That day, overwhelmed with possibilities, but flooded with fears of incompetence, she had agreed to run.

Now, even though elected, Stephanie rarely felt competent.

She sighed. Without a doubt, the quake victims needed help to rebuild their lives. The oil spillage must be cleaned up. Not since the Deep Horizon oil spill let loose the oil into the Gulf of Mexico had anything this massively destructive coated the sea and threatened the environment so shamefully. However, Babco Oil (which had donated heavily to her presidential campaign) claimed that the disaster was not their responsibility, because they saw the earthquake as an act of God.

The problem was money. *How am I going to find eighty billion dollars to pay for the cleanup without raising taxes?* she wondered. *I can't renege on my promise to loan Wakembezi money for medical schools and agricultural training. President Sibaba is not the type of man you double-cross.* Her thoughts shifted between fear and suspicion. *How can I guarantee Americans that he won't funnel the money into weapons or more nuclear bombs?*

She had no answer to the questions churning in her brain.

Maybe Philip had been right to scoff at her plans to make decisions without him. Sometimes she felt like a baby learning to walk, unsteady and uneasy, often tripping over her own feet. She had found the path of the presidency strewn with obstacles, which she often stumbled over as if they were boulders. As president, she took the brunt of criticism from both parties, and that often left her indecisive.

Stephanie wanted to do a good job. Without a doubt, she loved America and its people. She was grateful to be their president. However, she now realized these things had not qualified her to lead the nation.

Chapter 23

While thoughts of indecision tormented Stephanie, Adam was in the galley drinking coffee with the steward. Emptying the cup, he set it on the table and strolled to the president's airborne office. After a light knock, he cracked the door open to peer inside. Stephanie waved him in, so he entered eagerly. "I thought you might be resting."

A smile tipped her lips. "I did. I dreamed of Africa in the good ol' days."

He nodded, his eyes concerned.

She slouched in a seat by the window, her head resting against the cushioned headpiece. Her honey blonde hair glistened in the sunlight steaming in through the window. Adam thought how beautiful she looked. She had the flawless skin of a woman half her age, and a smile that often made him weak in the knees. Even after fifteen years together, she was still the most beautiful woman he had ever seen.

She broke the silence first. "You expected me to have my face buried in those articles, didn't you?" She pointed to the pile of periodicals and newspapers on her desk.

"No, I know you need to rest."

The plane began its slow descent towards Maryland. The pilot's voice came over the speaker, asking them to put on their seatbelts.

Adam sat in a large cushioned chair. Stephanie stood and seized the blue jacket she had draped over the desk chair. She turned to the mirror, quickly straightened her collar with the blue trim, and buttoned the jacket that accentuated a slim waist. In seconds she had turned her blue skirt and the cream blouse into a designer's ensemble. No wonder she had been on more magazine covers than any other woman in history.

Stephanie jumped back into her seat, secured her seatbelt, and stared out the window.

"You're trying not to look at me, Steph."

"You're imagining it."

"No, you always avoid eye contact when you have bad news to tell. You have the same look right now that you had in Africa—when you had to tell me about my parents being killed in a wreck."

She leaned her head back on the seat rest. "Yes, that was hard for both of us. We were on another continent and there was nothing you could do."

Adam studied her face. "What I remember most about that evening was the two of us crying together in each other's arms. I knew that night what a special friend you are. A decade or so hasn't changed that."

She offered a feeble smile and turned again to survey the terrain below.

Through the years Adam had learned to recognize mannerisms and spoken phrases as signs of what Stephanie was thinking. One day he realized that he probably knew her better than anyone alive—even better than that all-too-polished rascal she called her husband.

Today was no exception. He guessed what Stephanie had on her mind, and he wasn't happy about it. He waited for her to speak. When she didn't, Adam broke the silence. "You should know by now you can tell me anything."

"I'm thinking about calling Philip Lowe," she said guardedly. Her eyes spoke another message—fear that she had disappointed him.

"You can't trust him, Steph. You know that."

She gazed out the window again. "But his advice was usually right."

"His advice always had ulterior motives. He's just a pathetic old man who never could be president. He's a leech feeding off you. Do you want him sitting at home, patting himself on the back because he's running America?"

Stephanie sighed. "I'm tired of being ripped to shreds by the press." Her anxiety filled the room like a vapor. "In the old days everything printed about me was nice."

"Lowe had nothing to do with that, Steph. I wrote most of those articles." He waited until she looked directly at him. "Besides, you weren't president then. Criticism comes with the office."

"Just tell me you believe in me, Adam."

He touched her hand, a reaction more of affection than of comfort. "I do, Steph. There's no reason to ever question that."

"I know. I just need to hear it sometimes." She paused, biting her lip.

For a moment Adam feared she might cry, but she swallowed away the tears and became more assertive. "This job is over our heads, Adam. Surely you see that."

"Every president has had feelings like that at one time or another."

Her eyes darted away. She said the words again, this time with more determination. "I'm going to talk to Philip."

Before Adam could stop her, Stephanie pressed the buzzer for her administrative aide.

Adam raised his voice. "You promised not to call him."

She turned away, her face flushed.

"You know how I feel about that lizard. He's trying to make a puppet out of you—and he's nearly succeeded."

York Benson entered, interrupting them. "Is there anything you want me to do before we land?"

Stephanie started to answer, but Adam spoke first. "The president wants to meet with Senator Lowe." Sarcasm crept into his voice. "At three o'clock? Is that your desire, Madam President?"

She reddened.

They waited.

"Okay! I know you're right. I've been president for over two years now. It's time I stood on my own two feet." She took a long breath, long enough to scrabble her confidence. "But how am I going to get the Wakembezi bill through Congress without Senator Lowe on my side? And how will I deliver an aid package to Alaska without taxing the American people?"

Adam's sharp eyes fastened on her. "Don't you think you should lean on God instead of Philip Lowe?"

She grimaced, as if he had slapped her. "That was a low blow."

"Well, have you prayed about it?"

Her eyes dropped. "Well, not today." When she raised her face again, she voiced the words Adam hoped to hear. "Cancel that call to Lowe."

York remained silent, but Adam detected a frown. "Is something bothering you, York?"

The aide hesitated, taking a deep breath before verbalizing his concerns. "Since you asked, I'll tell you. Your conversations with the president are often too unconstrained for my liking. Even if you've known her for a long time, I don't think you should be calling President Franklin by her first name—and certainly not a nickname."

Adam and Stephanie stared at each other. Adam stifled a laugh.

Now that York felt free to express his views, more flooded forth. "No one else talks to her like you do, Adam. Look at the way you humiliated her a moment ago. That's something that no one else in the White House would ever do. She's President of the United States and you need to respect that."

Adam's tone conveyed his irritation, but he remained cordial. "Thanks for sharing that. If it bothers you, I'll work on it.'

York sat and secured his seatbelt.

Stephanie pushed a thatch of hair off her forehead. "York, you have to understand that Adam and I are very close. That's why I ask his opinions. I know he'll always be truthful with me."

"I like to think I am too, Madam President."

"Then tell me what you think of Philip Lowe," Stephanie said.

York didn't hesitate. "He's a seasoned politician. He's smart. He's got a lot of power—maybe too much power."

A panic flickered in Adam's chest. He refused to let Stephanie be caught again in Lowe's trap. "You have plenty of advisors. A cabinet. A vice president—"

Stephanie gave a limp nod, but her tone was unusually decisive. "Vice President Chang would be the better president. We all know that."

Adam hated to see her hobbled by a lack of confidence. *What do I say?*

Stephanie didn't wait a beat. "If I had been killed, Chang would be president right now. America would be better off."

Adam could tell that York agreed. However, this time the aide didn't say a word.

Chapter 24

Willy parked his white Bronco behind the senator's house. Maybe Lowe wouldn't notice he was late. Jumping out, he slammed the car door and darted to the residence. He found Lowe still at breakfast.

Lowe chewed heartily. In front of him were the remains of egg-battered bread smothered in powdered sugar.

"I like this French toast," he told his wife, wiping his mouth. "Be sure and make it that way again." He pushed away from the kitchen table.

She said nothing, but simply stared down at a sink full of suds.

Lowe turned to greet Willy. "Good morning," he said. "Let's go to my office."

That meant he didn't want his wife to overhear. Something was up. Without a word, Willy followed Lowe down a dark corridor to a bedroom that the senator had converted into a home office. Lowe pointed Willy to the desk and plopped into a nearby chair. "It's time for you to write another letter."

"It's only been two months since the assassination attempt," Willy said.

"It's been enough time. By now they're starting to believe the threats are over, and the shooter and the letter writer were the same man."

"Why send a letter now?"

"I want Stephanie frightened and intimidated. Remember she's already had someone shooting at her. I want her miserable, trusting no one."

Willy ran his fingers over his balding pate. "Do you think that'll turn her back to you?"

Lowe's mouth twisted in a half grin. "I'm just getting even. I no longer want her in office. I'm working on a plan to ruin her."

"How do we do that?"

"Somehow we need to destroy her friendship with Sibaba. Their relationship got her elected. If she no longer has influence over him, her voters won't continue to support her."

A light tap on the door interrupted them. The senator's wife opened it and leaned in. "Do you want the rest of the coffee in the pot before I wash it?"

Lowe eyed her critically. "No. Don't interrupt us again."

She muttered something unintelligible under her breath and closed the door.

Willy had long suspected theirs was not a happy marriage, probably because of Lowe's domineering personality. Pushing those thoughts aside, he reminded himself that it was none of his business.

He opened the desk drawer and retrieved a pair of work gloves. He hunched forward, slipped the gloves on, and under Lowe's watchful eye, started scribbling another hateful letter.

Willy wondered how many of these letters he had written, but he had lost count. He preferred to type it, but Lowe told him that was risky. "The cops can retrieve everything you write on your computer, even if it's deleted," he had said.

Willy attempted to make his printing illegible. As he concentrated on the rise and fall of the uneven letters, he thought about his first grade teacher. *I bet she'd think a child wrote this.* He smiled. If he could hoodwink the Secret Service like that, it would be the highlight of his day.

"Spell something wrong," Lowe said. "Make them think you're uneducated."

Willy snorted a laugh. For a moment the dark, block letters became bigger than the page. Written in black Marks-A-Lot, the words shouted rage and a dire warning.

"Tell Stephanie you demand that U.S. money not be spent on the Wakembezi nation." Lowe leaned forward, his eyes taking on a wicked hue. "Use the word *Africans* instead. No, change that to *niggers*. That way you'll appear to be a prejudiced psycho."

Willy smirked as he scribbled down Lowe's dictation. The boss enjoyed playing mind games with the FBI profilers, creating new traits for the unknown writer. He felt himself drawn into the charade. "How about tossing in a word from a foreign language? That will confuse them some more."

"Wasn't your foster mother Hispanic? Did you learn any Spanish?"

Willy scrawled a few words on the sheet of notebook paper, and handed it to Lowe for appraisal. Lowe leaned over and read without touching it.

"*Yo mataria tu.*" Lowe muttered in unskilled Spanish.

"It means, 'I'm going to kill you.' How's that, boss?"

Lowe smiled indulgently. "That's just like you, Willy, learning a phrase about killing."

They shared a victorious laugh.

Lowe's cell phone rang. Retrieving it from his pocket, he frowned. "It's my secretary. I've got to take this." He rose and strolled into the hall.

Willy read over his brief ravings one more time. Amid the misspelled words and venomous language was a finished product that delighted him.

Im sad today. I saw you on TV hiding from bullets.
To bad the guy missed you. Im a better shot. Yo mataria tu.
Then I be happy.

P.S. You want to live? Don't give no more American dollars to those Africa niggars.

He placed the letter inside an envelope and sealed it, not with his saliva but with a dab of water from the faucet in the adjoining bath. He was always careful not to leave any DNA from his spit. He had learned that the hard way—his DNA had been evidence against him at his trial. Now his fingerprints and DNA were in criminal databases.

He ambled into the kitchen. Spotting Lowe outside on the deck, he pushed open the patio door and peered out. Lowe, buried in his telephone conversation, gesticulated with his free arm and plopped on a bench without noticing him.

As he waited, Willy remembered the first time he wrote a letter for the senator. He had felt stupid doing it—but not anymore. As he slipped the stamped envelope into his jacket and headed out to the mailbox, he felt more powerful than death. He chuckled aloud. Maybe he would assassinate the president one day. In the meantime, his words were killing her slowly.

Willy hoped this was the last letter. He didn't like sticking his neck out. He knew Lowe had protected himself by having someone else write them. That was okay. Willy only wished he knew the ultimate plan. The senator had come up with one scheme after another to kill the president, but he kept changing his mind, saying he was being careful. Willy had never complained, but all the delays irritated him. He wanted to kill the broad. His preferred weapon was not a pen. He considered himself a killer, not a letter writer.

He checked his watch as he opened the lid of the mailbox. The mail carrier wasn't due for an hour. He dropped the letter inside and journeyed back to the house. He passed Speedy, a skinny greyhound that Lowe had rescued from an animal shelter. He patted the dog on his head and sat on the steps to the deck, waiting for Lowe to finish his call.

In a few minutes, Lowe flipped the phone shut and called for Willy to join him. "What did you do with the letter?" he asked.

Willy stood at the end of the table. "I mailed it."

"From my home?" The senator's eyes crinkled and he waggled a finger. "You know better than that."

"I thought this once—"

"I don't pay you to think. Go get it. We'll drive to West Virginia and mail it there."

Willy moaned deep in his throat and scurried to retrieve the letter.

Chapter 25

For weeks protestors filled the streets around the White House. Although limited by high fences and stern-faced guards, the demonstrators came armed with picket signs and shouted slogans that proclaimed their right of free speech. One large green banner with white letters screamed out their declaration: "Put America first…We can't feed the World!"

Other signs complained about the Alaska oil spill and demanded an environmental cleanup. They all echoed concerns about American dollars being spent abroad.

From the president's West Wing office, Stephanie and Vice President Chang watched the parade marching back and forth on the sidewalk.

Concern tinged his gentle voice. "You know what's causing this, don't you? It's about your devotion to Wakembezi."

The truth stabbed her heart. She said nothing.

Chang diverted his eyes from the scene outside to Stephanie. "They're like a bomb ready to explode. We've got to do something to defuse it."

When she still didn't speak, Chang strolled to a leather chair a few feet away. She could feel his eyes probing her from behind. She knew he wanted an answer. Frustrated, her head and her heart still at war, she said a quick prayer.

When she left the window at last, she felt haggard and drained. With a strained smile, she poured two cups of coffee and lowered her trim frame into a chair beside him.

He studied her with interest. This time he spoke bluntly. "Do we plan to run for reelection, Stephanie?"

The question puzzled her. "Certainly. We planned for that when I picked you to run with me."

"That was nearly four years ago—and if you recall, it was Philip who picked *you* to run with *me*."

Stephanie flinched. Her face crumbled into a sheepish grin. "Yes, I suppose that's the way it really was."

"I have no intention of backing out of our agreement," Chang reassured her. "Right now I only plan to run for vice president."

She eyed him quizzically. "Have you thought of running against me?"

"That's what Philip wants, if you don't cooperate." He set his cup on a nearby end table. "What you need to understand, Stephanie, is that promises were made—plans were made—and Philip Lowe is the only one of us who has the power to make things happen."

Only yesterday, Stephanie had said the same thing to Adam and York. Weakened by temptation, she had nearly reached out to Lowe. Today she felt stronger. "We can do it without Philip," she replied with a stubborn set of her chin.

Chang's dark eyes widened. "My goodness, Stephanie! Be realistic! You don't know the first thing about the job! Lowe got you elected."

"I'm tired of hearing that!" Stephanie snapped. "He used me, Ken. Did you know his cousin designed the new nuclear-powered drone that Congress funded last December? I was totally against funding weapons, but I didn't veto it. Lowe convinced me it would save pilots' lives."

Chang's only response was a slight shrug.

"He manipulated me. He knew my first husband's plane was shot down. I felt like a fool. I had to read about his cousin in the newspaper!"

Chang sat quietly, finishing his coffee while Stephanie composed herself. When he did speak, he talked in a moderate tone, his voice calm. "I don't always agree with Philip's tactics. There are always compromises in politics. You should have learned that by now."

"That doesn't mean I like it."

Silence hung between them like a curtain. Standing, Stephanie walked slowly over to the silver coffee pot and refilled Chang's empty cup. "We both know you're more qualified to be president," she admitted in a weak voice.

"But I couldn't get elected. I couldn't win the primaries. Remember?"

She nodded, embarrassed to admit that Americans would vote for a woman president before electing an Asian one.

"You were my ticket into the national spotlight," Chang continued. "It was a good arrangement—still is. The time was right for a woman. It was your time. But one day I will be president."

She sat again. "When you are, are you going to keep licking Philip's boots?"

"I never do that."

"Of course you do."

"I want to be president! You've no idea what it's like to be an Asian politician once you leave Hawaii."

"What'll we do?"

"For one thing you need to quit flaunting your piety. Most Americans don't equate that with being a good president."

"I don't agree." Defiant, Stephanie crossed her arms. "I'm not ashamed of being a Christian. That's who I am."

"There's nothing wrong with being a Christian," he said. "Many presidents have been Christians, but they didn't wear it on their sleeves. It's an ingredient for disaster."

Her brows knitted.

"When necessary, a president needs to be hardboiled, and not always fueled by brotherly love." He crossed his legs. "That's your weakness. You need to stop worrying so much about the needy in Africa, or we'll get voted out of office."

She pressed her lips together. They were never going to agree, so she changed the subject. "What else would you do?"

He didn't shirk. "Cut off moneys to foreign powers."

Stephanie's jaw tightened. She didn't like it, but he made a lot of sense. Her nervous fingers tucked a strain of wig hair behind one ear.

Chang paused for an answer, but getting none, he continued, "Look, this is *me* talking, Stephanie—not Lowe. Cutting foreign spending is the only thing that makes sense. Your bill for Wakembezi aid won't pass, anyway. There's no way Congress will approve giving money to Sibaba, especially now that he's building bombs."

"But I gave Sibaba my word. He gave me his word there would be no war."

Chang leaned so close Stephanie could feel his breath. "Listen to me." His eyes bore into her. "Just because you believe in peace, it doesn't mean everyone wants peace. You give Sibaba ten million dollars and you'll cause a nuclear war."

Pulling away, Stephanie retreated to the window again. It seemed to her that the crowd of demonstrators had grown. Chang's words surged though her mind.

Both Tony and Philip Lowe fooled me. Am I misjudging Sibaba, too?

The vice president softened his tone. "Look, I know what your intentions were years ago, but times change. We've got to change with them or our political careers go down the drain."

"You haven't told me anything I haven't heard before." A sullen pout covered her face. "The Cabinet told me the same thing."

"Why don't you listen to them?"

Outside the protesters continued to wave their signs.

"Okay," she said. "I'll break the news to Sibaba the next time we talk."

Chapter 26

~

Stephanie had another sleepless night. Although she had slept, sedated, until three a.m., she awoke in a sweat, anxious and apprehensive. She had dreamed of Sibaba sitting on a throne made of human bones, tossing bombs over his shoulder and laughing as he leveled cities and burned up human beings. Now, as she tried to shake the grotesque images from her mind, Stephanie knew that she could no longer delay talking to Wakembezi's leader.

For two months she had allowed herself to be distracted by Tony's infidelity and her mother's death. With the exception of the one webcam conference—which had been very brief—she had made no other attempt to converse with Sibaba. She doubted she was the able negotiator that Americans believed her to be. Her publicized relationship with the African leader had gotten her elected, because everyone, even Adam, believed that the woman who saved a whole tribe from Sibaba's exterminators could keep him in check. The truth was that Bantu Sibaba only compromised with people who gave him what he wanted and did what he required.

He had already murdered thousands. Now that he was building bombs, the press characterized him as a twenty-first century Adolph Hitler. Stephanie feared that she could never stop him from global destruction.

Turning over in bed, she pounded her pillow. She tried to go back to sleep; but whenever she closed her eyes, thoughts of Wakembezi seized her, and memories reeled beneath her lids like old film.

She remembered now that July afternoon when she first met Sibaba. On that day she had driven Adam's jeep into Kinshasa, formerly the capital of the Democratic Republic of Congo before it was overrun by Sibaba's troops. There, in the marketplace, she had joined a group of French nuns while they treated the citizenry for head lice. While Stephanie dabbed ointment on the heads of children, a boy and three men wearing military uniforms approached her.

The tallest soldier, over six feet tall, was a stocky man, solidly built, with friendly brown eyes and a shaved head. In his native tongue, he introduced the boy as Tumelo Rudo, the nephew of President Sibaba. As a family member, he had been sent to invite her to the presidential residence, where he said she would meet the president.

Stephanie studied the boy, about ten years old, with an ebony complexion and smiling eyes. She guessed the dictator had sent him so she would not feel threatened by accompanying soldiers to his home.

Looking down at her dusty shorts and dirty knees, Stephanie hesitated to accept.

"Please come," the youngster pleaded. "He very much wants to thank you for helping our people."

At dinner that evening Stephanie sat in a giant room, with smoky gray marble floors and tapestry on the walls, eating goat cooked in wine sauce. From the moment they met, she found her host to be charming and polite. Throughout the meal President Sibaba had talked unceasingly about his plans for the economy of his new nation, once separate countries torn by war, now unified by martial law.

To Stephanie, Sibaba seemed genuinely concerned about the quality of life in his new nation. His dream, as he explained it then, was to boost the economy by establishing trade among the Wakembezi states. While some had gold and platinum resources, but barren and rocky terrain, others had cattle and vegetation.

"Starvation is unnecessary," he said. "There will be proper management."

"Isn't there anything you can do for the starving now?" Stephanie asked. "How about the Kennel tribe?"

The nephew, whom she had nicknamed Ruddy, stopped eating. With anxious eyes, he studied his uncle. Stephanie, pretending not to notice the tension at the table, continued to verbalize her concerns.

She was not ignorant of the prejudice against the Kennel tribe. Regarded as an inferior people, because they were a mixed race fathered by French and German ancestors, the Kennels were treated with disdain by their fellow Africans. When their lands were taken from them by the civil war in the early twenty-first century, the tribe had settled on the Congo River. They became fishermen, until their homes were burned and they were driven away by competitive fishermen. Now they had pitched their tents on the fringes of the Kalahari Desert.

Stephanie said a quick prayer. "When I visited the tribe several weeks ago, I found malnourished children and adults with AIDS. The road to the nearest town has been blocked by soldiers, so the Kennels are trapped with a desert at their backs and no way to bring food into the village."

Sibaba stared at her, saying nothing, a hint of amusement in his eyes.

She kept talking. "Those who have tried to travel by foot on the road to Blew have been denied passage by your soldiers. Some have been beaten."

Still no comment. Sibaba sipped his wine.

"It's unfortunate that people can't live together without hatred." Stephanie spoke from the heart. Emotion choked her throat. "Without your help, I fear the tribe will die out."

"I can help you," he said, a smile curling his lips. "And perhaps you can help me. If I am to establish relations with the Western

World, I want to be taken seriously. I wish to speak English without an interpreter."

That evening Sibaba proposed that Stephanie teach him and his nephew English. In return, he promised sufficient food for the Kennel tribe, and a policy protecting them from intolerance. Impressed, Stephanie had left the mansion that night eager to begin the English lessons, and regarding Bantu Sibaba as a reasonable and forthright man.

At nine o'clock when she returned to camp with a military escort, Adam met her outside her tent with a furrowed brow. "Were you arrested?"

She grinned. "No, I had dinner with the president."

Without delay he sat her down in the mess tent. "You need to stay away from him, Steph. He's not what he seems."

"He listened to me. He agreed to help the Kennels."

"He's up to something. He's nothing but a selfish tyrant. I've been watching him for years and he's never done anything humanitarian."

"I believe him, Adam."

"Do you know what the villagers say about him? They say, 'he can charm the shirt off you—but if you don't give him the shirt, he'll rip it off.'"

Stephanie believed none of it.

Despite Adam's warnings, Stephanie continued to return to the mansion whenever Sibaba sent his limo. The next day and the next, in the mid-afternoon, a uniformed officer would drive into the camp and toot his horn. For several hours, Sibaba and Ruddy would repeat English words, learning conversational English one phrase at a time. They would have dinner before Stephanie returned home.

One afternoon Sibaba told Stephanie that trucks loaded with bread and cattle would be delivered to the Kennels by the end of the week. When Stephanie told Adam about the supplies, he grunted that the dictator was "nothing but an arrogant swine;" however, when the day arrived, Adam grabbed his camera and rushed to the site to witness the delivery.

They watched Sibaba's limo escorting two trucks, one with crates of food and one transporting the cattle. When the president made his exit from the car, the people cheered him. Women kissed his boots. Children placed a garland of multi-colored cloth on his head.

The result was a spread of pictures in *National Geographic*. Adam's accompanying text told about Stephanie teaching English to President Sibaba. Her concern for starving Africans had influenced him to bring peace between the tribes.

Within a week, $100,000 in food and supplies arrived, donated by charities in the U.S. Two weeks later a member of the Nobel Prize committee flew to Zaire, Wakembezi, to tell Stephanie of her nomination for the Peace Prize. Surprised, and almost overcome with emotion, she said, "If I win, the prize money will be spent on the people of Africa."

"What a quote!" Adam exclaimed, running to his laptop to write more stories for more publications. In a few short months, Stephanie and Sibaba were news all over the world.

Months later, Stephanie saw the Sibaba that Adam had warned her about. One afternoon, as she strolled into the front room for their English lesson, she saw Sibaba sitting on a sofa with a pistol pressed against a woman's throat. Only a few feet away, two dead peasants sprawled on the bloody floor, both shot in the head. The woman, her face bleeding and bruised, screamed, "You're a demon!" and Sibaba snarled, "Yes, and I'm sending you straight to hell."

Stephanie stood frozen, undetected by the dictator, trying to decide what to do. Someone moved in the shadows of a far corner. It was Ruddy. He came forward, his embarrassed eyes locked on Stephanie.

The woman sobbed. "Don't kill me. I have three children."

"You should have thought of that before you turned traitor."

She shivered in fear. "Please! I don't want to die!"

He emitted a wicked snort, and spit in her face. "You'll be begging to die before I'm through with you." He began tearing off her clothes.

Stephanie gasped and darted for the front door. Outside, she found the limo without a driver and no keys in the ignition. Frightened and confused, she leaned against the car and stared at the dozens of soldiers spread like human fence posts along the perimeter of the estate. While she tried to decide what to do, she spotted Ruddy running toward her.

"It's all right," he assured her. "Those are traitors. They plotted to kill my uncle."

A shot echoed from inside the house. Stephanie shook with fear, crying.

"Uncle must make an example of them to others," Ruddy added, opening the car door and honking the horn for his driver. "Would you like me to take you home?"

Stephanie crawled into the back seat. "What about a trial?" she whimpered.

"They were tried by the president," he said matter-of-factly, sliding into the car beside her. She continued to cry. "Try to understand," he said, putting his hand in hers as the driver started the engine.

She didn't understand. She never saw Sibaba the same way again.

After that, Stephanie stayed away from the mansion. Unable to tell even Adam what she had seen, she told everyone the English lessons had ended.

One day Sibaba arrived in camp and asked in perfect English to speak to her in private. While Adam and several of her friends hovered curiously outside the mess tent, Sibaba explained to her in a quiet voice: "You will get the Nobel Peace Prize. I wrote a glowing recommendation to the committee."

Stephanie stared at him in astonishment.

"You helped me with my English. I wanted to help you," he said in Swahili.

There was kindness in his eyes. For a moment he was the man she once knew—but she reminded herself that he was also something else. Beneath the surface was a vicious creature who tortured and killed.

He sat at a wooden table. "I miss you. I want you to come back to us."

"I can't condone violence."

Sibaba's eyes narrowed. "The ancient ways of our tribes demand retribution, Stephanie. I will not apologize for doing what my people expect of me. Doesn't your God also demand an eye for an eye?"

Stephanie frowned. "That was before Jesus said to turn the other cheek."

He bent closer. "You are also a recipient of retribution." When her eyes widened in surprise, he continued, visibly pleased to have captured her attention. "The Wakembezi tribes return good for good, evil for evil, favor for favor. That is our way. That's why I wrote the letter for you."

When the Nobel Prize money arrived, Stephanie felt obligated to return to Sibaba's mansion, but she only went twice a week. During their first lesson in months, Sibaba reminded her of her promise to spend the prize money on the African people. Without hesitation, she signed over the $1.4 million check to a government agency that built hospitals.

For five more years, she fooled herself into believing that she could influence Sibaba to be a kinder leader. He continued his humanitarian efforts under Stephanie's guidance—but only when Adam was around to generate publicity. Only two of the four hospitals were actually built by then, and Stephanie began to hear rumors that Sibaba had purchased weapons with her donated funds.

One day the dictator asked Stephanie's help to get aid from the American government for his poorer tribes "You are a lady from a distinguished family. They will listen to you," he said. "After all, you are a Nobel Prize winner."

Suspicion stabbed her. Staring into his dark, intense eyes that day, Stephanie saw Sibaba as the master manipulator he was. *Retribution. Favor for favor.* At that moment she decided to return to America.

A year after she arrived in Maryland, Sibaba embarked on a great expansion of his realm. In the next ten months, his depredations evicted several tribes from their lands, setting off large-scale migrations and clashes with neighboring nations who refused the refugees. Using the gold and mineral resources from the southeast region, he purchased the most advanced weapons from mercenaries. The war he waged against Algeria raged for months with thousands of people dying of starvation because of food shortages. With the formal surrender of Algeria, Wakembezi took control over much of the continent's petroleum production, which caused ripple effects throughout Africa.

Soon Sibaba's dictatorship stretched across the continent, his new nation splitting the northern and southern regions into two isolated worlds. He maintained his power with an extensive military and rumors of a nuclear bomb.

Stephanie's worries about the bomb—and the man ruthlessness enough to use it—had caused tonight's nightmare. She turned over and looked at the clock. *Three a.m.* "I've got to get some sleep," she muttered, tugging at her pillow.

In time sleep replaced insomnia.

When Stella opened the door at seven a.m., carrying a breakfast tray, Stephanie felt like she had just closed her eyes. Moaning softly, she pulled herself up in bed and propped herself against a pillow.

"I haven't had breakfast in bed since you went on vacation," Stephanie said, accepting the pancakes the maid thrust at her. "No one spoils me like you do. Did you enjoy San Antonio?"

"It was too hot," she answered, opening the drapes. "We shouldn't have gone in the summer."

An explosion of sunlight flooded the room, blinding Stephanie. She winced, and looked down at her breakfast tray.

"You didn't tell anyone about Mr. Franklin sleeping in another room, did you?"

Stella pouted. "No, I'd never do that. I told no one, not even my husband."

Stephanie offered a sheepish grin. "I'm sorry. I didn't mean to sound like I doubted you. I worry about it getting into the newspapers."

She nodded. "Shall I take a morning tray to Mr. Franklin?"

"No. He's still in Cancun."

Without another word, Stella slipped from the room.

Stephanie took a sip of coffee and tried not to think about Tony with Macy. She reminded herself to stay focused on Sibaba. The state of the world was in her hands today.

Chapter 27

~

Stephanie trekked to her personal office to talk with Sibaba. He had requested a conference at two p.m. Wakembezi time. She had ten minutes.

She sat, staring at the blank monitor of her computer. She had tried to put this off, but it was time to face Sibaba. Breathing heavily, she ran through a preplanned dialogue in her mind.

Please God, let him be reasonable.

She pulled up the security protected URL and switched the webcam on. Technology has become so amazing, she thought. Now anyone could reach someone anywhere in the world and talk to them face to face.

She clicked the webcam icon. She had never really understood the many features of the security URL, which had been used for multimedia conversations since the George Bush administration. Though she had not used the streaming device often, she knew if she followed the easy instructions on the screen, she would chat with the dictator in high-quality audio and video within minutes.

She navigated her web browser to the list of countries joined to the website, and finding Wakembezi, clicked on it. She chose Sibaba as the person she wanted to contact.

She had a quick response. "Wait. When the party accepts your webcam invite, your live feed will launch."

There was a long delay.

Stephanie guessed someone on the other end was searching for the dictator. Surprising, since he had selected the time of their conference. Was he sending her a silent message that she was insignificant compared to other pressing issues?

Sibaba was a master at mind games. He had forced her to tolerate them when she lived in Africa, so she knew what to expect. It would be tricky. He never hesitated to bully, belittle or blame in order to manipulate someone.

She realized for the first time how much Sibaba was like Philip Lowe. Both had played on her insecurities, never allowing her to forget they were the one in control. She resolved to handle things her way this time.

Finally, dark, bold letters filled the screen. *What is your security pin?*

Smiling, Stephanie typed the password. As the websites connected, a whirling kaleidoscope of colors replaced the words on the screen. Stephanie waited until the colorful fanfare dissolved and the smiling face of President Sibaba appeared.

"Good morning, Stephanie," he said in Swahili.

"Good morning, Bantu."

"You look well. You have recovered from the assassination attempt?"

"Yes."

"Your bodyguards should be more efficient. You should have them shot."

She blinked twice, unsure of what to say. After an awkward pause, he sported a toothy grin.

She forced a smile of her own and teased back. "I decided to let them live. I spanked them and sent them to bed without supper."

He seemed to miss the joke. "A leader who is murdered is martyred. You must not let fear of death alter your ability to rule."

Stephanie's mouth went dry.

He continued in English. "We have investigated. There is no evidence of any conspiracy by foreign powers. I believe your CIA and FBI will have similar findings."

"Yes, that's true." He had made himself the expert again. While Stephanie pondered how to bring up the loan, he took the reins of the conversation.

"I've considered your proposal about the summit. My advisors tell me it is a way to establish myself as a world leader. I will put it on my calendar."

"Good. I'm pleased." Stephanie quickly changed the subject. "I've got a problem here that you need to know about."

"How may I help you?" His tone was more patronizing than concerned.

She tried to ignore his piercing eyes. "I'm being forced into changes, Bantu. My country needs our moneys concentrated more at home than abroad."

"I see." Annoyance filled his eyes. "What does this mean for my people?"

"I don't know yet," Stephanie replied. "If you hadn't built the bomb, Congress might have allowed the loan. But now—"

Sibaba interrupted, his impatience escalating. "You put yourself in a dishonorable position, Stephanie. Am I to no longer trust the promises of Americans?"

His patriarchal badgering reminded Stephanie more and more of Philip Lowe. She bit her lip, trying to suppress her anger. "I haven't made any decision yet," she replied. "I'm simply making this call as a courtesy to you."

His white teeth bit at the air as he spoke. "A leader is only as good as his word—or *her* word."

Stephanie retaliated. "I remember a time when you promised me you had no interest in nuclear weapons. I gave you money. Now my sources tell me that you already have a bomb. You gave me your word."

"You misunderstood. I said that to help you get elected."

"You lied to me?"

"You can't expect my country to sit by and allow other nations to make us a sitting duck." A scowl flickered on his face. "Why should your country have the bomb and no one else?"

"We've stopped producing nuclear weapons, Bantu."

"We haven't. I have two already." He leaned into the monitor. "If you keep your promises about the money, I might not build the third one."

"How can I trust you after you just admitted you lied to me?"

"If you don't deliver, I will consider it an act of hostility."

Her eyes narrowed. "Don't threaten me. Don't threaten my country."

"I will do as I wish." His voice became hard and demanding, allowing no dissent. "There is nothing a little wisp of a woman like you can do to stop me."

Stephanie exploded. "Don't degrade me, Bantu. I have enough of that at home!" With one punch of a button, she terminated the transmission.

Everything was beyond reason. She sat staring at the blank screen, shocked at what she had done and wondering what to do next.

* * *

Panic-stricken, fearing she had sabotaged the summit, Stephanie tramped towards Dr. Pierce's office. As she raised her fist to knock, the door swung open. It was Nate Bobbitt.

He eyed her curiously. "Anything I can do for you, Madam President?"

She shook her head. "I came to see Dr. Pierce."

He stepped into the hall. "I'm leaving. I've got a bad case of athlete's foot—I can't seem to get rid of it."

"That cream I gave you should work," the doctor said, appearing in the doorway. She shifted her gaze to Stephanie. "You did say I could see other staff as patients. Is that still okay?"

Stephanie sat on the exam table. "Certainly. Why should you hang around here all day with nothing to do?"

Debra stuck a cold stethoscope against Stephanie's back. "Breathe deeply."

Like a typical doctor's office, the White House medical facility had an examination room, basic medications, and a crash cart for emergency resuscitation. Since the president's doctor needed to be accessible at all times, a former president had situated it down the hall from the Oval Office; that way the commander-in-chief would stop each morning for a checkup after getting off the elevator.

Stephanie stared out the window and took a deep breath. Outside two puffed-up robins perched on the branch of a tree, huddling together as the rain fell.

The doctor strapped the blood pressure cuff to Stephanie's arm and pumped until it tightened. "Your blood pressure is up," she said. "Are you taking the medication I gave you?"

Stephanie nodded, making no effort to hide her sullen mood. Her gaze drifted to an old nest on a branch above the robins. Last spring it had been full of tiny hatchlings; but now, abused by the weather, it was falling into ruin. It reminded her of her presidency. Her approval rating was now thirty-eight percent.

The doctor broke into her thoughts. "Are you having any side effects?"

Stephanie turned from the window. "I'm irritable. I'm not sleeping."

"What's upsetting you?"

Stephanie hesitated, not because the physician lacked her trust, but because she did not understand the watershed of events well enough to articulate them.

She made an effort. "I'm too moody. I wish I could blame it on being pregnant—"

"You know that's not it. Remember what the last blood test showed."

Stephanie forced a slight smile. "I was talking about when I fainted. Did you see how excited everyone got? Imagine their faces if they had found out the truth." She paused, her voice dropping. "We're going to beat this disease."

The doctor squeezed her hand. "Yes, we will."

Stephanie considered Debra Pierce a good friend. They had met five years earlier, while Stephanie was still living at home. She had tripped on the staircase and tumbled to the marble below. Aunt Catherine had rushed her to the emergency room of a small, rural hospital not far from the Taylor estate. With a broken ankle and several bruises, Stephanie had limped through the clinic doors with the help of her aunt's chauffeur.

Debra rushed into the waiting room. Like most people who read Adam's articles, she recognized Stephanie instantly.

"My grandparents moved here from Chad," she said. "I always wondered what it's like there."

Stephanie took a closer look at her. She had friendly eyes almost as dark as her ebony skin. "Why did they leave there?"

"Religious reasons." While she mixed the ingredients for a cast that day, the doctor had asked Stephanie questions about life in Africa.

Now Debra Pierce's voice pushed Stephanie back into the present. "I can't help you if you don't tell me what's troubling you," she said gently. "Remember, I have a confidentiality clause in our contract."

She didn't have to remind Stephanie of that—not after the two women sat through an hour-long lecture by Philip Lowe, who explained the terms for being the future president's personal physician. For the privilege, Lowe offered Debra twice the salary that she made at the Maryland clinic, and she agreed to endorse Stephanie's candidacy to African-American groups. The contract also stipulated relocating to D.C. and traveling with Stephanie during and after the campaign.

As for the confidentiality clause, Lowe had been very precise: none of Stephanie's health problems and no information about Stephanie's personal life could be shared with anyone. If the doctor found it necessary to speak to the press, she would only do so after a briefing with White House officials.

That was years ago. Now, as they sat together, the doctor waiting for her to open up, Stephanie saw genuine concern in her eyes.

Debra ventured a guess. "Is Senator Lowe still badgering you?"

Talking was hard. She found herself having to push words out of her throat. "He still causes me a lot of anxiety. But there's more… so much more."

As she spoke, the events of the last few months spilled out like a spewing fountain. Stephanie told her about Tony's infidelity, her tantrum and termination of the conversation with Sibaba, and her constant depression about the negative comments in the media. By the time she was finished, she was crying.

Debra picked up the president's medical chart and studied it. "I think you're having side-effects from your new prescription. Some patients have depression and mood-swings. It's just a matter of getting you on the right medicine." She opened a cabinet and took out a small bottle. "I want you to take these pills for a week."

Stephanie fingered her wedding band.

"When is Tony coming home?"

"I don't know."

"You haven't spoken to him since he left?"

Stephanie shook her head, too choked with tears to speak.

Digging into her desk, the doctor found a tissue and offered it to her. "I'm not going to minimize what's going on—with your marriage or anything else. It's a lot for anyone to handle. But I think the correct medication will help you deal with all the stress."

Stephanie wiped her eyes and blew her nose. "I wish I'd known before the election that life would be like this."

Chapter 28

The Cancun sun hammered against Tony's back, making his shirt sticky and wet with perspiration. The actress playing his girlfriend had kissed him twelve times, and Tony wondered how many more times it would take the camera operators to get the shot right.

"Cut!" the director yelled. "Wardrobe change!" He waved one cameraman to follow him. "Let's get a shot of the crumbled wall where they find the Mayan artifacts."

Relieved, Tony headed for his trailer and dry clothes. Trailing after him were his new bodyguards Frank Stanley and Dan Baker, and Macy whom the entire crew believed was Agent Karen Kelsey.

Inside the trailer, Macy pulled off her hat and sunglasses. "This heat is terrible," she grumbled, running her fingers through her wet hair.

"We're losing the sun behind us," Tony said, changing into a red polo shirt. "We'll wrap up soon. The hotel will be cooler."

"I heard the director say the rest of the filming will be done in New York," said Agent Stanley, who had come inside to share the air conditioning.

"Yeah. We'll fly back as soon as I can get a private plane."

Stanley pulled a folded copy of *Scoop* from under his arm. "One of the crew bought this at the New York airport. I picked it up to read while you were filming."

As Tony opened the tabloid, his eyes widened with surprise. On the front page was a large picture of the First Couple smiling and clicking glasses in a toast. Below the picture was the headline: "President Expects a Baby!"

Stanley beamed, interpreting the news as good. "Mr. Franklin is going to be a daddy," he announced with a toothy grin.

Tony sank onto the sofa, numbed by surprise, and wondering why Stephanie hadn't told him.

Snatching the paper, Macy plopped onto the sofa next to him. As she hurriedly scanned the article, her lips locked in a pout. They both knew everything had changed.

* * *

After sunset, Tony and Macy ate dinner on the balcony of their hotel room. Macy loved the gentle winds that cooled things down after darkness wrapped around the town. If it rained, as it had done the last few nights, they would retreat inside. For now they lazed in patio chairs and sipped drinks Macy had mixed with bourbon and bottled water.

Macy placed the plate with her half-eaten steak on the tray from the kitchen.

"Finished already?" Tony asked.

"I'm not hungry."

Standing, she looked over the railing. With the heat vanishing and the concrete sidewalks cooling, more and more people cruised the streets below, trafficking with vendors whose carts were heaped with Indian-made jewelry and shawls for the tourists.

Across the street three scantily clad women stumbled out of a bar. One leaned her back against the white building, with one knee bent and her foot propped against the plaster. The other two tottered to the curb, sharing puffs on a cigarette. The trim one wore a pink halter and low-cut shorts that exposed her navel. The other one, darkly tanned and pudgy, wore a sundress too short to hide her thick thighs. She whistled and shimmied as the men passed.

Prostitutes, Macy thought.

A van screeched to a halt and more girls hopped out. There was a brief exchange between the driver and the chubby whore, and he handed her a bag. *Probably dope.*

"This neighborhood has become a haven for drug dealers and prostitutes," she said, her back to Tony.

"Stanley told me about a raid on the south side last week. I guess they've relocated here."

Macy turned to see Tony watching her as he chewed the last of his meat. "Want another drink?" She stepped back into the bedroom without waiting for an answer.

Picking up the bottle on the bedside table, she glared down at the tabloid. Tony had left the paper laying open like a proud father ready to pass out cigars. Angered, she refilled her glass, this time with straight booze.

Tony followed her inside. She tried to decide what to say. She knew they had to talk about it.

He beat her to it. "This puts a wrinkle in things, Macy," he said, fingering the article again. "I won't kill my child."

"Sometimes the *Scoop* stories aren't true," she grumbled.

"But there could be a baby."

"Stop it, Tony. If it's not one thing, it's another!" Macy pushed past him to return outside. She leaned against the balcony rail, staring back down at the street.

Tony wrapped his arms around her. "Be patient. It'll all work out," he whispered. "At least Stephanie isn't keeping us apart."

Macy took a long gulp from her glass and said nothing. Below them, three more prostitutes had camped out in front of the bar. The streetlight on the corner shined down on them like a spotlight.

"I can give you children, Tony."

"I won't kill my unborn baby!"

"Every time we talk about Stephanie's accident you find an excuse. Now you want me to wait nine months?" Macy finished off the drink. "If you wait much longer, she'll divorce you. Then where are we? No money!"

Tony shook his head. "She doesn't want a divorce or a scandal. She'll keep me around until she's out of office, especially if we have a kid."

Macy began to feel the effects of the liquor. "See those whores down there?" she raved, pointing at the women on the street. "You make me feel like one of them."

"That's nonsense. You know how I feel about you."

"But we sleep together and that's all it is for you. I'm feeling more and more like a whore all the time." Again she stared down from the balcony. Two of the women were flirting with a vendor who had set up his cart directly under the streetlight. The one in the pink halter stared up at the balcony, as if she felt Macy's eyes touching her.

With the light flooding down on her, it was a familiar face Macy saw.

"Tony!"

"What?"

"Look at her! The girl in pink!"

Tony's eyes searched the street. "Oh, wow! Can you believe this?" Leaning over the rail, he strained to get a better look.

The woman had long brown hair, teased and flamboyantly styled. She wore too much makeup and clothes that a proper lady like Stephanie would never even try on. Otherwise, she was a dead ringer for the president.

Chapter 29

∽

As the 747 began its descent to Washington, D.C., Tony studied the prostitute seated in the leather chair across from him. She had said her name was Emilia. She looked more like Stephanie now that Macy had dyed her hair blonde and removed the gaudy makeup. She appeared almost stately in Macy's blue suit. The resemblance to Stephanie was remarkable.

Tony smiled, remembering Emilia's startled reaction when he showed her a picture of Stephanie. After a brief meeting in his hotel room, she had agreed to trade her complicity for a handful of American dollars and the promise of more. Tony's plan was simple. Emilia would impersonate the long-dead twin of Stephanie, collect her half of the inheritance from Amanda Taylor's estate, and split it with him.

Macy had exploded when Tony scrapped her plan. She raised her voice, cursing. "Why are you doing this? All you have to do is get rid of Stephanie!"

He glanced at Emilia, whose eyes widened with interest. Fearing Macy might blurt out their murder scheme, he pulled her onto the balcony and shut the patio door.

"I still want to get rid of Stephanie," Macy repeated, her lips in a pout.

"No. How many times do I have to tell you? Not while she's pregnant."

Macy plopped into the wooden chair, her arms folded across her chest. "What if there's no baby?"

He wasn't yet ready to terminate a marriage that kept him in the public eye. "I still like my idea. This way I can get some of the inheritance, and it will still be millions." He stared down at her gloomy face. "Come on, babe. We can always kill her later."

That seemed to appease her. Tony still felt uneasy about committing murder. He would cheat and steal to get what he wanted, but not take someone's life. For now, his plan was the better way. Perhaps finding the "twin" would earn Stephanie's forgiveness.

Before leaving Cancun, Tony had telephoned Stephanie to tell her things were over with Macy and he wanted to make their marriage work. Although Stephanie sounded cautious, she had agreed to meet him at her aunt's home.

"I have a present for you—for both of you," he said.

"What is it?"

His heart pounded in his throat. "It's a surprise. I know you'll like it."

Her words had rippled with interest. "I'll see you soon. Have a safe trip."

Now, as the plane touched down, Emilia caught Tony staring at her. "What are you smiling at?"

"You're absolutely perfect."

Her eyes glimmered. "I know."

"I meant you look just like my wife."

The plane slowed. Before it stopped, Tony stood up to get his bag. "You did a good job," he told Macy. "She could really be the twin." Eyeing the security team at the front of the plane, he whispered so no one heard. "We're going to get away with this."

"Emilia's eyes are the wrong color," Macy grunted.

"No, Stephanie's are brown too. She wears blue contacts because she thinks they show up better in pictures."

"I'm worried what to say," Emilia said. "I don't know a thing about your wife. How do you expect me to get away with it?"

"If you had been away from your family for forty years you wouldn't know anything about them anyway," Tony said. "I'll be there to help you through it. If you don't know something, just say you don't remember."

* * *

Getting through customs became a hassle when travelers mistook Emilia for the president and halted them repeatedly. That was unforeseen by Tony but completely understandable, because Emilia was with him and the Secret Service.

A fat woman with double chins and chubby cheeks approached them first. "It's really you!" she squealed. "I can't wait to tell everyone that I met President Franklin!"

Emilia stiffened. She said nothing, only smiled and offered her hand in a friendly shake. Tony tugged her arm and they continued the pace. "Relax and enjoy it," he whispered.

"Do I tell them I'm not her?"

He barely had time to answer with a shake of the head. A thin woman wearing thick, horn-rimmed frames interrupted them. "I voted for you," she chirped.

Emilia sugarcoated her words. "Thank you. I'm pleased to meet you."

As the Secret Service ushered her through a stunned, gathering crowd, cameras flashed. Excited voices shouted, "It's the president and Tony Franklin."

The gathering grew and grew.

In the next few minutes, Tony studied Emilia with interest as a transformation took place. The tension in her shoulders disappeared. Smiling, she approached people with an outstretched hand. She asked their names. She hugged their children.

Agent Stanley touched his elbow. "Shouldn't we tell people she's a twin?"

"No. The president needs to know first, before the press gets hold of it."

Stanley nodded. He remained close to Tony as they inched through the crowd.

When Emilia's brown eyes caught his, it was a self-assured confidence he saw. She swept back her blond hair from the line of her shoulders, and continued offering her hand. *She's enjoying the charade,* Tony thought, guiding her towards a short line at a customs desk.

For the first time he realized he had not thought things through. All this attention had put him in a precarious position. Everyone thought Emilia was Stephanie, but her passport said otherwise. He worried about the legal ramifications if caught in a lie.

While he was pondering what to do, a tall man with a close-shaven skull dashed over and identified himself as a supervisor. "Please come with me," he said, quickly leading them through the blockades to the exit. In minutes, the look-alike and her entourage were inside Tony's limo with no one the wiser.

Now, as they sped through traffic towards the Taylor estate, Tony closed the glass partition for privacy. He poured two vodka tonics and offered one to the new Samantha. "Where'd you learn to speak English?"

"I was the mistress of an American for ten years. He couldn't speak my language, so I learned his."

"Well, you sound like someone raised in the States. I don't hear an accent."

"I decided I wanted to be an actress, so he hired me a diction coach. I dropped the accent after several months."

"Are you a good actress?"

She giggled. "You'll find out in a few minutes."

"You did a good job at the airport."

"My acting career never worked out. Maybe you can help me get into American movies."

Tony leaned closer, as his words bit the air. "Forget that. You're already cast in the role of your life." He changed the subject as he filled his glass to the brim again. "What happened to your lover?"

"He left me." She sipped the drink, staring over the rim at Tony. "Did you ever love your wife?"

He frowned at her bluntness. "No. Why should that matter to you?"

"Your lady went home in a cab. She didn't look at all happy."

"Macy's impatient by nature, and she likes doing things her way. But she'll come around."

"I guess you're using her, too."

"Actually I love her." His voice was firm and sure. "We're doing all this because I want to be with her eventually."

"So how do you see this playing out? You get half the inheritance and then get a divorce?"

"Something like that."

"And what about me?"

"You can remain part of the family if you want—or fly back to Cancun. I don't care. Right now let's worry about getting the money." He paused to peer out the window as the limo began its journey up the winding asphalt road of the Taylor estate. "Remember I need you to help me with Stephanie. Keep assuring her that I love her, okay?"

She nodded, but he suspected she didn't hear him. "I have a queasy stomach."

"Try to relax."

"It's just the thought of meeting wealthy people." At that instant, as she noticed the mansion looming above them on the hill, her eyes glimmered. "Oh, my goodness," she muttered breathlessly, the words barely escaping her lips. "They are *very* rich."

The excitement in her voice tickled him. He pointed to the Secret Service standing on the front steps. "Stephanie is already here."

Chapter 30

Tony shifted in his seat to scrutinize his companion again. Emilia appeared nervous, but then so was he. This had to work. He had bet his future on her.

"Ready?"

She took a deep breath. She stared silently through the light tint of the bulletproof glass until the agent in the front seat hopped out and opened the door. She took his offered hand and stepped out, with Tony close behind.

The sunlight forced them to squint, but Emilia shielded her eyes with her hand and craned her neck upward. "How many rooms do they have?"

Before Tony could reply, Dalton descended the steps to greet them. "I thought you were inside," he said to Emilia.

Tony smiled. "Dalton, this is President Franklin's sister. Her name is Samantha."

"A twin?"

Tony laughed, feeling more comfortable in his deceit. "How'd you guess?"

Dalton opened the front door and they entered. Emilia gasped as she surveyed the ornate staircase and the marble floor in the massive entry. "I've never seen a place like this."

Hearing voices in the sitting room, Tony took Emilia's hand and led her there.

Stephanie and Aunt Catherine reclined near the fireplace in matching wing-backed chairs. As Tony and Samantha made their dramatic entrance, Stephanie stopped in midsentence. Stunned, she rose and walked cautiously across the room. "It's like looking in the mirror," she muttered, her voice an unbelieving whisper.

Emilia's eyes widened too. "Yes, yes, it is."

Tony grinned. "I found Samantha!"

"Come here child," Aunt Catherine harped from across the room. "I have arthritis or I would rise and greet you properly." She motioned Emilia to the chair where Stephanie had sat only minutes before. Her polite tone changed. "What makes you think you're Samantha?"

"I don't know that I am," Emilia stammered. "I just met Mr. Franklin—and he said I might be."

"Look at her Catherine," Tony prodded. "It's obvious."

Stephanie hovered close, her eyes locked on Emilia. "Auntie, you told me you never had a body to bury. I think it's her. Aren't twins supposed to have some sort of connection? I feel it's her."

Tony beamed. His plan was working.

Catherine studied the woman closely. "You're certainly a facsimile, except for that nasty scar on your hand," she said. "Lift your hair. I want to see if you've had plastic surgery."

Emilia leaned forward, pushing her hair away from her face. "I was grazed by a bullet when I was tiny," she said, offering her hand for Catherine to inspect. "I really don't remember it much—just the pain and the blood and the people screaming."

Stephanie gasped. "The assault on the embassy."

"Maybe. A blood test will tell us," Catherine replied, her eyes cautious.

Emilia stared up at the portrait of Ian Franklin over the mantel. Her eyes took on a thoughtful cast. "I remember a man with gray hair like that. He carried me on his shoulders."

"Yes, yes, he did!" Stephanie interrupted excitedly. "He's our grandfather."

Catherine ignored Stephanie's outburst. Her eyes continued to search Emilia's face for answers. "I don't mean to sound rude, young lady. There's a great deal of money involved here, so I need more proof."

"I just want to find my family," Emilia replied. "I grew up in an orphanage."

Pleased with Emilia's performance, feeling cocky and confident, Tony inched close enough to Stephanie to smell her perfume. Then he put his arm around her waist and pressed his body against her. At first she responded to his touch, but then he felt her back stiffen and she moved away, a silent gesture that warned him not to expect forgiveness yet. However, she was happier than he had seen her for a long time.

"Enough of this interrogation," Stephanie said. "Until I know otherwise, she is Samantha."

Catherine's eyes signaled a warning.

Stephanie didn't seem to notice. "Come with me, Sam."

Holding hands, the look-alikes began to climb the grand staircase with Tony only a few steps behind.

"This is your family," Stephanie said, making a sweeping gesture towards the gallery that lined the staircase. "They were industrialists, politicians, and manufacturers. Good people. They worked hard to make this a better nation."

"They tell me you are the American president," Emilia said softly.

"Yes."

"What is that like?" she asked. "Do the men obey you?"

Tony chuckled.

Stephanie flashed a smile. "America isn't a dictatorship. You have a lot to learn about this country."

She pointed to a picture of the twins, retrieved from the attic and now added to the family gallery. The twosome, looking like happy cherubs, stood behind an oak tree, each peeking out from different sides of the trunk. "Aren't we cute?" Stephanie turned to her sister for a response.

"Which one is me?"

"I wish I knew. Aunt Catherine thinks I might be the one on the right, but she's not sure."

Tony peered over Emilia's shoulder. "I can't see a difference."

Emilia touched the glass in the frame, running her fingers over the girls' lacy white dresses. "We dressed alike."

"Yes. There are more photographs in an album. We're wearing identical clothes in all the pictures. Want to see them later?"

Emilia nodded.

They continued their journey down the wide corridor and stopped in front of the first bedroom. "This is my old room," Stephanie said, pushing the door open.

Inside was a queen-size bed with a bedspread that matched the blue and cream curtains. Samantha, obviously impressed, wandered around the room, touching things. On the dresser, her curious fingers fondled a sterling silver hairbrush. "I never had anything like this," she said, her eyes bulging with expectancy.

"Keep it." Stephanie opened the walk-in closet to exhibit a row of suits and dresses in assorted colors. "What's mine is yours. I couldn't take it all to the White House."

"Really?" It was more of a squeal than a question.

"We're twins. Twins share," Stephanie replied, giving her new sister a hug.

While Emilia scurried into the closet, Tony and Stephanie had a moment alone. He smiled at her with affection.

"Thank you, Tony. This is a miracle." She hurried towards him and gave him a gentle hug. Somewhat disappointing, he thought, and devoid of emotion, as if thanking a stranger for a Christmas gift.

"Where'd you find her?" she asked, stepping back.

"On a street in Cancun." He managed a dramatic chuckle. "I kept following her. She thought I was a stalker."

They laughed together. He decided it was the right moment to bring up her pregnancy. "I saw the *Scoop* article—"

"Your clothes are beautiful," interrupted Emilia, unaware that her return had sabotaged Tony's attempt at reunion.

Stephanie shifted her attention to her new sister. "Did you find something to try on?"

Tony waited for another opportunity to be alone with her. He wanted to tell her that her pregnancy was a blessing. He needed to win her back. He intended to convince her that this baby would strengthen their marriage and they needed to raise it together.

Emilia picked a green silk blouse, and holding it against her chest, viewed herself in the full-length mirror.

Stephanie dashed into the closet and returned with a gray suit. "These go together, Samantha. What do you think?"

"I usually wear flashier clothes." Emilia stared at the reflection of the two of them in the mirror. "Do you think we enjoyed dressing alike as kids? I don't remember."

Stephanie returned to the closet, talking. "I hope we did. Twins dressed alike are always so cute."

This time she came back clutching a red dress with leather trim. "I loved wearing this." She thrust it towards her sister as a love offering.

"It's nice, Stephanie." Emilia flushed and ducked her head. "I've worn hand-me-downs all my life. I'd like for us to wear something alike. We never got to do that growing up."

The idea appealed to Stephanie. "Okay. Let's get you settled in here; then we'll go see my designer. Pick a suit you like and I'll get her to make you one like it."

"Can I have blue eyes too?"

"Sure. First thing tomorrow. Then I want you to come to the White House."

Tony smiled. Emilia had done a good job.

He excused himself while the *sisters* tried on the selected garments. Returning downstairs, he lingered in the foyer, eavesdropping on Catherine and Dalton in the sitting room.

Catherine sounded worried and suspicious. "I want you to investigate this woman," she told Dalton. "I want a blood test."

"Certainly, Catherine."

Tony grimaced. *Oh, no. That can't happen.* He stepped closer to the archway.

"Dig deep. Stephanie isn't the best judge of people." She shot a glance of reproach at Tony.

The security chief nodded. He tossed a stern gaze at Tony and then bolted from the room.

Unable to ignore the barb, Tony stomped toward Catherine. "I love your niece. You've got to know that."

"You loved her so much you cheated on her," Catherine snapped, her voice dripping with hostility.

Her stare caught and held him captive. For a second he imagined that he saw his sins recorded in her light eyes. He tried to think of something to say. Then he remembered a role he had played in a movie and the memorized words came trippingly off his tongue: "I made a mistake. It won't happen again. I'm a changed man."

Catherine shook her head in disbelief.

"Look, Catherine. If Stephanie forgives me, why can't you?"

"Has she forgiven you?"

"She will. Didn't you raise her that way?"

"In church, you mean?"

"Yes. She's a very good person. That's one reason I love her so much."

"Jesus loved everyone, too, but he rebuked the Pharisees when he saw them for what they were. All they wanted to do was kill him."

The truth unnerved him. He retreated, leaving her alone by the fire.

Chapter 31

~

The next morning a mob of reporters swarmed into the Press Briefing Room in the West Wing. Seated in blue theater seats that faced the podium, they chattered among themselves, waiting for the press conference to begin. In the hall, peeping through the opened door, Stephanie postponed her entrance until everyone found a seat.

Tony came along out of curiosity. He could have watched the gathering on TV, but he wanted to be there to assist Emilia through any awkward moments. He squeezed past Roberta Gibbs and her aides, closer to the alleged sisters.

"I'm going to field their questions before I introduce you," Stephanie told her twin. "It'll be about fifteen minutes."

Samantha nodded. "I'm going to sit down." She strolled into the adjoining Press Staff Room, empty now of journalists.

No one seemed to hear her. Adam dotingly fixed Stephanie's collar. "Finding Samantha is just what we needed," he said. "It's going to give you lots of favorable publicity."

Tony stood nearby and watched them. In other circumstances, Stephanie and Adam would be a nice-looking couple. There was a spark between them that no one could miss.

Tony wasn't concerned. He had long ago come to grips with their affection for each other. Any other husband would be jealous to see Adam putting his hands on his wife. But not Tony. He felt nothing, except a slight irritation at being ignored.

Bored, he whirled around and strode towards the door. He intended to go to the Oval Office for a highball, but he spied

Samantha sitting alone, squirming nervously in her chair. He darted just inside the door.

"Don't worry. All you have to do is smile." He glanced back into the corridor to see Stephanie and Roberta deep in conversation. His absence had not been noticed.

"Did you see my blue contacts?" Samantha asked. "I look in the mirror now and I see this woman with blonde hair and blue eyes. I don't recognize me."

Tony squeezed her hand. "You look beautiful. Just do what you did at the airport." He lowered his voice to a whisper. "How'd you come up with that stuff yesterday about old man Taylor—and about being wounded in the hand?"

"It just came to me."

"It was brilliant. Listen, they're planning on giving you a blood test—"

"It worked out fine." Samantha stopped talking as an agitated Dr. Pierce scurried past the door. "She must be here about the DNA test results. I wonder what's wrong."

Trouble lines surfaced on Tony's brow. "You gave them your blood?"

"I was smart about it. I got her to take a hair sample." Her smile became a smirk. "I had Stephanie's brush from the mansion in my purse."

Bedlam broke out in the corridor. By the time Tony and Samantha rejoined the others, Dr. Pierce was crying. Stephanie, whimpering, dropped a copy of *Scoop* onto the floor. "Why does she hate me?"

"I don't know how you put up with Cheri Eastley. I'm going to sue her," Dr. Pierce said through gritted teeth. She swung around, eyes blazing, and stared at Tony. "She says I gave the president an abortion."

Someone in the room gasped.

Fuming, Stephanie stalked into the press conference. The others followed on her heels, but Tony lingered behind, wondering if Stephanie had killed their child.

* * *

As Stephanie approached the assembly of journalists, nearing the platform, she slowed her pace, trying to conceal the agitation in her gait. Taking her place behind the podium, she took a deep breath and vowed to stay calm.

Reporters jumped to their feet and shouted questions. One voice swelled to a crescendo above the rest, so Stephanie pointed to her first.

"Madam President, what is your reaction to Wakembezi exploding a bomb last week? Do you feel President Sibaba is using this test to pressure you?"

Stephanie frowned. "Why would he pressure me?"

"For money." The woman sat, pen in hand, ready to take notes.

"I'll do anything to prevent a war," Stephanie replied, "but I won't be blackmailed or forced by any other county to do something that is detrimental to America. Sibaba and I spoke recently. He understands that."

A man on the front row questioned next, his tone scornful. "Are you going to help the Africans finance their cattle enterprise again?"

"No, I'm not." Stephanie had not expected all the questions to be on Sibaba. She wondered if anyone had seen the *Scoop* article. Her eyes landed on a friendly face. "You're next," she said to the reporter from *USA Today*.

"Have you talked to Sibaba about possible environmental hazards caused by his bombing?"

"I will. I'm concerned about the contamination of the water. The Nile is used by the entire continent."

Cheri Eastley jumped up without recognition. "There are those who say Sibaba has a hold over you. Is it true you lived in his house and had an intimate relationship with him?"

There was no way to remain presidential. Stephanie exploded. "Where do you get that stuff? Have you ever heard of journalistic integrity?"

"Take it easy," Roberta whispered a caution. She handed her the *Scoop* edition. "Confront her with this. Crush the rumors."

Stephanie held up the front page for all to see:

"President Scorns Motherhood!"

"Miss Eastley, I think being a parent would be a wonderful experience, but God never blessed me with the opportunity. I was never pregnant, in spite of what you printed. I certainly didn't change my mind and have an abortion. Your column is malicious."

Stephanie spied Tony leaning against the wall. Disappointment flooded his eyes. For the first time she realized how much he wanted a child. *I should have told him there was no baby,* she reflected. Last night she had been so busy bonding with Samantha that it hadn't occurred to her.

Now was not the time to linger on regrets. She reminded herself to stay focused and kept talking. "Everything you print is a lie, Miss Eastley."

"I print what my sources tell me."

"How about checking your sources."

Bemused tittering echoed around the room.

After experiencing momentary embarrassment, Cheri's temper flared. "There'll always be someone sniping at you if you're going to be president." She glared at the network cameras, now pointed at her, and proclaimed through gritted teeth, "Why are you picking on me?"

"On the contrary, it is you who are picking on me. One article of lies after another. Why you hate me so much I cannot imagine."

Cheri's cheeks reddened, but she offered no response.

After a moment of dead silence, Dr. Pierce approached the microphone. "This morning I was threatened by anti-abortionists outside my home—all because Cheri Eastley named me as an abortionist! I'm frightened. I would appreciate the help of credible press to get the truth out. The president was never pregnant. Even if she had been, I'd never have terminated the pregnancy." She glared at Cheri. "I've discussed your article with my attorney. The president may have to put up with the creative writing that you pass off as news, but I won't! I expect a full retraction or I'll sue."

The crowd jeered. Stephanie smiled for the first time and asked security to remove Cheri from the White House grounds.

Agitated, Cheri made her way out of the row of chairs. Before she could retreat up the aisle, an agent blocked her exit. He pointed her towards the French windows leading to the South Portico.

"Miss Eastley, you will no longer be allowed at press conferences," Stephanie called after her.

Cheri's angry eyes flashed hatred. She ran for the exit.

The crowd fell silent, all eyes scrutinizing the president. Stephanie seized the moment. "Relax," she laughed. "I called you here today for another reason. My husband just returned from Cancun. Let me show you the present he brought me."

Samantha entered, escorted by Tony. The voices of the reporters registered surprise in unison. Their cameras flashed, focusing on the twins, who stood side by side in identical lavender suits.

"This is my twin sister Samantha," announced the president. "My family thought she was dead. It's a long story. I'll let you hear it from her."

Samantha stepped forward, visibly delighted by the attention and her new life in front of the cameras.

Chapter 32

Philip Lowe and Kenneth Chang watched the press conference on a flat screen TV at the vice president's residence. At present, Samantha was a little tearful, but the very picture of energy and excitement as she told about seeing Stephanie for the first time.

"Look at that!" Chang settled back in a plush chair to watch the broadcast. "Stephanie's improved her popularity twice in just a matter of minutes."

Lowe accepted the drink that Lily Chang handed him. "Twice? What are you thinking?"

"First she proved Cheri Eastley's stories were crap, and now the twin angle. People love that sort of thing."

"Oh, yeah." Lowe passed it off with a swat of his hand. "She just got lucky."

Chang's squealing daughter scampered through the room, pursued by her brother. Rising to his feet, Chang rattled off a stern warning.

Lily handed him his usual mineral water and headed for the door. "I must apologize, Senator Lowe. Our children are restless; they've been cooped up inside for the past few days. I do wish the rains would stop."

She disappeared, the kids trailing behind her. At first the screeching and laughter penetrated the shut door, as did Lily's high-pitched voice, but now all was silent again.

Their attention returned to the television. Samantha told reporters that she had been raised in an orphanage. "That pulls at the heartstrings," Lowe grunted.

"I've told you all along—Stephanie is no idiot," said Chang. "Want some coffee?"

Lowe didn't seem to hear him. "She's going to fall on her face without me."

The vice president tuned out the rest. He had tired of his companion's tirades on Stephanie. Lowe had said the same thing three times since they sat down. Chang wondered how many drinks the senior senator had before he arrived unexpectedly at their residence.

"I tried to get Stephanie to see you, Philip. Sorry."

Lowe gulped down his drink and unleashed a string of cuss words. "She seems to believe she swung the election herself."

Chang remained silent. Disinterested, he glanced from time to time through the window at the inky sky. When he diverted his eyes back to the TV, he noticed that the news conference had broken up, with only a few reporters remaining in the Press Briefing Room.

Lowe continued venting his anger. "Who groomed her for the press? Who spent millions on her publicity?"

"Who encouraged her to marry Tony Franklin?" Chang snorted a laugh.

"Did I? I don't recall." His mouth turned into a sly smile.

"Of course you did. You manipulated her and the women of America. Voters were swept up in her romance weeks before the election. You staged a public courtship, much like Stephanie just staged this touching reunion with her sister."

"She's learning, I admit." Lowe pointed to the TV. The twins stood side-by-side, holding hands. "She's going for the public's emotional jugular again."

"That will boost her popularity in the polls."

"Sure, but in a few weeks interest in the twins will die out. Then the incompetent Stephanie will reappear in the news."

Chang turned off the TV. "I've noticed lots negative press lately. You're behind that, aren't you?"

Lowe answered with a smirk.

"I figure you're trying to destroy her popularity with the American people, so she won't be nominated by the party again."

"Bingo."

"I can see why the abortion story would be detrimental. But what was the point of the earlier article? Why say Stephanie was pregnant?"

"She had to be pregnant before she could be accused of having an abortion."

Chang swallowed hard. He had learned more than he wanted to hear. "I'm the one who told you she fainted and she might be pregnant. I feel responsible for what you did. That's not the way I play the game, Philip."

Lowe's face took on a fiendish determination. "I promised you that you'd be president—and you will."

Chapter 33

Leaves fell on the lawn, gathering in drifts outside the Taylor mansion. Inside, in the enclosed swim area, where seasons had ceased to exist, the residents enjoyed the pool and hot tub year-round, even on a chilly October morning.

Samantha squatted and dipped her fingers in the tepid water. "I'd never heard of a heated pool before I came here," she said to her aunt, who today had decided to watch her nieces swim while she lazed in the hot tub.

Catherine steadied herself by holding Karen Kelsey's hand as she eased into the tub. Her face relaxed as the hot water swirled around her. "The warmth is nice. It helps my arthritis."

Standing, Samantha ran her fingers down the sides of her new one-piece bathing suit, something uncharacteristically modest for a woman accustomed to flaunting her body. The "proper" Taylor look took some getting used to—the truth was Samantha preferred a bikini. Wanting to please Catherine, she had resigned herself to a whole wardrobe of conservative attire, much like Stephanie wore.

"Is Stephanie here yet?" Catherine asked.

Samantha nodded. "She's changing into her suit."

Delaying her plunge into the water, Samantha sat on the diving board, hugging her legs close to her chest and staring through the glass walls at a world exploding with color. Fantastic gold and red foliage clung to the branches of the trees near the driveway.

Nearby two squirrels frantically dug at the yard to hoard nuts for the hard times ahead. Startled, they scampered up a tree trunk as Dalton jogged by on his morning run. As he passed, clad in heavy gray sweats, he turned to wave at the two agents stationed outdoors. They stood against the transparent wall, probably trying to escape the crisp autumn wind. After a while, one returned to his car and pulled a heavy jacket out of the trunk.

At last Stephanie entered the pool area. Samantha studied the entourage that doggedly followed her sister, and then she dove from the board into the water. Coming to the surface, she swam to the edge of the pool and hung on, watching Stephanie doff her thick robe and slippers. Stephanie waved, beamed, and hurried toward her.

Left behind, the president's bodyguards plopped into loungers and chairs as Stephanie slowly descended the ladder into the pool. Samantha wondered about all the devoted watchers whose eyes followed the president everywhere—you'd think the world would end if anything happened to her. *Do they do it for the money or do they really care about her?* Samantha wondered. *Maybe I'll shake things up and find out for myself.*

She felt someone's eyes on her. Shifting her gaze, she found a handsome, auburn-haired agent staring at her. Surprised since Stephanie was always the center of attention, she winked at him before she could stop herself. Old habits were hard to break. She had always found her worth, her self-esteem, in the arms of a lustful male. It was hard to lead the Puritan life expected of the Taylors.

"Hi, Sam." Stephanie glided through the water with a slow breaststroke.

"I'm glad you came." Samantha answered without looking at Stephanie, her interest still captured by the agent with copper hair. He had broken eye contact and now sat at a fiberglass table with Karen Kelsey. They sipped coffee and loudly discussed the last Redskins game. Samantha watched them, befuddled that intelligent grownups could be so enthusiastic over a silly game with a ball.

Stephanie placed a wet palm on Samantha's shoulder. "We're both wearing the same blue bathing suit. How'd that happen?"

Samantha snapped her head around, smiling. "Isn't that odd, that we picked the same suit?"

"I've heard of twins doing things like that," Stephanie replied, her eyes charged with excitement.

That was easy, Samantha thought. Stephanie had become easy to manipulate, so eager was she to embrace the girls' duplicity. She would never know that Samantha had hunted through her dresser drawers, found her suit and shopped in three stores before she found one exactly like it.

Samantha, treading water away from the edge, changed the subject. "Tell me about the agent sitting with Karen. I've never seen him with you before."

"His name is Tim Burnside. He rotates." Stephanie looked as if she would go further, but she stopped, studying her twin, deliberating the question. "Sorry. He's married, Sam."

"Too bad. He's a stud." Samantha sighed. "I like his hair."

That settled, the look-alikes swam to the center of the pool, each clinging to opposite ends of a floating raft. In minutes Stephanie was laughing, kicking and splashing her sister with waves of water. They giggled together like schoolchildren, Samantha retaliating, and Stephanie returning fire, as they continued a war of spattering water.

"I want the float," Samantha squealed, pulling it with one hand while she struggled to paddle away.

"What was it we decided about sharing?" Stephanie teased, holding tightly to the inflated lounger.

Without warning, Samantha released the float. She pulled herself out of the pool and ran, dripping water all the way to the diving board. "Bombs away!" she shouted as she tucked her legs to her chest and jumped on Stephanie below.

Stephanie went beneath the lapping water. She clung to the float, struggling to keep her head above the surface. Samantha, showing no mercy, swam beneath the surface and tugged her legs from below. Again she sank. They came up together, spitting water, their drenched heads cresting above the churning waves.

The startled agents rushed to rescue the president. Paying no heed to their panicked shouts, Samantha forced her sister's head underwater again.

"Which one is the president?" shrieked Karen. She pulled off her shoes and ran to the edge.

Stephanie's head was back above the water. The girls, laughing, continued to spray and splash each other relentlessly.

"They're just being sisters," Catherine said.

"That new niece of yours is too competitive." Burnside whirled around to address her, annoyance in his tone. "Watch it, Samantha."

Samantha cocked her head and glared at him, her eyes registering the same hostility as her voice. "Do you think I'd hurt my sister? You're crazy."

Burnside shrugged and returned to his seat. "I'm just doing my job, ma'am."

Stephanie appeared uncomfortable. "I wouldn't expect anything else from my protective detail. He's a good agent."

"Sure," she scoffed. "I understand now. These guys just work for you. It's a job—that's all it is."

Stephanie's eyes took on a baffled cast. "These agents would die for me, Sam. Burnside could have been killed at the airfield. He protected me from the assassin by covering me with his body."

"He can get on top of me anytime."

Stephanie splashed her playfully.

They were both giggling as Dalton arrived, his footsteps echoing on the tile. Forgetting the conversation, Samantha put her chin on the edge of the pool and watched his hurried gait. He walked straight to Catherine and helped her out of the hot tub.

"Tell me about Dalton," Samantha asked Stephanie. "He's over here a lot."

"He's probably lonely. His wife and child died in a car crash a few years ago. Catherine likes him, I know."

Samantha treaded water as Stephanie stepped out of the pool.

"Interested?" Stephanie asked in a tired voice.

Samantha laughed. "I can do better. Come on, I'll race you to the other end."

"Not today. You wore me out." Stephanie breathed deeply. "I've got to get back to the White House."

Catherine donned a terrycloth robe and sat with the agents. "I want to talk to you girls before you leave," she called out.

Samantha climbed out of the water and the twins, dripping on the tiles, moved together like bookends towards the table.

"Your birthday is next week."

The twins exchanged excited smiles.

'I know you have a lot to do, Stephanie. Since you're here today, I thought I'd give you girls your gifts now, unless Stephanie can come back for Allison's three layer birthday cake."

She looked from niece to niece, her eyes revealing her uncertainty which woman was the president. Relief covered her face only when Samantha spoke.

"When is our birthday?" she asked. "I never knew."

As she awaited an answer, Samantha found herself staring at surprised faces. She couldn't overlook the sadness—or perhaps pity—in everyone's eyes.

Catherine reached out for her wet hand. "October 20."

"We'll be forty-five," Stephanie added. Her breathing still labored, she dropped into an empty chair and towel dried her hair.

Dalton stood and offered Samantha the seat next to Catherine, who still clung to her hand. Samantha allowed Catherine to pull her into the cool chair, shivering, while Dalton ran to fetch her some towels. Grateful, she released Catherine's hand and wrapped one towel like a turban around her long hair. A second one she draped like a blanket around her quivering shoulders.

Catherine pressed her warm palms against Samantha's cheek. "Ooh, you're like a block of ice!" She asked an agent to fetch Samantha some hot coffee from the bar. Karen returned promptly with a full Styrofoam cup.

Stephanie gasped, seeing a clump of blonde strands on the towel. "I'm losing my hair!"

"That can be caused by your thyroid," said Karen. "My mother took medicine for that."

"That would explain your lack of energy," Dalton added.

Catherine chimed in. "But wouldn't that have shown up in your last blood test?"

A slow shadow passed over Samantha's face. Stephanie had managed, as always, to steal the attention away.

Unaware of her pout, Catherine captured Burnside's gaze and waved him over. "Did you bring it?"

He dug into his pocket and handed Catherine the key to a new Jaguar.

"It's red," Catherine beamed. "It's parked by the kitchen."

Samantha's eyes lit up like fireworks. Her voice hit a jubilant squeal. "You're serious? For me?"

"I hope you have a Happy Birthday."

Samantha snatched the key from Catherine's hand. "Can I go drive it?" Not waiting for an answer, she scampered toward the kitchen.

A smiling Stephanie turned to her aunt. "I'd say she's happy, wouldn't you?"

They shared a laugh.

"She's like a child in a candy store. She's really quite delightful to watch," Catherine said. She reached into her purse for a velvet jewelry box. "Your gift is less extravagant, but more practical, Stephanie. Happy Birthday."

Inside the velvet-lined box was a gold pin embossed with the presidential seal.

"I had it handmade for you."

"I love it. I'll wear it every day!"

"You'd better. That way I can tell the two of you apart," Catherine laughed. As soon as the words escaped her lips, she realized it wasn't a joke.

Chapter 34

∼

Samantha stirred restlessly. In her dreams a woman emerged from a thick fog and trudged slowly to the end of a rackety dock. Her arms clung tightly to a curly headed child with a bloody rag wrapped around her tiny hand. The little girl's lavender dress was splattered with blood—perhaps too much for all of it to be the child's blood.

A fat Latin pinched her little cheek and she began to cry. Without hesitation, the woman handed her over to him, trading the girl for money. Then she hurried away. Left alone, the child began screaming, frightened by the cries of other children, and repelled by the rough grip of her captor.

There was a burst of light. The girl was now in the hull of a ship, sandwiched between two older children. She cried softly. As the ship rocked and pitched, a darkly clad man holding a flashlight slapped her and ordered her to stop crying. She stared up at his twisted brown face and cried some more. He hit her again.

Samantha screamed as she came up in the bed. Sweat spotted her face and neck and her throat was dry. Breathing heavily, she struggled to her feet and went into the bathroom to splash her face with water. As she dried off with a towel, she noticed her scarred right hand reflected in the mirror. She stared at it thoughtfully, pondering, while she wrapped herself in her robe.

As long as the vision of blood and terror plagued her mind, she knew that she would not sleep. A multitude of questions raced through her brain. Samantha sensed that what her mind had given her was not a dream but an actual memory. The realization snatched her breath away.

She wandered into the dark hallway and down the creaking stairs. From the entryway, she could hear a fire crackling in the sitting room. She strolled inside and stood for a moment in the dark, studying the portrait of Ian Taylor lit up by the flames in the fireplace. She continued her journey to the portable bar and poured herself a straight shot of bourbon.

"Hello."

Samantha jumped. Aunt Catherine leaned around the side of the wingback chair, watching her gulp down the drink. Samantha emitted a nervous laugh. "You scared me. What are you doing up?"

"I often sit by the fire when my arthritis bothers me. The warmth helps."

Samantha poured another drink and then settled by the fire. "I'm having dreams. This is the third tonight. It's all so strange. But I'm remembering things—I don't think they're just dreams."

"What are you remembering?"

"I think it's a war." She stroked her scarred hand. "I'm bleeding. I'm with a nurse or nanny. In the first dream, she protected me from men with guns. Tonight she gave me away to people in a boat. She told me not to cry, but I did. I cried a lot."

"That could explain how you survived the massacre." Catherine turned her gaze to the doorway. "This could be the last part of the puzzle, Dalton."

For the first time Samantha saw the security chief, his arms laden with logs for the fire.

"What are you doing here at three in the morning?" Samantha asked.

"Someone has to guard the two of you. It might as well be me."

Catherine smiled. "Dalton was kind enough to build up the fire for me. He often keeps me company on the bad nights."

Dalton strolled to the fire, now truncated to glowing embers, and laid one of the logs on top. "Do you remember if the twins had a nurse, Catherine?"

"Of course. There were lots of servants." She paused, as if trying to lift the curtain that separated past and present. "I still have Amanda's letters in the attic. Maybe you can find something up there."

Samantha's mouth felt surprisingly dry; her chest tightened. "It sounds like you're investigating me."

"I am. But it's standard procedure." His voice was demanding, not allowing dissent. "Anyone near the president has to be cleared. With the summit planned for next month—"

Something in Samantha's brain snapped. "Are you protecting *us* or protecting Aunt Catherine from *me*?"

"Nonsense, child. You're family." Catherine's voice held genuine concern. "I asked Dalton to put a rush on this, so your mother's estate could be settled. I want you to have your inheritance."

"I don't want you digging around in my past. There are things I'm not proud of."

Dalton and Catherine exchanged a glance, but it was long enough for Samantha to see a communication without words. She wasn't sure why she felt panic, but she did.

After a short pause, Catherine asked Dalton to bring her the family album from the bookshelf, and she flipped through the pages with Samantha.

Samantha was puzzled. "I've seen these pictures before, Auntie."

Catherine studied her with an intensity that disturbed her. "How do you feel about being part of such a distinguished family?"

"I feel cheated." Her tone was surprisingly bitter, but she made no effort to control it. "There was a life I should have had."

"Life isn't always fair, Samantha. I've felt cheated, too, by not having children. Your mother was cheated. She loved you and never knew you were alive."

Samantha fell silent. A sudden, flash of memory took her again into the past. She saw herself cowering beneath a pool table. With striking clarity she remembered the stinging pain in her bloody hand. Men with guns circled around the walls of the giant room, working in from the outside, allowing no chance of escape. People screamed and raced around the room, looking for a way out. A woman fell near the table, a crimson spot growing on the white bodice of her dress. The child covered her eyes and screamed.

At that moment she knew she was indeed Samantha Taylor.

"God wouldn't want you to be resentful," Catherine said softly.

"Since when does God care about me?"

Catherine's fingers curled around her shoulder. "God loves you no matter who you are. We all sin and God never stops loving us. Whether our sins are large or small, he helps us through the tough times."

Samantha was dumbfounded. She wasn't sure she even believed in God.

"Every family has a black sheep or two, Samantha," her aunt continued. "You won't hear me admitting this outside the family, but the Taylors have had our share of horse thieves and Confederate spies."

Samantha stared into Catherine's penetrating eyes. Uncomfortable, she glanced over at Dalton, who stood with arms crossed, a smug smile in his lips. Their faces gave them away.

Samantha moaned. "So you know. I had to live somehow." She swallowed nervously, remembering her agreement with Tony. "Don't blame Tony. He knew Steph couldn't handle the truth and I was afraid no one would accept me."

"We Taylors can handle lots of things."

Bitterness escaped from Samantha's lips again. "I sure had to."

Catherine's eyes searched Dalton's face. "Samantha obviously wants her file to be confidential—unless the president has to see it, of course."

Nodding, Dalton stoked up the fire. "She never sees the records unless there's a security problem. But I need to complete this file, Samantha."

She nodded. "It's not important to me. I know I'm Samantha."

Dalton strode towards the foyer. "I'll read those letters from the attic. If I get a name for the twins' nurse, I'll push the CIA to find out if she's still alive." He turned to gaze at Samantha. "Somehow you ended up in the hands of a Mexican pimp. Let's complete the puzzle."

"I don't see how that's possible. It's been forty years."

Catherine chuckled softly. "You underestimate the power of the Taylor family."

Chapter 35

New England's worst winter of the decade had reached out to capture even the Washingtonians in her icy grip. For two weeks traffic edged up the snow-laden streets, tires spinning, drivers peering through windshields into a pure white blanket. Now the snow was melting. Tree branches, once drooping from the weight of the storm, had now escaped their icy imprisonment.

From inside the White House, Stephanie noticed the snowdrifts, plentiful as they had been, had turned into little ponds. Outside the traffic had resumed its morning routine. The world, still white in shaded areas, shouted that life would go on as usual today.

Normally Stephanie would have joined the throngs outdoors, overjoyed to escape the prolonged isolation and to travel the streets once again. She always felt a psychological edge with the warming of the sun—but not today. After a few hours of vomiting into a White House toilet, she was weak and disheartened. She staggered slowly away from the window and lowered herself weakly back into bed.

Dr. Pierce arrived and placed her medical bag on the bed.

"Thanks for coming," Stephanie said. "I'm feeling worse. And look at this—I'm losing more hair." She indicated a small bald patch on the top of her head.

"I warned you it might happen," the doctor said. She checked the president's pulse. "Chemo does that."

"I've been telling everyone it's the stress. I had to order some wigs. I can't show my face looking like this."

The doctor patted her shoulder. "Try to stay calm." She went to the bathroom, filled a glass with water and handed it to Stephanie with a pill. "I'm going to help you through this."

She watched as Stephanie gulped down the tablet. "It's time to tell them, Stephanie."

"No. If I tell one person, before you know it the whole country will know. I have work to finish. Give me anything. Just get me on my feet so I can meet with the Wakembezians next week."

A light tap on the door interrupted them.

Samantha swept into the room. Seeing Stephanie, she froze. "You look awful."

Stephanie forced a slight smile. "Thanks."

"I want you in bed for several days," the doctor ordered. "I mean it. Rest."

"I'm supposed to visit a children's ward in the inner city today."

"Let someone else go," Dr. Pierce insisted. "What are vice presidents for?"

"I'll do it. Let me, Steph. I want to do it," Samantha offered, plopping down on an old trunk pushed against the wall.

Stephanie cringed. "Please don't sit there, Samantha. That trunk is priceless. It belonged to Eleanor Roosevelt."

Samantha popped up. Her eyes studied the oak trunk, decorated with shipping labels from the former first lady's travels. "If it's that valuable, you need to put a sign on it or something."

"It belongs in the Smithsonian," Stephanie answered. "Aunt Catherine purchased it at an auction in the 1960s. When I was elected, she had it shipped here. She thought it was appropriate for it to be on display with the other White House relics."

Samantha ran her palm over the leather strips that secured the lid. "Don't give it away, Steph. It belongs to us."

"I can't without Aunt Catherine's permission anyway."

Samantha shrugged and returned to the previous discussion. "You rest today, Steph. I'll go to the children's ward for you."

Stephanie gave her a feeble nod. "Thank you, Samantha."

In an instant, Samantha was gone.

"That's odd," muttered Dr. Pierce. "She never asked what was wrong with you."

* * *

A few hours later Dr. Pierce returned to check on Stephanie. The president, wrapped in a red wool robe, sat up in bed, propped against her pillows. She busily clicked through the TV channels with the remote control.

Debra wrapped the blood pressure cuff around Stephanie's arm. "Do you feel as good as you look?"

Stephanie forced a weak smile. Her eyes settled for the afternoon news.

The anchor reported on the president's visit to the Rainbow Children's Center. The camera followed Samantha and her security guards as they made rounds in the hospital. Looking regal in a teal suit, she made her way to a recreation room decorated for a Valentine's Day party. There she hugged the children who flocked to her arms.

"They don't seem to know that's not me," Stephanie uttered, her eyes glued to the TV.

A montage of pictures appeared, each image quickly replaced by another. Samantha embraced a tiny tot with a brace on his leg. She pushed a girl in a wheelchair and handed out valentines and candy to bedridden children. In a close-up, Stephanie saw the gold presidential pin on Samantha's lapel.

"How did she get my pin?" She stared at the doctor with shocked eyes.

Before Debra could speculate, Samantha bounced into the bedroom. She flopped on the bed, grinning like a child who had tasted ice cream for the first time. "I had a great time!"

"So it seems," Stephanie answered, visibly annoyed. "I saw *me* on the news."

Samantha's joyous face crumbled into a sheepish grin. "Did I do something wrong?"

It was the worst attempt at pleading innocence the doctor had ever seen.

Stephanie's pressure rose like a rocket. "Why did you pretend to be me?"

"I thought that's what you wanted me to do." Samantha gazed at the two puzzled faces and blurted out a defense. "Do you want people to know how sick you are? There was press everywhere. Why panic Americans?"

Stephanie cringed. "You're right about that. I guess I should be thanking you for helping me."

"Anytime. I had fun." Her eyes took on a far off glaze. "I felt what you must feel every time you mingle with the people. You're fortunate to have such love, Steph." She blew her sister a kiss and danced out the door.

Debra pursued her down the corridor. "Samantha!" she called, "Wait a minute."

Samantha whipped around, her eyes puzzled.

The hallway was empty, so Debra talked openly. "Sam, I've watched you for months. You've changed your hair, your eye color, your style of clothes—"

Samantha interrupted, a territorial edge to her voice. "I'm a Taylor now."

"More precisely, you're a twin now."

"Well, what of it?"

"Even twins have their own identities, Sam."

Samantha's eyes shot daggers. "What are you doing, psychoanalyzing me?"

"I have the name of a colleague I'd like you to talk to—"

Samantha exploded. "Why would I need a shrink?"

All of a sudden a maid appeared, carrying a vase of roses into the president's bedroom. Afraid she had heard the outburst, the doctor seized Samantha's arm and pulled her into another bedroom. "It's very normal to be proud of a sister who has accomplished what Stephanie has. But you seem to want to be her."

"You just don't understand twins," Samantha challenged her.

Debra inhaled. "You need to return the presidential pin that you took from Stephanie's jewelry box."

Samantha's jaw locked. She dug into her pocket and slapped the pin into the doctor's waiting hand.

"I want the very best for your sister. I need to know that you do too." Debra waited for a reply, but received none. "Did you tell the security men with you that you were the president?"

Samantha turned and left without answering. The doctor remained standing in the long corridor, watching a troubled woman make a further escape from reality.

Chapter 36

The sun streamed into the Oval Office, coating the carpet with its rays. Roberta and Stephanie sat together, chief of staff and president planning the week ahead, when Roberta asked unexpectedly, "When are you going to take a vacation?"

Stephanie, who had worked flat out since becoming president, had repeatedly delayed her holidays. When Tony left for Cancun, she spent two weeks with her aunt and Samantha on the Taylor estate. It wasn't a vacation really, because she ran the nation from there. When her stay in Maryland was finally over, she found herself more tired than rested.

"I worry what the newspapers will say if I go without Tony. I have enough negative press as it is. I don't want them speculating about my marriage."

Roberta's eyes drilled her with questions, but she didn't ask the obvious. "Why don't you take off somewhere with Samantha?"

Stephanie hesitated. "I'll think about that."

Her hesitation was difficult to explain. Of late she had experienced tension whenever she was around Samantha—something Stephanie couldn't put into words.

She felt her energy failing more and more each day. She had accepted that she was dying, and wanted to make the most of the time she had left. She aspired to leave a legacy of peace behind.

"If you're not going anywhere, why don't you work out five days a week?" suggested her chief of staff. "Can you squeeze that into your schedule?"

"Certainly." She lied, sure she wouldn't have the energy.

"I'm glad you're doing this, Madam President. You've been looking...frail."

Stephanie's brow netted. "You think so?"

"I mention it out of concern. I hope I didn't hurt your feelings."

Stephanie finger-combed an unruly strand of wig behind her ear. "It's the truth. Don't ever apologize for telling me the truth."

Roberta shuffled through a pile of papers. "Oh, dear."

The president waited.

She swallowed hard. "Do you want the good news or the bad news first?"

To Stephanie, the choices seemed magnified, even threatening. She felt like someone asked her to walk through a minefield. "Just say it outright."

"We have received a letter from Bantu Sibaba. He says he's not coming to the peace summit."

Stephanie moaned. "We need him here." She wondered if he was punishing her for hanging up on him.

"He says he never leaves Wakembezi. But he's sending his vice chairman."

Stephanie took the letter from Roberta's outstretched hand, read it, and paused to consider. "That will be okay. At least he shows some interest. If his representative is here, my critics won't have any reason to worry about a rift between us."

"Maybe you can get Sibaba to change his mind."

"Is that the good news?"

"No. We've had acceptances from nine counties that have nuclear weapons."

Stephanie smiled. It was hope that kept her going.

Chapter 37

After months of meticulous planning, the small delegation from Wakembezi arrived. Vice President Chang and a group from their embassy greeted them. The U.S. Marine Band played their national anthem as Vice Chairman Udo Wasswa strolled with Chang on a red carpet leading to the microphones. There were speeches about each country's respect for each other. Little was said about the missing president, except she was recuperating from a virus. Everyone assumed it was protocol for one vice president to greet the other. Afterwards the foreign visitors were ushered around the city on a tour of the nation's capital.

That next evening Stephanie greeted Wasswa and all the visiting delegates at a ball in their honor in the State Dining Room. She wore a beaded and sequined white silk chiffon evening gown, hoping the folds of fabric flowing from the empire waist hid her tiny waistline and her recent loss of weight. Tonight she had refused to dress like her twin, telling a disappointed Samantha that it would not be appropriate at a government function where the president was the hostess.

When Samantha arrived, she looked sophisticated and chic in a lime green floor-length gown with an alluring halter neck. Immediately half a dozen men surrounded her, vying for her attention.

At present, Stephanie danced a slow waltz with Vice Chairman Wasswa. As they floated across the room, he complimented her on her remarkable command of the Swahili language.

"I lived among your people for ten years, you know."

"When I talk to everyone else, I have a translator to help me," he said, pointing out a young man in a gray suit. He had turned his chair around, his back to the table where the rest of his delegation had clustered.

"I noticed him. He's very devoted," Stephanie said. "Is he a bodyguard too? He hasn't taken his eyes off you."

Wasswa chuckled. "No, my lady, it's you he's watching." The music ended and they clapped politely before the vice chairman continued. "He hasn't stopped talking about you all day. Come." He led her by the arm to his countrymen.

The young man with mahogany eyes smiled. He stood to greet the president and kiss her hand. "Lady Stephanie, it is good to see you," he said in perfect English.

She eyed him inquisitively. "Are you enjoying your stay in our country?" His smile reminded her of someone, but she couldn't remember who.

"Yes. We saw lots of monuments today," the translator answered. "One for Lincoln. Another for Washington. Will you have a monument too?"

"Of me? Because I'm president?" She laughed, but paused to contemplate the possibility. "That's flattering, but I think you have to be dead first."

At that moment Tony joined them. Clutching his hand, she began the introductions. "This is my husband Tony Franklin—"

"She doesn't recognize you," the vice chairman said to his translator in their native tongue.

Stephanie spun around. Her eyes pierced the face of the man, whom she guessed was little more than a teenager. "Who's this? What is your name?" she asked, lapsing into Swahili.

He offered a familiar smile. "Tumelo Rudo. You always called me Ruddy."

Surprised and overjoyed, she hugged him. "My goodness, little Ruddy, after all these years." Excited, she tugged at Tony's coat sleeve. "This young man was thirteen years old last time I saw him. He's Bantu Sibaba's nephew."

Tony and Ruddy shook hands. Then Ruddy turned his attention back to Stephanie. "Because you taught me English, I have a nice job traveling with government officials."

"I'm pleased it worked out for you."

Wasswa interrupted her and requested that they not converse in English.

Stephanie complied. "What a nice surprise," she said. "Ruddy, can you stay in the White House with me? We can catch up." She stopped, seeing Wasswa shaking his head. "Of course, the vice chairman needs you to translate. But I hope to see more of you while you're here."

Stephanie noticed that Tony had slipped away to converse with a group of senators.

"I think we drove my husband away because we weren't speaking English," Stephanie remarked. She felt dizzy. "Let's go sit and talk some more."

Chapter 38

While Stephanie and Ruddy caught up on the lost years, Cheri pranced off the elevator and through the pressroom. She had written her article on the flight from NYC, after borrowing a laptop from another passenger. Now she headed to her desk, slipped the CD into the computer, and printed the manuscript. Spotting Ed Marrow returning to his office, she sent the file to his computer, seized the pages and followed him there, arriving in time to prevent him from closing his door.

"Read this," she said, proud of her undercover work. "I've got an exclusive on Stephanie Franklin's sister."

He skimmed the first paragraph and handed the article back to her. "Cheri, this vendetta has to stop. You're beginning to look foolish."

"I sell newspapers, Ed."

"I won't deny that. But Dr. Debra Pierce's lawsuit has changed things. I told you last week to lay off the president and write about someone else."

"This is about her sister."

"That's the same thing and you know it."

"You're not letting me tell you what I did."

He sat on the edge of his desk, his arms folded.

"I shadowed a FBI agent to New York. He found the nurse of the Taylor twins when they lived in Columbia. Imagine, she's still alive and living in the States!"

"I expected you at the meeting this morning," Ed said bluntly. "I wanted you there. I'm not paying expresses for a trip I never approved."

"Are you listening to me, Ed?"

"We won't print anything without solid proof."

"It was a good tip. I had to check it out."

Ed breathed a sigh. "Look Cheri, I've always liked your spunk. You write exciting stories that sell papers. But you have to let go of this. Whatever is going on with you is about to cost you your job."

Cheri frowned. "I see."

"I'm just the editor, Cheri. I've been told no more stories on the president unless you have a verified source." Ed sat behind his desk. "Lay off! I'm not going to lose my job over your stupidity."

"But I've got strong proof! I've got my interview of the nurse on tape. I took pictures on my cell of her talking to the FBI investigator."

"The president is very powerful." Ed warned through gritted teeth. "Why do you hate her so much, Cheri?"

Cheri's head dropped for only a second, but when she raised her eyes again, they were damp with tears. "My boyfriend saved the president's life and what did he get for it? The president's bodyguards blew him away!"

Her voice grew louder. Ed rushed to close the door as Cheri's outburst rose to a crescendo. "What did Madam President do? She showed up for five minutes and gave Manny's parents a dumb, meaningless medal that's supposed to whitewash a Secret Service blunder!"

She wiped tears from her cheek with her palm. By then Ed had fumbled in a desk drawer and found a tissue box. She blew her nose as he placed his hand lightly on her shoulder. "Cheri, this has got to come to an end. I'm putting you on a two week vacation."

"No," she protested, "not with the summit going on."

"Someone else can cover that. You need a rest."

She gripped her hands into fists. "I'm not backing down from the best story of my life. If you don't want this, I'll sell it to someone else—and you'll miss the biggest scoop of the year."

Ed's eyebrows knitted. He picked up the article again and read silently. "Samantha Taylor was sold as a child into prostitution? You can prove that?"

She handed him the cassette tape.

"Okay," he said at last. "If the guys in legal approve this, we'll run it."

Chapter 39

∼

The next morning *Scoop*'s headlines sold a record number of papers.

"Lady Sam was a Prostitute!"

The banner shouted Cheri's discovery in bold, black letters. The picture of the agent and the nurse covered two columns.

Someone at the embassy handed the tabloid to Vice Chairmen Wasswa while he ate breakfast. Willy saw it in a rack at a gas station and shared it with Senator Lowe. Vice President Chang was already in his office when a staff member arrived with the tabloid. York Benson snatched it up in the supermarket, while Dalton Mercer read it in the barbershop.

At the White House, Adam overheard the secretaries talking about it with Dalton.

"Do you think it's true?" Nancy asked. "*Scoop* makes up things."

"They have a picture. And they quote Samantha's nurse." Dawn glued her eyes to the tabloid. "Either way, this will embarrass President Franklin."

"I checked the FBI report. It's true," Dalton said.

Adam hurried towards them. "What does it say?"

Nancy stared at him with skeptical eyes. "Samantha's nurse saved her during the embassy massacre. Then she sold her into child prostitution."

Adam moaned deep in his throat like a dying animal, snatched the paper away from Nancy, and went to find Stephanie.

In Maryland Aunt Catherine was enjoying lunch with Samantha when Timothy Burnside told them about the article.

Samantha's reaction surprised them. "That should singe what's left of Steph's hair," she snickered.

"Why are you behaving like this?" Catherine asked. "You know how much the *Scoop* stories upset her."

"She was bound to find out," Samantha scoffed, finishing her coffee.

Catherine looked at Burnside. "Are the facts right?"

"Your niece is the one to tell you." He moved behind Samantha and placed the tabloid on the table beside her. She read it and simply shrugged.

Burnside rubbed his chin. "It says the nurse talked to a FBI investigator before Cheri Eastley interviewed her."

"Ask Dalton to see if there's something else the family should know."

Burnside nodded and waited.

"One of us needs to talk to Stephanie." Catherine's eyes focused on Samantha's face.

Samantha pushed away from the table. "You mean me, of course. Okay, I'll go see her." She glanced out the window at her Jaguar in front of the house. "I'll drive us, Tim. Come on. I'm not facing her alone."

"Stephanie is going to be mad at me too, for not telling her the truth," Catherine said. "But she needs to understand that we all wanted to protect her."

The remark didn't register with Samantha. She hurried through the arch, across the foyer, and outside to her Jaguar. Burnside was close behind.

They were doing 50 mph before they left the drive.

Burnside gripped the dash. "Slow down, Samantha."

She pushed the pedal to the floor. "Who's going to give the sister of the president a ticket?"

* * *

After reaching the White House, Burnside and Samantha made their way through the halls amid a barrage of stares and whispers. Unnerved by the cool reception, Burnside deposited Samantha in the president's chambers and went to find Dalton.

Alone, Samantha busied herself by stuffing her hair inside one of Stephanie's wigs. She stared into the mirror at Stephanie's image staring back at her, and broke into an imaginary conversation with her sister.

"So I'm a whore. Live with it."

She mocked Stephanie in a prudish voice. "That really wasn't a proper way to live, Samantha."

"It was fun, though."

"You're not sorry?"

"No. I had lots of men in love with me."

"Are you at least sorry that you ruined my political career?"

"Come on, Steph. Isn't Washington filled with people prostituting themselves for political gain?"

Samantha threw herself on the bed and laughed hysterically.

Chapter 40

With the *Scoop* article in his hand, Adam journeyed in search of Stephanie. After checking the Oval Office and the chapel, he texted her. "Where are you?"

No response.

He wondered if Stephanie was hiding somewhere, feeling humiliated. Lately she had been disappearing for hours at a time, sometimes with Dr. Pierce. Now, because Stephanie was unreachable, he felt helpless and unsure what to do.

As he passed a conference room, two of the president's image consultants ambushed him.

"Have you seen President Franklin?" the senator from Indiana asked, backing Adam against the wall. "We want to talk to her about this." He waved the malicious article in his chubby hand.

"I don't know, sir. I can't find her either."

"Did she see the article?" asked the female senator.

"I don't know. As I said, I haven't talked to her."

"It sounds like she saw it and went into seclusion."

Adam cleared his throat, unsure what to say.

The woman's eyes flashed. "People are known by the company they keep. You tell her to send her sister back to Mexico."

Adam glanced at his watch and lied. "I have another meeting. I'll tell the president about your concerns."

He escaped around the corner, hurried to the White House, and climbed the stairs to Stephanie's private chambers. Finding the living room was empty, he moved slowly towards the bedroom, dimly lit by a light reflecting from the walk-in closet. Cautious, he peeked inside.

"Steph?" He saw Samantha standing in the closet. She modeled a fur coat in front of a full-length mirror. Mistaking her for Stephanie, he asked, "Going out?"

She didn't answer, only floated toward him. He could see her face clearly from the light streaming from the sitting area. She smiled, something she had not done for weeks. He guessed she had not seen the article. "You need to read this," he said, indicating the tabloid.

"I saw it."

"I talked with Dalton. He said the story is true. What do you want to do?"

"Why don't we let Dalton handle things?" Samantha leaned closer, nuzzling her lips against his neck.

He stiffened. "Steph—what are you doing?"

She pressed against him and he felt her breath on his face. "Anyone can see the way you look at me. I want you too. Tell me you love me. Tell me."

"I love you. I've always loved you, Steph."

Rooting fingers in his hair, she grinned up at him until his eyes grew misty. "We've waited too long. Come to bed."

Adam hesitated, glancing at the door. "But Tony—"

Samantha tossed the coat away and curled up on the satin sheets. "Forget about Tony. We're over. I've filed for divorce."

He believed it was true. Stephanie would never cheat on her marriage.

"Tony never deserved you," he said, advancing towards the bed.

Framing her face in his hands, he kissed her gently at first. Soon the kisses became intense and passionate. He had waited for this—dreamed of it. The pent-up desire of ten years burrowed through him.

"Are you sure about this?" he gasped in breathless anticipation.

She answered by removing her skirt and blouse. "Shhhh. Just love me."

He heard a whimper of alarm in the doorway. He shifted his gaze to see Stephanie, a silhouette with the light behind her.

Her voice hit a high pitch. "Samantha—in my bed!" She switched on the overhead light.

Adam jumped away from the bed, alarmed. "Samantha?" He stared down at her scarred right hand.

Samantha smirked at Stephanie. "You once said we'd share everything."

Adam's face twisted up in shock. "I'm sorry, Steph. This is humiliating."

"It certainly is," Stephanie replied, glaring at Samantha.

"You don't understand. I thought she was you. She let me think she was you!"

Stephanie stared at him. He watched awareness crawl into her eyes as she realized for the first time the depth of his feelings.

Samantha was no longer smiling. "Quit blubbering, Adam. You'd think I raped you."

Stephanie threw Samantha's clothes at her. "Get out!"

"I was just having a good time."

"At my expense," Adam snarled.

"I want you out of here!" Stephanie fought tears. "You're everything the tabloid says you are!"

Samantha giggled as she slipped on her shoes. "Where am I supposed to go? Oh, I know—I'll walk the streets. I'll start with Pennsylvania Avenue!" Garments bunched in her arms, she stalked out the door without looking back.

Stephanie slumped on a sofa and the tears flowed. "She lives to embarrass me. I wish they'd never found her."

Adam sat next to her, unable to talk. At last he put his arm loosely around her. "I feel terrible about what happened. I'm sorry."

"I blame her." She gave him a careless pat. "I still love you."

Adam seized her hand. "Don't make light of it. When I say it, I mean it."

Stephanie flinched and he released her.

"I wish I could say what you want to hear. There's no future for us, Adam."

"What future do you have with Tony?"

"None." Stephanie's voice softened. "I care about you more than you could possibly know. The truth is hard."

Puzzlement stabbed at reason. "What's going on, Steph?"

She took a slow breath. "I have leukemia. I don't have much time."

The news landed like a lightning bolt. He held her tighter.

"I'm having chemo in secret," she said softly.

"Is that where you were today?"

"Yes." She turned to him with an urgent expression. "I'm dealing with it pretty well. I can even handle dying. I worry more about what the newspapers are saying. I don't want to go down in history as a lousy president."

He tried to remain stoic, but his voice cracked. "Steph—"

She set her jaw. "Please, Adam. Be strong for me. I'm having a hard enough time as it is with Sam around."

"I'll have security lock her up somewhere or send her back to Cancun."

"No. Somehow, I'll have to forgive her for what just happened. I need to walk carefully around her. Doctor Pierce says I might be saved by a bone marrow transplant."

His jaw dropped with the weight of hope. "Yes! You've got to do that."

"Sam hasn't agreed yet to help me. After what just happened, she probably never will."

Adam sat silently, unable to talk. Finally, she buried her head in his chest, crying uncontrollably.

"This is the worst day of my life," she moaned.

Mine too, he thought.

Chapter 41

As she entered the sitting room, Catherine's gaze fell on the fireplace, where a healthy fire crackled and spit. The heat beckoned her aching limbs, so she parked herself in her usual wingback chair, near the sofa that held Dr. Pierce and Samantha. She kept wondering about this mysterious gathering in her home.

Allison, the housekeeper, brought them tea on a silver tray. She offered the doctor a cup as Tony breezed through the archway.

He greeted Catherine with a squeeze of her hand. "It's nice to be here again." He took a cup of tea and two lumps of sugar. "What's this about, Catherine?"

"It's my doing, Tony," Dr. Pierce said. "I could have talked to you at the White House, but I wanted to see the three of you together."

Catherine motioned for Allison to leave.

"Please make sure no one's in the foyer," Dr. Pierce called after her.

Placing his cup on the coffee table, Tony strolled to the arch and peered out. "Why so serious?" he asked the doctor when he returned.

She took a deep breath. "Let me start by saying the president knows nothing about this—and what I'm doing is a breach of my confidentiality agreement with her. I've asked to see you because you're her family and you need to know…She's dying."

Catherine gasped. Tony, his face twisted up in surprise, flopped on the sofa next to Samantha.

"What is it, Doctor?" Catherine asked.

"Leukemia. We've known for six months. But she swore me to secrecy. She was afraid of the media at first, and we thought we had her in remission until recently. She wanted to run for reelection—which now will most probably be impossible." She paused. She eyed Samantha warily, and scooted closer to her. "When you were found, it changed everything. You are, of course, the perfect donor for a bone marrow transplant."

"Because I'm a twin, you mean?"

"I've told her time and time again that we need to get the two of you into the hospital."

Samantha squirmed in her chair. "You mean the day I first came here—when she accepted me so easily—she was planning this operation?"

"Now don't get the wrong idea. She's not like that."

Catherine's stomach dropped in a sick free fall. She fought tears. "Samantha, you can save her life."

Samantha fell silent. Her lips parted slightly but no words escaped. She stalked to the window and stood there in profile, shifting her weight from one foot to the other.

Catherine's pale eyes locked on her. *Why is she hesitating*? Icy fear raced through her. Behind her niece, through the windowpane, her elderly eyes caught sight of snowflakes swirling out of the sky. It occurred to Catherine that Samantha's heart was as cold the world outside.

Doctor Pierce turned to Tony. "Stephanie didn't want you to come back to her because she was ill."

He nodded, seemingly upset.

Catherine's eyes burrowed into him. When she dug beyond the surface, lifting his layers of deceit, what she saw was a grief-stricken actor's face. She wondered, *Am I the only one besides the doctor who really cares*?

"She refused hospitalization because she doesn't want the news leaked," the doctor continued. "She had chemo in secret. She wants to finish her term in office, but I'm worried about her now. Really worried. I've pumped her up with experimental drugs for weeks to keep her going."

Samantha turned from the window to see everyone staring at her. "I won't do it," she said with a stubborn jaw.

Catherine's brow lifted in reprimand. "Samantha!"

"I'm not a pound of beef to be carved up."

"This is your sister we're talking about. Have you forgotten what it means to be a Taylor?" Catherine scolded.

Samantha avoided eye contact.

The doctor was insistent, but gentle. "There's nothing to be afraid of, Samantha. It doesn't hurt. These days, we lure stem cells out of the bone marrow by a regimen of drugs. Your blood will be filtered through a machine and the cells skimmed off."

Samantha's lips pressed together defiantly. "I don't like hospitals."

Dr. Pierce sighed. "Frankly, Stephanie was afraid of this. That's why she has never asked this of you. I know you two have had your problems of late, but she's going to die unless you do this."

Samantha hesitated. "I've got to think about it," she said at last.

"Stephanie would walk off a cliff if it meant saving you," Catherine said.

"She's not me."

Catherine's gaze shifted to the doctor. "I've heard patients can use their own stem cells."

"We've already tried that."

Catherine's eyes locked on her niece. She waited.

Dr. Pierce tried another approach. "Surgery has to be delayed until after the summit anyway. The president is determined to solve this thing with Wakembezi first. Before the transplant, Stephanie must receive high-dose chemotherapy and radiation therapy to destroy leukemic cells. That will make her too sick to negotiate, so she chooses to wait."

She paused, scanned the dismayed faces in the room, and turned again to Samantha. "Do you think you can make a decision by the beginning of next month?"

No answer.

Catherine fingered her cane nervously. "If you don't do this, Samantha, I will disinherit you."

"Come on, Catherine," Tony laughed. "Sam got a huge inheritance from her mother. This isn't about money."

"No, it's about family."

"What do we do, Doctor?" Tony asked. "Do we tell Stephanie what we know?"

"Well, that's what I planned when I called us together. I feel Stephanie needs your support. But now, if Samantha isn't going to help—"

"I said I'd *think* about it." Samantha turned again to stare at the white blanket outside.

Chapter 42

∼

The next day Tony decided to meet Macy at a recreation area near Luray, Virginia. Agent Ted Vincent pulled off the road near a picnic table. He and Dan Baker, the other half of the Secret Service detail, waited outside the government car, while Tony completed his disguise.

Tony changed into jeans and a heavy flannel shirt. As usual, he had with him the baseball cap to obscure his face, but today, he decided to add facial hair. Looking into the mirror on his visor, he glued a fake mustache to his upper lip. It was quite the monstrosity—bushy and broad, with its ends sweeping upward. With the cap on his head and the monstrous mustache stroking his cheeks, Tony looked a lot like baseball pitcher Rollie Fingers.

He stepped out into the cool air. "Wait here," he told them.

"No, sir," said Agent Vincent. "We're supposed to stay close."

Tony frowned. "It's the off season. There's hardly anyone here."

Vincent scratched the side of his nose. "I'm aware that you've cut agents loose in the past, but I follow regulations."

A moment passed, gazes clashing. "What would you call an agent who ignores a direct order?" Tony demanded, teeth clenched.

Vincent poked his glasses higher on the bridge of his nose and said nothing.

"Fired!" Tony told him. "Then you'll really be cut loose."

Vincent's gaze didn't waver. Tony felt stumped. He reminded himself to get Bobbitt and Stein back on his protective team.

Tony swung around and headed towards the lake with the agents keeping up.

He hid a sigh. "I'm meeting Macy." He dropped on a bench under a tree. "Can't you guys step back and give me some privacy?"

A solemn frown wrinkled Vincent's raisin-dark face. He turned and waited for Baker to answer.

Tony sensed a weakness. "Come on, Baker. Can't we do what we did in Cancun?"

Baker's voice filled with chilly authority. "Okay, but you need to stay where we can see you at all times. That's Dalton's orders."

Tony gritted his teeth. "Great. Dalton is trying to ruin my sex life."

Vincent purchased hot chocolate for Tony at a nearby concession stand, and the three waited together in silence at the picnic table. When Macy arrived, the agents retreated twenty yards away.

Tony barely recognized Macy with her hair tied up in pigtails. She wore a floppy, oversized plaid shirt, an aqua jacket, and pink tennis shoes. Tony laughed. "Hey, beautiful."

"You don't look like Prince Charming either," she teased, her eyes focusing on his upper lip. "Promise me you'll never grow a mustache like that."

He laughed. "Come here." He gave her a long kiss. "I've missed us together."

"Me too."

He spoke in a near whisper. "It won't be long now. Stephanie is dying."

Her eyes gleamed. "What are you doing, poisoning her?"

He chuckled. "No, I'm going to let God take care of it."

Macy breathed heavily, visibly puzzled.

Nearby Tony noticed two teens returning a paddleboat. "Perfect for privacy," he said. "Let's lose these guys."

He tossed his empty cup in a tall garbage can and they darted to the boat. He glanced over his shoulder to see his protective detail running to catch up.

"It won't take them long to find another boat," Tony said. "Paddle fast."

They jumped into the boat and traveled into the middle of the pond before he spoke again. "Doctor Pierce says Stephanie has leukemia. It's perfect. I sit back and wait, she dies, and I inherit."

"How long, Tony? I'm tired of being without you."

"I don't know. She's very sick. Dr. Pierce wants Samantha to give her stem cells for a transplant. That seems to be Steph's only chance."

Macy frowned. "You can't leave this to chance, Tony."

"The transplant will probably kill her," he whispered, ducking his head as another paddleboat passed by. "Besides, Samantha refuses to be a donor."

"You can't leave this to Samantha. She's flaky. She might change her mind."

"I know. Sometimes I wonder how stable she is."

"Amanda Taylor's will was probated weeks ago. When is Samantha going to give you your cut of the money?"

"I'll be very rich anyway when Steph dies."

"That's not the point. You trusted Samantha to honor her promise. She didn't. She's not dependable."

After silence reached its limit, Macy cleared her throat. "Samantha knows too much about us, Tony. What if she gets Stephanie to change her will? She could end up with all of it." She paused briefly for Tony to absorb her words. Then came a bold proclamation: "I think we should have it all."

Tony, continuing to paddle, chuckled to himself. "Aren't you wicked!"

Macy rubbed her hand on his leg. "There's a dump of a motel up the street."

"We can't afford to take any chances now, Macy. We'll be together soon."

Glancing cautiously around, Macy opened her purse, revealing a gun.

"Take it, Tony. You've got to get rid of Samantha."

Tony frowned. "Put that away."

"If Stephanie dies, Samantha will inherit part of what's yours. Do you want that?"

Tony fell silent. He watched his bodyguards paddling towards them with a procured boat.

Macy slammed her purse shut. "If you can't do it, I'll handle it," she declared through gritted teeth.

Tony sighed. As always, she was determined to have her way.

Chapter 43

~

While Philip Lowe hunted a good book in his library, his wife came into the room to tidy up the clutter of newspapers and empty the mounds in the ashtrays. When he stuck a cigar in his mouth, she exiled him to the outdoors, reminding him not to smoke in the house.

Now he sat at a picnic table on his lower deck, bundled up in a fleece-lined jacket and puffing the cigar. After a few minutes, Willy opened the patio door and joined him. Lowe offered him a cigar from the pocket of his coat.

Still standing, Willy lit it and puffed heavily. "Is this from Cuba?"

"Sure. I have my ways of getting what I want."

As Willy leaned against the wooden rail, enjoying the aroma and the flavor, he noticed a red Jaguar coming up the drive. "You've got a visitor," he said, pointing out the fast moving sports car.

The driver parked, waved, and exited the vehicle. As she approached, the presidential pin glinted in the sun like a big chunk of gold on her crimson collar.

Lowe beamed. Stephanie had come to her senses at last. Excited that his banishment was finally over, he tried to stand, but arthritis pain anchored him to his seat.

He welcomed her with a smile as she slid onto the bench across from him.

"What a pleasant surprise, Madam President. This is Willy. He's my bodyguard." He shifted to a businesslike tone. "What can I do for you, Stephanie?"

"I'm not Stephanie," said the woman wearing the presidential crest. "I'm Samantha."

Lowe's eyes pierced her face. "Of course. Stephanie wouldn't have come—and certainly not without the Secret Service." He feigned a casual nonchalance, although her deceit irritated him. He would not allow her to know how foolish he felt that she had tricked him. "What can I do for you, Samantha?"

A smile tipped her lips. "I've heard a lot about you."

Lowe sneered. "Oh, really? Don't believe everything Stephanie says." He sipped his coffee, eyeing Samantha over the cup. She was an exact replica of her twin, but there was a hardness that he never detected in Stephanie. "I've heard about you too. People say you and Stephanie are exactly alike, except for one thing." He leaned close. "Show me."

Samantha removed her glove and laid her scarred hand on the table. "Did you think I was Stephanie playing games?"

"Just being careful." He paused and asked again, "Why are you here, Samantha?"

Her face was serious. "I'm not going to mix words with you. I understand you want to be president. So do I." She pointed at the presidential pin. "It's a copy I ordered from Catherine's jeweler. Looks good on me, don't you think?"

Lowe's eyes became tiny slits. "Go on."

"I'll be your figurehead president for you. You want to run the country, so run the country. I could care less. Just let me finish Stephanie's term. You can rule the world as far as I care."

The elderly senator was not prone to making impulsive decisions. He asked Willy to pour Samantha a cup of coffee. He sat in thoughtful contemplation while his bodyguard lumbered into the kitchen and returned with a steaming mug.

Lowe fingered the rim of his cup. "What do you intend to do about Stephanie?"

"She'll be dead in a matter of months. Leukemia." She accepted the cup Willy offered her. "Her doctor wants me to give her my stem cells, but I'm not going to."

Lowe studied her with an intense stare. "You're hard as nails, Samantha."

She spoke through gritted teeth. "I feel nothing for her. I was raised the daughter of a whore; her mother left me to die."

Lowe took another puff on the cigar, considering the possibilities. "What if I don't want to wait months for her to die?"

"Whatever. You're the boss. Handle it anyway you want."

"Do you think you can fool the people who know her best?"

"I've been playing games with them for months. I fooled you, didn't I?"

"I like your openness, Samantha." Lowe paused to ponder the possibility. "We'll have to switch you before it's obvious she's ill. Who else knows about the leukemia?"

"Her husband and Aunt Catherine."

"No staff? No one else?"

"Doctor Pierce has kept it very quiet. Stephanie didn't want people to know."

Lowe downed a big gulp of his coffee. "Do you expect me to believe you're going to be happy being in the spotlight for just a little while?"

"If things had happened differently in Colombia, Steph would have been the one left behind and I'd be president today. I want the lost years back. I want everything she's ever had—her position, her money, and even her husband—for a while."

"You don't want to run the nation?"

"No."

As he stared into her earnest eyes, he believed she could actually pull it off. "No problem. I'll contact you." He offered her his hand without struggling to stand.

As the two men watched Samantha return to her car, Lowe felt a surprising admiration for her. "I like her spunk and her cooperative spirit, Willy. Things would be different today if Stephanie were like that."

Willy stood, hands crossed, silently waiting for his instructions.

"Forget about shooting the president," Lowe said at last. "I think Samantha's plan may be the safer way. The doctor must die, of course, and anyone who knows too much."

"How fast do you want it done?"

"Fast."

Chapter 44

Samantha shoved one hand through her hair and moaned, trying to clear the cobwebs from her brain. Where was she? She couldn't remember how she got here.

Gradually she became aware of her pounding head and an odd taste in her mouth. She lay on something flat and thin, with sheets. Her back was stiff and her hip was sore, as if she had been clobbered with a sharp hammer.

Hugging the sheet for warmth, she forced herself to focus on her surroundings. At first everything was foggy and she drifted in and out of sleep. Finally she woke with the nasty thought that she'd like to hit somebody.

Adam was the first one she saw. He sat in an armchair by the door.

Then she remembered.

She had been at the Taylor mansion, listening to rock music, when the phone rang. At first she left it for the housekeeper, but when it rang several more times, she scooped up the receiver.

"Samantha?" It was Adam's husky voice.

"Yes." She steeled herself for his usual tongue-lashing.

"I need to see you. It's urgent."

"What's going on?"

"Do I have to spell it out for you? I'm excited just talking to you."

Samantha smiled. She had that effect on men. "Where are you?"

"At my office."

She had dashed to her Jag. She didn't remember the drive to the White House. Nor did she know how she got into this bed. However, she did recall Adam escorting her to the West Wing. She closed her eyes again and let the memory return.

She had come here to meet Adam. She found him standing by the door to the reception area. Her heart pounding, she had hurried towards him, expecting him to grope her without delay. Instead, he had given her a quick kiss and whisked her down the hall towards the elevator.

"Where are we going?" she giggled.

"To my office."

"Are you going to be a bad boy?" she teased.

He grinned. "Oh, yes. I'm going to be very bad."

She put her arm around his waist as they strolled in the direction of the Oval Office. Adam steered her to the first room on the right. The moment they stepped inside, Samantha knew something was wrong; it looked more like a doctor's office than the workspace of a press secretary.

Inside Dr. Pierce waited next to an examination table. She wore a cloth gown over scrubs, a cloth cap, a gauze mask, and latex gloves—like someone dressed for surgery.

Adam shut the door and locked it. "Samantha decided to give Steph her bone marrow," he announced, his voice full of sarcasm.

Alarmed by his deceit, trembling with trepidation, Samantha had whirled around to leave, but Adam had wrapped his arms tightly across her chest, holding her in his iron grip.

The doctor had hurriedly stuck a needle into her arm, a hard poke into the flesh that caused burning. As Samantha went limp, Adam had staggered under her weight. Then everything had gone dark.

Until now.

She studied the room, about twelve by twelve, and realized she was in a hospital bed.

Doctor Pierce patted her shoulder awkwardly. "There, now, you'll be fine."

Samantha drew back, took a deep breath, and frowned. "You won't get away with this."

"We already have." The doctor offered her something in a plastic cup. "Drink slowly."

Her dry mouth welcomed the wet liquid. "I'll tell the press what you've done."

Adam moved closer. "We'll all deny it."

Samantha cursed. Her hip throbbed with pain.

"Do you expect people to sympathize with someone who'd let her sister die?" Adam placed his hands on the edge of the bed and leaned closer. "You forced us to do this, Samantha. Did you think we would sit back and do nothing?"

Samantha glared at the doctor. "You said it wouldn't hurt."

"That would have been true if you had cooperated. This way I had to do it fast, while you were out. There was no time for the regimen of medicines. I had to go into the bone."

Samantha heard some shuffling from the other side of the room. It was Aunt Catherine. "No one meant you any harm, Samantha."

"You did this to me?"

Catherine's was an icy reply. "For days I waited for you to have a conscience. I gave you a chance to save your sister. I loved her too much to wait any longer."

Samantha stared in disbelief. "Nobody has ever loved me like that. Nobody."

"I love you, Samantha. I would have done the same for you. Of course Stephanie wouldn't have refused to help you."

The door opened, and the click of high heels on the tile floor interrupted them. Samantha turned her aching head to see Stephanie, who sported a tremendous smile. "I want to thank you for helping me," she said.

Samantha grimaced as another pain scissored through her hip. "I should have known. The all-powerful president can take anything she wants."

Stephanie, puzzled, turned to Adam for an answer.

He looked sheepish. "She had to be persuaded, Steph."

Stephanie's smile evaporated. "What do you mean?"

"They trapped me like an animal and knocked me out. They operated on me without my consent." Samantha's voice was full of hostility.

Stephanie stared at the doctor, then her aunt. "I wish you hadn't done this."

"Well, it's done now. We want you to live," Adam replied.

Everyone was silent.

Stephanie reached for her sister's hand. "I'm sorry things happened this way, Sam. Honestly, I didn't know what they were doing. I was told you offered to do this."

Samantha pulled her hand away and said nothing.

"I'll always be grateful to you—to all of you." Stephanie moved away from the bed and turned her attention to the doctor. "I can't have the surgery now, you know."

Doctor Pierce nodded. "I'll store the cells until after the summit. But I want you in here the moment the Wakembezi delegation leaves." She returned her attention to her patient. "You'll rest here tonight, Samantha. You'll be back on your feet tomorrow."

Before Samantha could answer, the doctor injected her with a sedative, and Stephanie entered the hallway, followed by Adam and Aunt Catherine.

Sleepy, Samantha allowed her head to embrace the pillow. Okay, so they have the stem cells for Stephanie. *That doesn't mean they've won*, she told herself. She would keep quiet about what happened as long as it was to her advantage. Now she would have to make sure Stephanie never had the operation.

Chapter 45

∼

Tomorrow was garbage pickup. After spending the night in her office with Samantha and not returning home until the next evening, Debra Pierce had forgotten that it was Friday. Remembering after dark, she ventured into the backyard, lifted the lid of the garbage can, and deposited a plastic bag of trash. As she rolled the large container out to the curb, she spotted a dark, stationary figure on the sidewalk across the street.

For the first time she realized how late it was. The street was empty of moving vehicles and neighbors walking their dogs. There was no one except a chunky-looking man who walked in the patches of darkness that defied the streetlight. He came to the corner, stepped off the curb, and crossed the street. He was coming towards her.

Alarm traveled up her spine. Then she knew. "What are you doing here?" she asked as Nat Bobbitt stepped out of the darkness.

"I miss you." He tried to caress her, but she backed away.

"Some people might call this stalking." Anger tainted her voice.

"Come on, Doc—"

"We decided it was over."

"No, you decided it was over."

He touched her dark cheek gently. "Let me come inside."

"That's not a good idea. Go home to your wife." She turned back to the house, but he was right at her heels.

She halted him at the gate. "I can't do this. I always feel dirty afterwards."

Staring into his lustful dark eyes, she felt her resolve melting. After all, *what difference did it make if they were together one last time?*

"Where's your car?"

"Around the corner. I'm being discrete."

She said no more, allowing him to follow her to the backdoor. As she reached for the knob, he embraced her from behind, whispering in her ear, "I love you."

"Will you stay until daylight?" she asked as they stepped inside. He didn't answer and he didn't have to. She knew he would be gone when she awoke.

* * *

Debra stirred about two a.m. Nat was moving around in the kitchen. She was chilly, so she found the spread and tucked it around her.

How long she lay there, she could not have said. She heard barking dogs and a garbage truck changing gears. She started to call to Nat to come back to bed, but decided that he was dressing to leave.

Moments later Debra heard the front door close. She turned over and pounded her pillow, trying to sleep away the guilt. She loathed herself for being so weak. One more time she vowed that she would never again commit adultery.

In a few minutes she heard someone in the kitchen again. "Nat?"

No answer.

"Hello? Is somebody there?"

Memories resurfaced of the threats of anti-abortionists. Cold and afraid, she wondered if Nat had locked the door when he left. Had someone else entered her home?

"Is anyone there?" she called out again, this time reaching for the telephone.

"It's just me." It was a man's voice, heavy with sarcasm.

He was at the bedroom door, coming closer.

In the light coming through the window from a street lamp, she saw the stoic face of a white man with long hair in a ponytail. In his hand was a knife.

She fled from the bed, running to the bathroom to lock herself in.

He was faster. He picked her up as if she were weightless and tossed her on the bed. She kicked at his arm and the knife went flying to the floor.

She screamed only once before he pressed her pillow hard against her face and left it there. She kicked again, blindly, making contact with his crotch. He cursed loudly and pushed harder on the pillow. Afraid and dizzy, unable to breathe, she wondered how long it would take to find her body. If her Volvo wasn't gone in the morning, would the neighbors notice? If she wasn't in her office for the president's morning checkup, would the White House be sufficiently alarmed?

Just as everything went black, she heard a gunshot and felt the weight of the intruder's body on top of her.

She moaned. Someone pulled the man off her and pushed the pillow away. It was Nat.

"Honey, are you okay?" He helped her to her feet and switched on the light beside the bed. "Who's this?"

She stared down at the blood splattered on her gown and carpet, and managed only to shake her head. Then the physician in her took control. She sank to her knees and checked his pulse. "He's dead."

"You don't know him?" Nat repeated.

She looked closer. He was young, perhaps 22, with silver rings in his nose and his ears.

"No." She could only whisper. She had almost died. *Why was he trying to kill me?* Chilled and terrified, she slumped on the bed and hugged her knees.

Nat squatted down and patted her shoulder. "Maybe he was a junkie looking for drugs."

"He didn't ask me if I keep medicines anywhere. He didn't search. He just came at me to kill me."

He helped her to her feet. Her mind began to claw out of the fog caused by fear. "You came back?"

"I realized I left my cell phone on your kitchen counter. When I drove up, I saw this guy stalking around in the shadows. Before I could get out of the car, he had fiddled with the door. So I followed him in."

She hugged his big frame and thanked him at least three times. "We have to call the police."

"I can't do that, Doc. How do I explain why I was here?"

Nat went into the kitchen and poured her a small glass of water from the tap. She joined him at the round table next to the windows. "Someone probably heard the shot." She downed the water in a single gulp.

He pulled out his cell and called Dalton Mercer. In thirty minutes Dalton arrived and the three of them had a story ready for the police. Dalton said that he had assigned Bobbitt to guard Dr. Pierce, because of the threats on her life. Nat told them that he had gone outside for a cigarette and returned when he heard Doctor Pierce screaming. He arrived in time to kill her attacker.

The police called the incident justifiable homicide. After they left, the three relaxed. For some time they stood on the front porch, watching the ambulance from the morgue pull away from the house. The last thin rays of moonlight were disappearing, replaced by budding rays of sun.

Dalton said what they all were thinking. "I guess it's still going to make newspaper headlines, but at least it won't cause a scandal that embarrasses President Franklin."

A solemn frown wrinkled Debra's dark face. "I would hate to see that."

Dalton leaned against a column, his eyes focused on Debra's face. "You need to remember you're a public figure. I'm trying not to be judgmental, but the tabloids would be."

"We'll be more careful," said Bobbitt.

Debra cringed at his words. *No way. No time. Never again.*

"I can't stay here," she said, holding her robe tightly against her body. "I feel violated. I don't feel safe anymore."

Dalton's eyes registered his concern. "Can I call anyone for you?"

"I want to go back to the White House. I have a hospital bed in my office. I need to sleep for a while."

Dalton looked at his watch. "Go on home, Bobbitt. Tell your family you saved the doctor's life before they hear about it on TV. I'm taking Doctor Pierce with me."

Debra watched Bobbitt pull away from the curb before she went inside to change clothes. She reminded herself to ask the president if she could stay in one of the White House bedrooms for a while.

Chapter 46

After several hours of sleep, Debra locked her office and went to hunt for President Franklin. Her body, used to seven hours of rest, was sluggish. Her head hurt like a hangover, even though she'd had nothing to drink. Worst of all, her heart was riddled with guilt and regret.

As she passed the chapel on the way to the Oval Office, she experienced an overwhelming need for absolution. Stepping inside to pray, she found the president sitting quietly on the front pew. Debra hurried up the aisle and slid beside her.

Stephanie smiled. "I'm glad to see you. I heard what happened."

"Did Dalton wake you?"

"No. He knew I'd be up early." Her face looked strained. "I asked him if the attempt on your life could be connected to the attempt on mine last spring. He didn't think that was possible, but I'd hate for you to be harmed because you're loyal to me." She closed the Bible on her lap and placed it between them. "Dalton suggested you stay with us on the second floor. I think it's a good idea. Actually, I've thought of it myself from time to time. I'd like having my doctor nearby 24/7."

"I appreciate this. I'm still afraid to go home."

"I'll send some agents with you to get your things. You can stay down the hall from me in the Queens' Bedroom. It's got a sitting room attached. How's that?"

"Thank you. If I can't feel protected here, I can't feel safe anywhere."

Stephanie stood and pulled the jacket of her two-piece suit down to fit her waist. "Do you want me to come to your office for a checkup?"

The doctor paused to consider. "Actually I came in here to pray. It's funny how a thing like this can make you go seeking God."

"I didn't know you were a believer, Debra."

"I haven't been a faithful Christian, but I grew up in the church. My mom took me every week. I learned right from wrong, but I keep straying from the path." She stared at the cross. "Do you think God will hear me if I pray after all this time?"

"Of course. God always listens."

Dr. Pierce breathed heavily, relieved.

"May I pray with you?" Stephanie asked.

What an amazing woman! Here was the leader of the greatest nation in the world, with problems that dwarfed Debra's own personal needs—and Stephanie Franklin still had time to pray with her.

"What do you want to say to God, Debra?"

"I need help. I want to be good—to do the right thing—but I keep committing the same sin over and over." She ran her fingers over the leather cover of the Bible beside her. In this setting with a godly woman, confession came easy. "I'm sleeping with a married man."

"You've tried to break it off?"

"Too many times."

"Are you in love with him?"

"No, but he's so persistent. He keeps proving I'm a pushover."

Stephanie opened the Bible to Matthew 12:31. "Jesus was against adultery, but he also said it wasn't an unforgivable sin." She placed the book on the doctor's lap.

Debra's eyes watered. Stephanie took her hand and prayed for the Lord to strengthen her friend. As she rose to leave, Debra grabbed her hand again.

"You're such a good person, Stephanie." It was the first time she had ever addressed the chief executive by her first name, but it had flipped off her tongue so naturally that the president didn't seem to mind.

Stephanie grinned. "I'm not running for sainthood."

"I admire you so much. I consider you more than a patient. You're my friend."

Stephanie embraced her. "Well, if you need to talk, girlfriend, I'll be just down the hall."

Debra chuckled, but she quickly grew serious. "How can you do this—care about other people when you're so sick?"

"I can't do anything about my illness."

"Do you pray for healing?"

"I used to. But I've come to accept that's not God's will."

"We have the stem cells. I want you to stay positive."

"I am positive. I know God loves me. Now I pray for wisdom to lead our nation. I pray for my marriage and for peace in the world."

After a few more minutes, Debra asked to stay in the chapel alone, and Stephanie headed for the exit. Remembering, she turned back. "Do you want to move in today?"

"Yes."

"Talk to Dalton about taking two more agents along with Bobbitt."

Debra flinched.

Stephanie stared at her with wide eyes. "Oh, that makes things harder, doesn't it?"

"I don't want him to lose his job, Stephanie. But I need my space."

"Have you had sex with him in the White House?"

Debra flushed.

"We can't have him coming to the Queens' Bedroom. Do you know what Cheri Eastley would do with a story about that?"

"I'm sorry."

"I forgive you. But it can't happen again." Stephanie stared at the cross above the altar, pondering the situation. "Instead of moving in, I want you to get away for a few days." Her voice was decisive. "Don't you have family in California? You need to be somewhere Bobbitt can't get to you."

"But I'm still afraid. What if there's another killer out there?"

"I'll send Karen Kelsey with you. I always feel safe with her."

"But with your illness—I can't go. I need to be here for your bone marrow transplant."

"After the summit, we'll do the surgery. Right now, let's take care of your spiritual health. The Bible says not to put temptation in front of those who will stumble. I'll be doing that if I allow you to stay. You need to get away from temptation, Debra."

Tears crowded the corners of the doctor's eyes. "I've sworn to take care of you."

"There are other doctors on your staff, Debra."

"But they don't know about the leukemia. You need me."

Stephanie's voice took on the tone of a general. "I'm ordering you to go. By the time you get back, Bobbitt will be assigned to other duties outside the White House. He will still have his job; but with God's help he won't have you."

"I won't be too far away. Will you call my cell if you need me?"

"Of course. I wish we could spend more time together, but that's impossible right now. The delegation from Wakembezi should be here any minute. Promise me to pray and lean on the Lord." She smiled, gave her friend a hug, and she was gone.

Debra sat alone in the quiet of the chapel, loathing herself, and asking God to forgive her weakness.

Chapter 47

～

Willy assembled the weapon that Lowe had purchased in the roadside park. It was a thing of beauty, he thought, attaching the silencer. He ran his fingers slowly down the cool barrel, stroking it gently, much like caressing the parts of a woman. Except no woman had ever given him the pleasure that killing did.

He sat on the bed on the eighth floor of the Hilton Washington Embassy Row Hotel, located in Dupont Circle in the midst of more than 170 foreign consulates. The room was luxurious and the king-size bed was comfortable, but it was more important to him that his room was across from Wakembezi's embassy. The hotel was only half a block from the metro station where he would make his escape in the midst of a throng of commuters.

His mind flew back to another time when he joined Special Forces. He had been a private in the Army, eager to serve his country. After he fought several months in Iraq, an officer informed him that he had been flagged for sniper training while in boot camp.

He remembered standing at attention as a captain patted him on the back. "What you're doing will shorten the war in the Middle East," he had told Willy. "Your file says you're a remarkable shot."

Willy concentrated on keeping his back straight. "Yes, sir, I am."

The captain sat at his desk and buried his head in a file. "Your profile also shows an affinity for killing."

"Yes, sir."

"Shooting a target is different from shooting a human being."

Willy said nothing. He didn't see any difference.

"Have you killed anyone face to face?"

"Yes, sir. Three." He felt pride crawling into a smile.

"Did you like it?"

He eyed the captain curiously. "Yes, sir."

"I'm recruiting you as a sniper. However, you'll be more than that. I want you to learn Arabic. I want you to be able to mosey into any room unarmed and make a weapon from things you see."

That sounded like fun. Willy was excited. "Thank you for the opportunity," he said.

Immediately he was sent to kill a traitor who had fled to Turkey. Then a sheik that hid in Kuwait while he headed al-Qaeda's propaganda operations. During the next few years, Willy went into Afghanistan and Iran where he assassinated several double agents. He was good at what he did—and proud of it.

When his tour was over, he bummed around, lost and bewildered. He had no idea what to do with his life. His killing skills weren't suitable for a resume. One day he wandered into a bar, and after three beers, killed another man by cutting his throat with a broken bottle. He served eight years for manslaughter in the United States Penitentiary in Lewisburg, Pennsylvania. After he was released, Lowe hired him as his bodyguard. However, Willy was much, much more than that.

Today Lowe had ordered him to kill someone. Finally. At last. He felt a quickening in his blood, a flicker of that old excitement returning. He had missed the rush of adrenalin whenever he squeezed the trigger. He enjoyed watching the victim fold up like a scarecrow.

He pulled a chair to the window and watched the flow of people in and out of the embassy residence. Pulling a glasscutter out of his case, he carefully removed a square section from the window. It was just the right size to hold the barrel of the gun.

He braced the rifle on the windowsill, waiting. He never needed more than one shot.

In just a few minutes, he spotted his target, lined up the scope, and without thinking, pulled the trigger. Udo Wasswa was dead in seconds.

Chapter 48

Ronald Reagan Washington National Airport was usually spacious and quiet—but not today. People pushed and shoved to get on the planes. The pay-to-see TVs blared with predictions of a looming war with Wakembezi. Nothing since September 11, 2001, had panicked Americans as much as the violent death of the African vice chairman. Thousands had clogged the roads and highways, trying to leave Washington, D.C., but after hours of bumper-to-bumper tag, cars that were out of gas blocked the exits.

The president's secretary Nancy had fled to the airport like so many others, hoping to get a flight out. Unable to find an empty space in the parking lots, she had abandoned her Volvo in a red zone and fled into the terminal. From the moment she stepped into the building, she knew that she shouldn't have gone home to pack a bag. People pressed into the elevators and escalators like canned sardines. The restroom lines were so long that people were urinating in corners of the complex.

Nancy secured her place in line at the American Airlines counter and pondered the likelihood that the airport would be a prime target. She suspected that this same scene was being played out in cities all over the nation, with people heading for the small towns, believing that Sibaba would not target sparse areas.

As she stood there, the line inching along, Nancy tuned out the shouting and chaos, as she recalled the events in the White House that morning.

When word spread about the assassination, panic had invaded the calm of the government offices. People scurried up and down the halls like ticket holders trying to exit a burning theater. Petrified by fear, Nancy joined a nervous group forming outside the Oval Office, hoping for some encouraging word from the president. They had found their path blocked by Dalton Mercer, who stood immovable, like a sentinel guarding a pharaoh's tomb.

Kenneth Chang pushed his way to the front. "I've got to see her."

"She's with the Wakembezi delegation," Dalton replied, paused a moment, and added respectfully, "They're talking with Sibaba on the webcam, sir."

The secretaries chattered excitedly. "What will she do, do you think?" Nancy asked, her voice shaky.

"She's promised to stop a war." Dalton answered, but somehow that hadn't reassured Nancy.

"I need to be in there with her," urged Chang, but Dalton continued to block his entrance. "Tell her I'm here for God's sake!"

Without warning, the door opened and the Wakembezians departed. The president looked surprisingly calm, but tired. "Everything's going to be fine," she reassured the staff.

Her eyes shifted to the vice president. "Ken, take a plane from our fleet. Fly out of here with your family."

His eyes were dark slits. "My God, Stephanie, there could be a nuclear war."

"No, I won't let that happen."

"Shouldn't we get with the joint chiefs?"

Stephanie clutched the vice president's arm. "Look, if it comes to it, it's important one of us survive—you know that. Go now. I'm the expert on Sibaba. Go. Please."

Chang turned away, pushed past the wide-eyed secretaries, and rushed down the corridor. By the time he stepped into the elevator, he was already talking to his wife on his cell phone.

Nancy scurried to her desk and filled her arms with belongings. "It's not safe here," she told the other secretaries.

Dawn dropped into her desk chair. "But your job—"

"What job? After we're blown to bits?" Nancy had sprinted down the hall, joining the others who fled the White House.

Now she stood in line at a ticket counter in the airport, realizing how useless her escape plans had been.

"We have no more flights out," the ticket handler yelled to those in line.

The fat man in front of Nancy flashed a wad of money. "What've you got? Come on, find something."

Nancy moved away, dazed, ignoring the shouting and screaming, crazy chatter, and little kids crying; it all just floated around her like smoke.

Later she found herself in front of the windows in a waiting room, watching the departure of airplanes. Outside Kenneth Chang and his family were boarding the Boeing 747 designated to fly them to safety. With him were several dozen other passengers, whom Nancy recognized as Cabinet members and senators. She put her hands against the glass and wished she had asked him to take her with him.

She continued staring out the window, miserable and afraid, until the aircraft taxied away. She turned and aimlessly wandered the terminal. After a while, she spotted Adam Thorsten on television, so she stopped to view the press conference.

Adam read a prepared announcement. "The president is presently in meetings with the visiting delegates. There is some distress in Wakembezi because one of their leaders, here in peace, was violently murdered. This is understable. Our president is outraged and heartbroken at the loss of a friend. She wants to reassure the Wakembezians that those responsible for this terrible act of violence will be punished by our courts."

"Reassure the Wakembezians! What about reassuring Americans!" a tall man snorted sarcastically. "What about the dirty bombs being placed everywhere!"

Meanwhile Adam continued his report. "The White House wants to assure the American people that we are not in immediate danger. Do not panic. The president is not relocating her own family because she believes there's no reason to worry. In addition, most of the delegates from Wakembezi are remaining here to seek a peaceful solution to this tragedy. They are not leaving, at our president's request, as a symbol of the solidarity that still exists between the leaders of our two nations."

When he finished, Adam returned to the West Wing without hearing questions. As the broadcast continued, an anchor reported that the president would be traveling to Wakembezi on Saturday. "At that time, the body of Vice Chairman Wasswa will be taken back by Air Force One for burial," he said. "The president believes that her attendance at the funeral will illustrate American's peaceful and remorseful attitudes."

The TV news switched to pictures of rioting in central Africa. In the streets of Dallol Bosso, angry demonstrators burned the American flag taken by force from the American Embassy. The mood among the Wakembezi people was explosive everywhere, from South Africa to Kenya, with some military leaders looking at the assassination as an act of war. Three American ambassadors had quickly evacuated their homes and flown to Europe.

"We're going to be blown to bits any minute now," snarled the tall man.

Another man, wearing a black overcoat, stood on his toes and stretched to see the TV screen. "They'll talk to her first," he answered as if addressed.

The tall man spat out his words. "You're an idiot. She's just going home to her African friends where she'll be safe. She's leaving us all to die."

Nancy whirled around, no longer voiceless. "President Franklin is no turncoat. Besides, there's supposed to be a bomb shelter for her in Washington somewhere, so she doesn't have to leave to be safe."

A soft-spoken woman, probably the tall man's wife, mentioned that the president was waiting three days to leave. "That must mean something," she said. "That wouldn't make sense, if she was running away."

He frowned, but her logic seemed to calm him.

Another man, still agitated, pushed through the crowd, his blank expression revealing his uncertainty. Pulling a teenager by the wrist, he brushed against Nancy, seemingly unaware of the physical contact. "I forgot about my uncle's boat at Chesapeake Bay," he said, his voice flooded with relief. "We'll go out in the ocean as far as we can get."

Nancy watched them depart, envying them, until she remembered they couldn't travel the roads to get there.

Chapter 49

∽

With car horns blaring all around her, Nancy trudged five miles from the airport to the White House. She hitched a ride several times, but travel was repeatedly hampered by severe traffic congestion, so she continued her trek on foot. After several hours, shivering, with the cold rain beating against her back, she pushed her way through the crowd at the White House gate and showed the security guard her identification.

After stepping through a metal detector, she spotted the president's aide in the hall ahead. Darting after him, she called his name.

York swung round. "So you came back."

Nancy closed her umbrella and followed him eagerly. "I shouldn't have tried to leave. No one can go anywhere."

His eyes searched her face. "Is the traffic bad?"

Nancy nodded. "Cars are out of gas and blocking the streets. I walked here in the rain."

"Come with me."

She followed York down one corridor after another, the route twisting and turning at least six times. They were moving farther and farther away from the secretarial area in the West Wing. "Where are we going?"

"The East Wing."

They took an elevator to the second floor, moved off at a quick pace, and finally slowed as they reached a brightly lit corridor. They passed several offices, all empty of their occupants. At last they entered one. The décor was strictly feminine. Nancy stared at a coffee mug with hearts on it and bookshelves with streamers and stuffed animals. "This isn't your office is it?"

He shook his head. "This is temporary." He checked his watch. "Why are you here?"

"I'm scared." Nancy shivered, more from fear than the drenched clothing. "What is President Franklin doing about the bomb threat?"

"There's not going to be a war."

"How do you know?"

"The president says so, and I believe her."

"I remembered the president's helicopter and hoped we could get on it and leave."

"I don't have the authority to do that." He cleared his throat. "Don't be afraid. Believe me, you don't have to leave town. You don't see me running away do you?"

She stared into his stoic face. "It looks like all the other people on this wing are gone. Why did they leave then?"

He avoided the question. "Let's get that wet coat off of you." He helped her out of the sleeves and tossed the coat on a sofa. "You're safe here."

"I worry that they'll bomb the White House first."

He smiled, as if amused. "You haven't heard a word I said, have you?"

She just stared at him.

"As you know, I usually work in the West Wing." He kept his tone low and soothing. "That's where the president's office is. We're in the East Wing. Do you know what that means?"

She shook her head. "I've never been in this area."

"The bomb shelter is right below us."

A flutter ran through her chest.

"I still don't think it's going to be necessary. But the staff that remained behind brought their loved ones here just in case."

York opened the door. "I have to get back in case the president needs me before she leaves. I'll take you down to the shelter first."

"Thank you," she said, her tears released by relief. She shook the water off her coat and followed him. Finding a tissue in the pocket, she dabbed her wet eyes as they journeyed to the end of the hall.

President Franklin stepped into the corridor, and seeing Nancy, beckoned them inside. She smiled, but she looked tired. She directed them to nearby chairs, while she sat behind the oak desk.

"The joint chiefs don't want me too far away from the bomb shelter," she explained. "Tony isn't here today, so I'm working out of his office."

The president's measured words and calm demeanor reassured Nancy that everything was under control. Nancy tried to imagine the heavy burden on the leader's shoulders. "Since I'm here, what can I do for you, Madam President?"

"Thank you, but right now I want you to go to the bomb shelter." Her eyes locked on Nancy's face. "Don't be afraid. It's almost over." Her gaze shifted to York. "I want you to go there too."

"No. I won't leave you."

The corners of her glossed lips turned up a little. "I appreciate your loyalty."

York swung around to face Nancy again. "You really don't need to be down there yet. Sibaba has promised to do nothing until President Franklin pleads her case on Saturday. Do you mind staying underground until then?"

"I can't go anywhere else."

"If you'll feel safer, then you need to go downstairs," said the president. "It's really quite nice down there. York will show you."

"Thank you, ma'am."

Stephanie glanced at the doorway, where Adam waited quietly. "Right now, I've got to run to the Oval Office to pick up some things."

"Let me do that," York insisted. "You stay here."

The president paused at the door. "No, this is something personal I need to handle. You must quit worrying. Sibaba isn't going to bomb us."

Adam finally spoke. "Dalton says you can't stay long."

Stephanie chuckled. "People might think I'm not the boss around here." She winked at Nancy and disappeared into the hall.

"She looks exhausted," Nancy said.

"She has a lot to do. She's really wearing herself out. I hope after Saturday things will be different," he said.

They strolled to the end of the corridor. York used a key to open the elevator. Nancy stepped inside, but he remained in the hall.

"Aren't you coming?" she asked.

"I'll come down after the president leaves."

Chapter 50

~

While Stephanie and her escort trekked to the West Wing, Samantha wandered the empty halls with Agent Stein.

"Shouldn't you be in the bomb shelter at your aunt's estate?" he asked.

She studied him with a baffled stare. "You know about it?"

"Sure. I was there right after your sister became president. They were digging the hole."

"It's supposed to be well stocked and roomy too."

"You haven't been inside it?"

She shook her head. "I'll do it when Aunt Catherine says to."

They entered the Oval Office. Finding Stephanie absent, Samantha plopped herself into the president's chair and began exploring the items on the desk.

Stein looked uneasy. "Is the president expecting you?"

"Of course," she lied. "You can wait outside."

As he turned to leave, he spoke into his sleeve to his superior in the communications room. "Control, this is Stein. Lovebird is secure in the Oval Office."

"Lovebird? You call me Lovebird?"

He reeled around. "We don't mean anything by it, ma'am." His face grew pinker by the second. "Everyone we guard has a code name for security reasons. Someone gave you the moniker before we knew about your former occupation."

Samantha giggled. "It's appropriate. I like it. What do you call Stephanie?"

"Rosebud." He disappeared into the hall.

Bored, Samantha began exploring her sister's desk again. There were three letters in sealed envelopes, a thick document from the EPA, and a picture of the twins, which Stephanie had placed in a silver frame.

Dalton opened the door. He eyed Samantha with a raised eyebrow, breathed a sigh, and elected to wait outside.

Samantha laughed. "What are you afraid of, Dalton?" she hooted. When he didn't return, she picked up one of the letters, intending to open it.

* * *

When Stephanie and Adam entered the Oval Office, Samantha still fingered the letter. Alarm bounded through Stephanie. "What are you doing at my desk?"

"The secretaries were missing, so I let myself in."

Adam's antagonism was unrestrained. "What are you doing, Sam, pretending to be president again?"

Samantha smiled slyly. "What, no kiss for me this morning, my love?"

"I'd as soon kiss a cockroach." His lips curled in disgust.

Stephanie stared at the letter in her sister's hand. *She can't read that!* She raced to the edge of the desk. "Those are presidential papers, Sam."

Ignoring her, Samantha whirled around in the leather chair.

Stephanie's impatience surfaced. "What is it now, Sam? I have a lot to do before I leave on Saturday."

"I'm here to talk about sisterly sharing—you remember about that, don't you?"

"I don't want to talk about Adam."

"I don't either."

Stephanie stared, controlled, trying to discern her sister's intentions.

At last Samantha stated her case. "You owe me, Stephanie. I want something in return for my stem cells." She rubbed her scarred hand. "I hate the way this looks. I've tried gels and laser treatments and nothing has helped. Maybe a skin graft from your skin will work."

"Why not use your own skin?"

"Because I want yours."

Stephanie squelched the response forming on her lips.

"She's still trying to look just like you," Adam snorted.

"That's not why," Samantha argued. "How would you like living with this hideous scar?" She held up her hand, displaying the moon-shaped disfigurement that ran from her middle finger down to her wrist.

"Your timing isn't good. Let's talk about this when I get back."

Samantha sneered. "You're not going to do it, are you? I can see it in your eyes."

"I just said it has to wait. I didn't say *no*."

"I thought we'd do it before you leave, in case you don't come back."

"It's impossible right now."

The sisters stared at each other, neither willing to yield.

Adam opened the door. "You need to leave, Sam. All you do is think about yourself. Stephanie has the weight of the world on her shoulders. Your vanity can wait."

"There are legal ways I can prevent you from having the transplant," Samantha snapped back. "I suggest you and your flunky quit antagonizing me." Her eyes threw daggers at Adam as she strolled away.

Adam shut the door. "Why do you put up with that?"

"If there is any way we can be friends again, I need to try."

He glanced at his watch. "Dalton gave us five minutes."

"I'm not going back to the East Wing. I'm going to my quarters for the night."

Adam protested.

"I keep telling everyone that we're safe until Saturday. Who's going to believe me if I'm hiding underground?"

Stephanie glided to her desk and picked up the three white envelopes. "I have some letters here. I've written them to those I love the most." She handed them to him. "Don't open yours. None of them is to be opened until my death. I'll trust them to your keeping until then."

Adam looked puzzled. "Why this, Steph?"

She hesitated and turned away. "I wrote them one day when my leukemia worried me. I was afraid I wouldn't live much longer, so I wrote the letters like some people write wills. Just put them somewhere safe like you would a will."

Adam reached out and touched her shoulder, running one hand around the back of her neck. There was no way to ignore the love in his touch. She closed her eyes, melting into the moment. She felt the smooth sweep of his lips on her cheek, smelled the scent of his hair, and turned her head to welcome his kiss. As their lips met, she felt more alive than she ever had. She realized she loved him. As hard as it was, she made herself pull away.

He loosened his grip on her waist and eyed her in breathless silence.

"I can't." She spoke an indisputable truth. "I'm still married."

He ducked his head and inhaled sharply.

They remained inches apart without speaking. "Let's ignore what happened," Stephanie said at last. "Will you pray with me before we go to Wakembezi?"

He relaxed. "Of course." He tapped her nose playfully with an index finger. "I pray for you every day."

Chapter 51

～

It was a cool day, so Philip Lowe stayed indoors to drink his coffee. For an hour he sat in the warm kitchen, reading the morning newspaper and consuming most of the six-cup pot. He could feel himself smiling, a huge grin that grew larger with every written word about the assassination. It was impossible not to be happy.

Willy entered without knocking. "Good morning, sir."

"You've seen the news?"

"Yes. That's why it's a good morning." Willy flashed a smug smile and continued to stand a few feet away. "I didn't know I would cause a war, though."

"Don't worry about it. No one in his right mind is going to start a nuclear holocaust."

Willy reached into a cabinet for a mug and poured himself some coffee.

"I want everything solved and soon," Lowe said, taking a sip. "I'm getting impatient for Stephanie to die. How about taking another stab at killing her? Do you think you could blow up her plane? Everyone will believe it was Sibaba."

"There's no way I could get close to Air Force One. It's guarded like the crown jewels."

Lowe folded his arms across his chest. "You avoid taking risks. Good. I don't want to be caught." He paused to drink from the cup. "Let's keep being careful. No one's ever traced that Iowa hick to us."

"They won't now. It's been nearly a year. If they had any leads, we'd know it."

"What about the Wasswa thing?"

"I know what I'm doing, sir."

"That may be true, but some of the guys you hire are idiots—like the one you hired to kill the doctor."

"He was a good man, and capable. If that agent hadn't been there, she'd be dead."

"If he knew his business, he should have been aware of the Secret Service agent."

"From now on I'll handle the killings myself, sir."

They were interrupted by a knock on the kitchen door. Samantha had driven up the drive and parked by the back door without either of them hearing her.

Once inside, she tossed her leather jacket on a kitchen chair. "I'm here for tutoring." She glanced around. "Are we alone?"

Lowe nodded. "It's just Willy and me. I sent my wife to visit her sister in Indiana."

She raised perfectly plucked eyebrows. "Are you worried about the bomb?"

"Not much. But she feels safer." He dropped a spoon into his milky coffee and stirred. "How do you manage to keep shaking your bodyguards?"

"It's easy to sneak out. I keep my car in the drive by the front door. They're so devoted to Aunt Catherine they follow her from room to room. They'll fuss when I get back, but they've come to see me as a free spirit."

"How's the traffic between here and Washington?" Willy asked.

"Not bad. People must be listening to Stephanie and staying home."

Lowe peered at her over his spectacles. "Did you learn Swahili yet?"

"It's too hard. Why can't I just speak English?"

"Are you going to be Stephanie or not?"

"Okay, I'll work on it."

Lowe drained his cup. "How's Stephanie's health?"

"She's hanging in, but not for long. I'm about ready to make the switch."

"Not before Stephanie goes to Wakembezi. You mean after that, right?"

"When she gets back, she's having a bone marrow transplant. Neither of us wants that, do we?"

Lowe frowned. "They found a marrow match?"

"They drugged me and took mine by force." Samantha gritted her teeth, the anger growing with every word. "They're not getting away with it. So let's make the switch."

"I'll know when you're ready. You're not ready, Samantha."

She threw out a string of words in Swahili. "See, I know more than you think." She walked straight up to Willy, their faces so close together they breathed the same air. "What do you think? Am I ready?"

He stiffened. "That's not my decision."

"Ah, the ever-silent drudge. You never say anything. You never smile. But I bet you take it all in, don't you?" She ran her fingers playfully down the front of his shirt. "I've got you pegged as a man of action, Willy. You want some action?"

Annoyed, Lowe slapped the table, the impact splashing coffee from his cup. "Stop that, Samantha. I've told you repeatedly that Stephanie doesn't flirt. That's one good reason why you're not ready!"

Willy moved to wipe up the spill with a paper towel.

Samantha squirmed back into her seat. "It won't happen again," she promised. "Let's get on with my lesson."

* * *

After leaving Lowe's home, Samantha drove the quickest route to the White House. She made good time because most of the traffic was not traveling into D.C.

After her session with Lowe, Samantha coveted the power of the presidency even more. On the hour drive, she decided to destroy the stem cells. She wasn't going to take chances. *Stephanie had to die.*

After checking with security at the northwest gate, she trudged towards Doctor Pierce's office in the West Wing. She was eager to execute Step One of her plan.

The office was dark. Samantha closed the door and began scouring the room for her stolen marrow cells. She had no idea what kind of container to look for. She pulled open drawers and cabinets. She searched the little refrigerator in the doctor's office. She hunted for a safe or a locked cabinet. At last, discouraged, she sank into the chair at the desk and searched the computer for information on harvested stem cells.

A website read, "Stem cells have to be effectively stored until it's time to use them. The cryopreservation method freezes stem cells at low temperatures below 150 degrees C by immersing them in nitrogen vapor."

"What was I thinking?" Samantha muttered aloud. The doctor had frozen her booty at a nearby hospital.

Before she could leave, someone entered and flipped the light switch in the outer office. Samantha turned off the computer and strolled casually into the waiting room.

It was a dark-skinned man with a shaved head and brown eyes. Because he wore a white lab coat, she decided he must be part of the medical staff. "Dr. Pierce isn't here," she said. "I was just leaving her a note."

He glanced at her presidential pen and offered an obliging smile. "She's on leave. I'm filling-in."

"Good. I wanted her to take a few days off," Samantha said sweetly. "I wanted to tell her not to worry about going to Wakembezi."

"Yes, ma'am." His baldhead reflected the overhead light. "Do you need a doctor to go along? I'd be honored."

"I think that's handled. But thanks for offering." She intended a fast departure, but remembering her purse, scurried into the doctor's office to retrieve it. When she returned to the waiting room, she found the doctor blocking the door.

"Dr. Pierce told me to check your blood pressure and give you a checkup. This looks like a good time."

A flag of caution alerted her brain. "It's not a good time; not right now. I'm trying to prevent a war."

He looked like a child reprimanded by his teacher. His head bobbed up and down. "Of course—of course, Madam President."

Making a quick exit, Samantha glanced at her watch. She had wasted twenty minutes in an unsuccessful quest for the bone marrow. It was time to change her plan again. She'd go straight to Stephanie.

She trudged down a long corridor to the White House, and continued with quiet steps towards Stephanie's private rooms. In the West Sitting Hall, now used as a lounge outside the president's private quarters, she found Bobbitt and Stein sprawled on beige sofas beneath the elegant half-moon Tiffany window. She nodded a greeting and moved on to the bedroom.

"You're here late," Bobbitt said, standing as if at attention.

"I'm always here late," Samantha replied with a small laugh. She indicated the presidential seal on her lapel. "Did you think I was my twin?"

His eyes blinked twice. "When did you leave your rooms, Madam President?"

"About thirty minutes ago," she lied. "You guys were deep in conversation."

"I'm sorry," Stein stammered.

"Don't worry about it. I'm perfectly safe inside the White House. You don't need to hover over me every minute." She paused, pondering what she would say next. "I've got some personal things to take care of. I want more privacy."

The agents exchanged uncomfortable glances. "What are you asking?" Stein replied.

"Go to the first floor. From there you can guard the staircase so no one comes upstairs."

Stein shook his head. "We can't leave this floor."

She let out a sigh of annoyance. "Go across the hall to the kitchen. Have some coffee. This won't take long. I'll call you back in a few minutes."

"Dalton expects us to stay right here," Stein protested.

"To protect me from a bomb?" Impatience crept into her voice. "Does that make sense to you? How can you possibly do that?"

His eyes probed her. "We have to obey our orders."

Nerves prickled on the back of her neck. "Are you going to obey Dalton instead of your commander-in-chief?"

A stunned moment passed. Their gazes bore into each other, until finally Stein shrugged. "Madam President, we are ready to carry out any orders you have."

The agents scurried away as Samantha entered the president's quarters. She sneaked through the living room and peeked into the bedroom. Stephanie was on her knees next to the bed, praying, unaware that she was in danger.

Chapter 52

～

Stephanie finished her prayers and pushed on the bed to stand. From the end table she picked up a now cold cup of coffee. She debated whether to heat up the brew in the kitchen or toss it out.

A sudden voice broke the silence. "Evening, Sis."

She jumped, surprised by Samantha's soundless approach.

"Did I startle you?"

"Nothing about you surprises me anymore."

"You're not wearing a wig," Samantha observed. "You don't look like yourself without it."

Stephanie ran her palm over the fuzz on her scalp. "My hair's growing back. I just wear the wig when I go out."

She motioned for Samantha to sit. "I'm glad you're here. We need to talk about something." Stephanie seated herself at her writing desk and picked through the mail. "I just received this bill from a jewelry company." She passed it to Samantha with an outstretched hand.

"Oh, that." Samantha rolled her eyes and remained standing. "I just needed a nice piece of jewelry."

"Dr. Pierce seems to think you're developing a problem. You go places and sign my name. You charge—"

"According to Dr. Pierce you're the one with the problem."

Stephanie looked away, still talking, ignoring the jab about her leukemia. "You had no right to have a pin made like mine. You aren't *me*."

"Aren't you the super-righteous one," Samantha sneered. "You sit there like Queen of the World on your presidential throne…"

Stephanie, now disgusted, made a conscious effort not to lose her temper. She stood, confronting her sister at eye level. "Please—"

"…and you judge everyone," Samantha continued. "Who made you God?"

"Now you're the one who is unreasonable."

Samantha's outburst became a scream. "Me? You grew up rich. You don't know what it's like to struggle to survive. You've no idea what it is to be someone like me." She stalked closer, continuing her tirade. "You grew up with silk sheets and bubble baths. I grew up with rats and a roof that leaked next to my bed!"

Shocked by the bitterness flowing forth, Stephanie stared, trying to fathom the depths of her sister's pain. "I'm sorry, Sam."

"Don't talk down to me!" She hurled a handful of mail at Stephanie's face. "I hate you. I hate you for all the years I missed *this*!" She threw her arms wide, pointing to pictures on the walls of Stephanie's accomplishments. "I've had nothing!"

Stephanie tried to embrace her, but Samantha pulled away and, agitated, began stalking around the room. "Adam's not your property."

For the first time Stephanie recognized the depth of her twin's instability. "Why are we talking about Adam now?"

Her tone taunted Stephanie. "Why so upset, Your Highness?"

"Quit calling me that."

"You're just jealous," she hissed. "Adam told me he loved me. No one ever told me that before."

"He thought you were me."

Samantha's disturbed mind vaulted elsewhere. "I was forced into bed with a fat Latino when I was twelve." From the end table she snatched up the framed photo of Stephanie's inauguration and slammed it against the wall.

Feeling threatened, Stephanie backed away. "I'm sorry, Sam. You've made your point."

"Look at you and look at me. Tell me you don't owe me something for forty years wasted."

"What do you want?"

"I want to be you."

Stephanie stared at the presidential pen on Samantha's lapel. "You don't know what you're saying."

"Yes, I do." Her lips spewed enmity. "Quit looking at me like that."

Chilled by fear, Stephanie backed up to the writing desk and fumbled for her phone behind her back. "I can't let you be president, Sam. I was elected."

"Shucks, anyone can be president." With a haughty smile, she dusted her fingers over her replica of the presidential pin. "I can be you. I did it at the children's ward. I've done it lots of times with Adam and with the staff."

"Sam, you've got to stop—"

"Shut up, Your Highness. I can prevent you from using my stem cells."

"You can't threaten me, Sam."

"Do you want to live or not?"

"I'm not afraid to die." Stephanie pondered what to do. "How can you let me die without any conscience at all?"

Samantha sneered. "As you said, I'm not you." She took another malevolent step towards Stephanie.

Stephanie glanced at the door. The panic button in the sitting room was out of reach. "Sam, you're my sister. I know we missed out on growing up together and all that—what matters is we're sisters and we're together now."

Samantha leaned within inches of her face. "You *will* die."

Stephanie stared in disbelief. She blamed herself for this. *I shouldn't have let her substitute for me the first time.*

"I said you're going to die."

"I told you I'm not afraid!"

"That's good to hear!" Samantha screamed viciously, hitting Stephanie on the head with the base of the telephone.

Stephanie stumbled forward, bracing herself on the back of a chair. Samantha came at her again, grabbing her purse and hitting Stephanie with it repeatedly. The purse, battered by the blows, flew open, its contents falling to the floor.

Stephanie collapsed to her knees, staring down at a lipstick and Samantha's driver's license. Breathing deeply, she struggled to stand again. She knew she was in trouble.

Before she could recover, Samantha seized a lamp and clubbed her again.

The pain was so intense it felt as though an ice pick was stuck into her brain. She was grateful to land on the soft carpet. Dizzy, seeing double, she decided to lie still, so Samantha wouldn't hit her again.

After some minutes, Samantha seemed to come to herself. She glared down at the lifeless body on the floor, and calmly picked up a handkerchief that had fallen from her purse. Looking pleased with herself, she wiped Stephanie's blood off the lamp.

She thinks I'm dead, Stephanie thought. Too weak to move, she watched Samantha glide into her closet. She returned with a pink suit from Stephanie's wardrobe and tossed it on the bed. From the jewelry box, she picked a strand of pearls to hang around her neck.

After she dressed, she appraised herself in the mirror. "There is something missing," she muttered. She snatched one of Stephanie's wigs from its stand and stuffed her hair under it. Satisfied, she skipped to the telephone and dialed.

Stephanie felt herself slipping into an obscure abyss. *No, no,* she thought. *Fight it! Stay conscious!* Before she slipped into darkness, she heard Samantha talking to someone.

"This is your president," she squealed her delight. "Get over here."

Chapter 53

～

Damn you, Samantha. Lowe gripped his chest and tried to breathe normally. He refused to have another heart attack because of that stupid woman.

The cold air coming in through the opened car window filled his lungs and allowed him to breathe more easily. The knot of anxiety in his chest dissolved now, as they approached the White House. Willy had driven in excess of the speed limit at the senator's command. Now he slowed, stopped the limo, and waited for admittance.

"The president is expecting you," said a courteous guard. "She asks you to come to her private quarters."

Willy moved the car slowly up the circular drive to the North Portico.

"Good. She's followed my instructions this time," Lowe told his driver through gritted teeth. "Wait 'til I get my hands on her."

Willy parked the limo and said nothing.

As they walked the familiar route to the elevator that would take them upstairs, Lowe pondered the situation. What was happening with Samantha? Not even four hours since she pledged to obey his orders, and she had already failed him. She didn't have the kind of obedience he expected of her. Instead, she had acted on her own and ordered him to the White House like a flunky. On the telephone she said she was the president. *What did that mean? What had she done to Stephanie?*

Lowe received his answers when they opened the door to the president's suite. They found Samantha sprawled on a sofa in the bedroom with the crumpled body of her twin at her feet.

"What have you done?" Lowe bellowed.

"I'm president now," Samantha said, raising a haughty eyebrow.

"Are you crazy? How do you expect to get away with this?"

"That's why I called you."

He stared at her in disbelief, wondering what to do next. "Willy hadn't killed her before now because he has good sense. He listens to me. We were waiting for the right time."

She smiled playfully at Willy. "Well, I decided it was the right time."

"The right time is not in the jaws of the White House," Willy scoffed. His eyes scanned the room. Almost immediately he stomped to the old trunk and opened it. "This is empty," he said, propping the president up and heaving her like a sack over his shoulder. He stuffed her inside with her knees bent to her chest.

"What you did was stupid. I would've handled it," Lowe scolded again.

Before Willy shut the lid, Samantha bent over and detached the presidential pin from Stephanie's collar. "Now I have two of them."

"Woman, are you listening to me?" Lowe glanced uneasily at Willy. He grabbed Samantha's shoulder and whirled her around. "You're supposed to be working for me. I don't want you summoning me again to clean up your mess. Understand?"

Samantha shrugged and capered to the window. Lowe stared after her, wondering why he hadn't seen her instability before.

"How are we getting the body out of here?" Willy asked.

Silence.

Samantha's mind snapped back. "That trunk once belonged to Eleanor Roosevelt. Stephanie wanted to donate it to the Smithsonian."

Lowe studied the oak case. It was a large one, 36" wide x 21" deep x 24" tall. With Stephanie's tiny frame stuffed inside, it would weigh about 145 pounds. "It'll take several men to lift it," he said. "Call your friends, Willy."

Willy telephoned two cronies and ordered them to bring a van. Lowe could not assist with the lifting, so he suggested Samantha ask the president's bodyguards for help.

Willy's eyes boggled. "The Secret Service won't fall for that. These are trained security men. They're not going to let us take a valuable trunk out of here."

Lowe's mouth twisted in a half grin. "They'll do what their president tells them to do." His voice became commanding. "Samantha, you said you can fool everyone. Show me."

Samantha glided through the president's sitting room and outside the living quarters where she found agents Goldman and Vincent, who had replaced Stein and Bobbitt for the night shift. Bored, they were more than eager to help. In a matter of minutes, Vincent returned with a large dolly.

"What's in this?" Goldman grunted, as he and Willy lifted the weighty trunk onto the dolly.

"It's full of things that belonged to Eleanor Roosevelt," Samantha lied. "Some are books. I'm giving it all to the Smithsonian Institute."

Lowe noticed Goldman eyeing him suspiciously, probably wondering why the exiled senator was included in the transportation of a trunk. He felt uncomfortable until Samantha noticed the agent's expression. Her next lie came just as easy. "Senator Lowe is on the board of the institute," she said, "so he's got a truck waiting. Please assist him in any way you can."

Lowe was pleased. She had redeemed herself.

"May I get you a wheelchair, Senator?" Vincent offered.

Normally Lowe was adamant about walking. Now, wanting to remove Stephanie's body as fast as possible, he agreed. Vincent recruited the chair from a nearby office and pushed the elderly senator behind the moving dolly.

Samantha remained in her new quarters as the two unsuspecting Secret Service agents helped Willy with the trunk. Outside they loaded it into a waiting van and then headed back inside.

Lowe stepped inside his limo. "What are you going to do with the body? Bury it?" he asked Willy's friend through the rolled down window.

The man, perhaps 25, offered a smug grin. "My uncle's got a mortuary in West Virginia. We'll cremate it when he's gone home for the night."

Lowe liked it. No body to find. "Don't burn the trunk. It's got to end up at the Smithsonian tomorrow."

"No problem." The young man smiled at him with rotting teeth. "Who's dead?"

It occurred to Lowe they would recognize Stephanie. "Burn the trunk," he said. "If no one opens it and sees the body, you'll get an extra c-note."

"Don't worry. I don't want you sending Willy after me."

"Do you know who I am?"

"No, sir."

"Good. Let's leave it that way."

The man shook his hand and jumped into the van where two shadowy figures waited.

A few minutes later Willy slid behind the wheel of the limo and pulled away from the White House. In the backseat, Lowe planned the next step in a scenario kicked off by Samantha. "Willy, I need you to cover for Samantha."

"Something tells me we'll always be cleaning up after her. She's a fruitcake."

"I know. But it's too late to change the plan. Stephanie Franklin is gone and we're stuck with Samantha."

"Why not knock her off?"

"First things first. I need you to take care of the president's doctor before she realizes Stephanie is fully recovered. Kill Tony Franklin too. He'll be the first to spot Samantha."

Chapter 54

～

The blue van sped along Highway 290. In the front of the cab, three men guzzled beer and sang along with the radio. The driver was a beefy Hispanic wearing a backwards baseball cap. The one in the middle, a thin man in a black jacket, was very drunk. Their companion, a young man of college age with blackened teeth, kept pushing buttons to find a rock and roll station.

"You call that music? It'll burst your eardrums," said the driver. "Find a country station."

In the back of the van, the antique trunk bounced and shook with every pothole in the road. The leather straps that secured the lid had worked themselves loose.

The man with bad teeth tossed an empty beer can over his shoulder and accidentally hit the trunk.

The driver grinned. "Ain't ya got no respect for the dead?"

The three laughed and the young man popped open another beer. "This is it," he said, pointing out a gravel road. "This'll take us over the state line."

The radio blared with country music as they crossed into West Virginia.

"I gotta take a leak," the thin one announced. "There's a station up ahead."

Inside the trunk, Stephanie opened her eyes. Startled at first, touching the sides of the trunk in the darkness, she groped her way to find the top and lifted the lid. Peeking out, rubbing the dried blood on her wounded head, she tried to clear her mind. She stared at the backs of three men's heads, and sensing danger, slipped back down into the trunk.

The music was too loud and made her head throb more.

"I gotta take a leak," the man announced again over the blare of the radio. "Let's stop for grub too."

The van pulled up to a diner where the only other vehicle was a 2002 Pontiac. As two men stumbled inside the diner, the thin one made his way to the outside entrance of the men's restroom.

Stephanie raised the lid cautiously. She felt dizzy, but she climbed out of the trunk and crawled on stiff knees to the back of the van. At first, unable to get the door open, she was overcome with jumbled thoughts of her own survival and a war that was imminent. *I need to get away,* she thought frantically. *I have to be on that plane tomorrow.* Then she collapsed.

She was unconscious for only a moment. When her head cleared, she dragged herself to the front and pulled herself over the seat. She watched the intoxicated man leave the restroom and stagger into the diner. She slid out, at first losing her footing, but recovering, she headed for the side of the diner to hide.

Inside the women's restroom, Stephanie splashed water on her face and bloody scalp. After carefully examining the head wound, she turned around and leaned against the basin. For the first time, she saw the payphone.

Hope returned. She lifted the receiver but found no coins in her slacks or in the telephone's coin return. She moaned and sank to the floor, feeling faint again.

When Stephanie opened her eyes, a redheaded girl in a checkered shirt and denim pants stood over her. Stephanie guessed that the girl was about ten.

"Are you okay?" she asked.

Stephanie groaned. "I need help."

The girl squatted near her and stared, unafraid.

"I need to make a phone call. Do you have a cell phone?"

She shook her head.

"Do you have any change for this phone?" Stephanie asked, rubbing her throbbing head.

The wide-eyed girl dug into her pocket and handed Stephanie two quarters.

Stephanie groaned and managed to stand with the child steadying her. "Thank you. Where are we?"

"Reed's Diner outside Wardensville."

"What's your name?"

"Kristyn Gregg."

Stephanie put the coins into the phone and dialed. "Do you know who I am?"

Kristyn shook her head. That was a surprise to Stephanie until she remembered that she was not wearing her wig. Her head throbbed. She glanced at her bloody hair in the mirror as she listened for someone to answer her call.

The door opened and Kristyn's mother leaned inside. "We're waiting. Hurry up." She focused distrustful eyes on Stephanie. "Who are you talking to? You know better than to talk to strangers."

"This lady passed out on the floor. I just wanted to see if she was okay."

The color drained from her mother's face. "That does it. Drunks everywhere, even in the Ladies. We're not stopping here again. Let's go."

Kristyn left, never learning that she had helped the president.

Chapter 55

~

Tony decided to mix himself a pitcher of martinis. He contemplated taking it with him to the bomb shelter under the East Wing. He was stirring the ingredients at the portable bar in the president's living room when the bedroom door opened.

Samantha entered, sashaying across the floor. She lounged on the sofa and crossed her legs.

"I wasn't sure you were here," he said. "I thought you'd be underground."

"Haven't you heard there's not going to be a war?"

"You're sure we're safe?"

"Yes." She shot him a seductive smile. "Aren't you going to offer me a drink, darling?"

Surprised at Stephanie's unusual show of affection, Tony's spirits perked up. "The usual club soda and lemon?"

"Ick! We're celebrating. Fill the glass with gin."

Tony smiled and went to join her, carrying the drinks. "What are we celebrating?"

"Samantha is finally gone."

"How'd you manage that?"

"I think she felt safer leaving the country." She lifted her drink in a toast. "Hallelujah! Free at last."

Samantha's sudden departure puzzled Tony; but he sipped his drink and said nothing, until his eyes fell on a driver's license just inside the bedroom door. He went to pick it up. "It's Samantha's."

"She left last night. She's not going to need that where she is."

Tony stuffed it into his pocket.

She edged closer, so she was breathing right up against him. "I think it's time we put everything behind us. I want you to move back into our bedroom."

"I'd like that," Tony lied, leading her there.

She draped her arms around his neck. She clutched handfuls of his hair, breathless. "Make it like it was before."

Tony kissed her, but something didn't feel right. Then he knew. He pushed her away and she landed on the bed. "What are you doing, Samantha?"

She giggled and stroked the presidential pin. "I've got it all now." She paused, running her playful fingers down his cheek. "I'd like to have you as my husband. It would make it all complete."

He seized her wrist tightly and studied the scarred hand. "Where's Stephanie?"

"I told you my twin is gone. Don't push it."

"Is she dead?"

Samantha exploded. "Yes! You'll get your money if that's what you're worried about."

"Half?"

"Why not."

"You promised me money before. I never got it."

She stared at him as if that truth had never occurred to her. Immediately she reached for a checkbook in her purse. "I'm going to give you what's in Samantha's account," she said, scrawling a check and handing it to him. "I'll use Stephanie's money from now on. I've been working on her signature."

Tony stared down at the check and smiled.

"Enough zeroes?"

Five million. He nodded, astonished by her sudden generosity.

She shrugged. "I'll inherit everything from Aunt Catherine someday."

"Okay, we're in business."

"I want you to help with my charade. I get to be Stephanie. That's as important to me as the money is to you."

"You don't know one thing about being a president."

"Stephanie didn't either, so it'll be easy. Anyway, Senator Lowe will help me."

"Is he behind this? You just keep getting in deeper and deeper, don't you? Are you sure you can trust him?"

She sipped her drink, not answering.

"Stephanie didn't trust him. If you're not careful, you'll be caught."

"Why should my twin always get everything, while I've had nothing?"

He rolled his eyes.

"Stop belittling me. I know what I'm doing. Dr. Pierce has my stem cells."

He sat up straighter. "Why did you do that?"

"No one will suspect I killed her if I wanted her to have the transplant."

Tony's jaw dropped. Did Samantha realize she had just confessed to premeditated murder?

Chapter 56

The White House halls were empty as it neared eight p.m. Inside the security room on the first floor, Agent Stanley sat in front of hall monitors playing solitaire. On the screens he watched the usual maintenance crew vacuuming empty bedrooms on the third floor. Two cooks in the kitchen peeled potatoes for a meal the following day. It was the same every night, boring.

A burst of boisterous male laughter ended the silence. Stanley blinked at the top monitor. Dalton and Stein approached him from the West Wing, so he stuffed his iPod into his pocket.

The phone rang.

Stanley lifted the receiver and answered as the agents entered. "Security." As he listened, he rose to his feet restlessly and motioned for someone to trace the call. "Where did you get this number?" he asked.

"I'm President Franklin."

"Sure, and I'm Donald Duck."

The caller, her voice strained, went on. "You know me as Rosebud."

His mouth dropped open. He covered the receiver and spoke to Dalton. "She insists she's the president, sir."

By then Dalton had picked up an extension. "Hello. Who is this?"

Stanley continued to listen. It sounded more and more like Stephanie Franklin's voice coming over the line. "Dalton, thank

God!" the woman said. "I need you to come get me. I'm at Reed's Diner outside Wardensville."

Stanley's eyes followed Dalton's gaze to a monitor. Tony and the president had stepped off the elevator. "Madam, I'm looking at her right now. Are you aware that impersonating the president is against the law?"

The caller became more urgent. "Dalton, don't you recognize my voice? Do a voice check!"

Dalton continued to watch President Franklin and Tony. They stopped briefly to converse with another agent. When they separated, the president returned to the elevator alone.

As she jabbed the button, Dalton pointed on the screen to her presidential pin.

The call was a hoax.

Dalton's eyes flashed. "There are a dozen voice impersonators who do a better job!" He spewed out the words and hung up.

* * *

After Samantha went upstairs, Tony ambled down the corridor. Head bent, with no interest in his path, he scrolled through his text messages. One was a sexy text from Macy, sent an hour ago. Macy had been waiting for him in the parking lot all that time.

Tony's stroll became a trot. He waved as he passed by the security station. "How's it going, guys?" He said, not intending to stop.

Stanley answered him. "We just got a strange phone message. Some dame claimed to be the president."

Tony's eyes locked on the agent. "I was with her just a second ago."

"We traced the call," Dalton added. "Want to press charges?"

"Why bother? Unless she keeps calling."

A frown deepened in Stanley's brow. "Golly, she sure sounded just like the president," he said to Dalton. "Very few people have this number, and she knew about Rosebud."

The awful truth hit Tony like a jackhammer. *Stephanie is alive.* His stomach clenched but his gaze didn't waver. "It was Samantha, playing games. She's pretending to be Stephanie again."

Dalton nodded, but he gazed with suspicious eyes. "That would be it."

"Didn't she go back to Mexico?" Stein asked.

Tony didn't answer the question. His mind was loaded with uncertainty. *What's going on? Did Samantha really think Steph was dead? Or had she outright lied?*

"Look, this is a family problem," Tony said. "Stephanie needs to take care of this herself. Give me the address."

Dalton handed him the piece of paper.

"Wardensville. That's in West Virginia, isn't it?"

"She said a diner called Reed's," Stanley said. "Of course that's probably a lie too."

"I'll take care of this," Tony repeated, fingering Samantha's license in his pants pocket. *It's time to finish it.*

"Where is your security team?" Dalton asked.

"I left them with Steph." Not really a lie. They had no idea Tony planned to leave the White House. "I'm just going to get something from my car," he said, continuing his route to the parking lot.

Dalton ordered Stanley and Stein to accompany him.

Tony cringed. *They're going to be in the way.* He'd have to shake this protective detail too.

He texted Macy as he walked ahead. "Do you have the gun?"

* * *

An hour later Tony sped along, making good time in Samantha's Jaguar. He had left Washington on I-66, crossed into West Virginia on I-81, and then detoured on to VA-55 towards Wardensville.

Tense from anticipation, he gripped the steering wheel with the black gloves he'd worn to avoid leaving fingerprints. When he spotted a billboard for "Reed's Diner - 5 miles," he steered the car off the road and waited for Macy to show up. When she arrived in his Lincoln, braking fast on the gravel, he pushed down on the pedal and headed again towards the diner. There was no reason for the lovers to talk; they had everything planned.

In no time, they pulled up in front of Reed's. The diner was dark now and a *closed* sign hung on its soiled glass door. Slipping the gun Macy had given him inside his jacket, Tony exited the Jag. He prowled around outside the darkened building and peeked inside a window just in case. After finding the restrooms locked, he headed to the Lincoln.

Macy rolled down a window. "Where is she?"

He shrugged.

"What now?"

"Scoot over. I'm driving." He tossed the pistol on the seat between them.

They continued their quest on the dark country road, lit only by the Lincoln's headlights and a full moon.

Macy broke the silence. "You're sure it was Stephanie calling?"

"Had to be."

Macy picked up the gun and checked its magazine. "I thought Samantha said she was dead."

"Sam's not all there, you know. We've got to make sure."

A few minutes later, they spotted Stephanie staggering haggardly on the side of the road ahead. She turned, hearing the car, and blinded by the light, shaded her eyes from the glare.

Tony slowed down. "Get in back. Quick."

Macy threw her body over the seat and squeezed down low on the floor. Tony tossed the gun over his shoulder. Braking to a stop, he opened the door and leaned out. "Need a ride?"

The worry on Stephanie's face instantly disappeared. "Thank God it's you," she said breathlessly, stumbling to the passenger side and sliding in next to him.

"I heard the guards talking about your phone call and figured it out," Tony said, feigning concern. He turned the car back towards the diner. "Are you okay, Steph? What happened to your head?"

"Sam tried to kill me. She's crazy."

"I know. She's pretending to be you."

Stephanie put her face in her hands. "I need to straighten things out. I've got to be on that plane to Wakembezi."

As they slowed down, Stephanie saw the red Jaguar in the headlights. Alarm filled her voice. "Why is Sam here?"

On cue Macy rose up from behind the seat. She grabbed a handful of Stephanie's hair, too sparse for a good grip, and pointed the barrel of the gun at her throat. Stephanie fought, her feet kicking against the windshield.

"Macy, not in my car!" Tony yelled, stamping hard on the brakes.

The sudden lurch of the car catapulted Macy forward, knocking the gun from her grasp. It flew against the glove box, glanced off, and fell to the floor. In that jolting second, Stephanie pulled her head away and escaped from the car. She ran blindly back down the road.

"Get her!" Macy screamed, running after her.

For a second Tony gawked after the two women; then he grabbed the gun from the car and followed in determined pursuit.

By now Stephanie tired to a stumbling jog. Slowing, she glanced over her shoulder. As Macy bore down upon her, Stephanie threw up a hand to protect herself. A scream sprang from her throat, but it was stifled by a jarring impact that left them struggling on the ground. Macy pounded her nose. Frantically Stephanie fought to push her away.

"Tony, help me!" Macy shrieked, sitting on Stephanie. She raised her eyes to see Tony standing in the road, frozen in indecision, holding the pistol at his side. "Tony, come on! Do it!"

Tony refused to think about it; he just fired, barely looking at Stephanie. When he raised his eyes, he saw his wife's face covered in blood. Still frozen, he stared down at the body. Adrenaline coursed through his arteries. "I did it. I can't believe I really did it!"

"You closed your eyes. You could have killed me," Macy snapped.

"Is she dead?"

Car lights crested the hill. "Come on, Tony." Macy tugged on his sleeve. "We've got to go."

They pulled away from the scene of the crime, full of the thrill of the kill. Soon they had left the car lights behind.

"Do you think they stopped to see what happened?" Macy asked, looking back at the road.

"Probably."

"We can't go back that way now," Tony said, driving the Lincoln into the mountains.

They had gone only ten miles when Tony remembered Samantha's license in his pants pocket. He tossed it on the seat next to the gun.

Macy picked it up. "What's this?"

"I wanted everyone to believe Samantha died there. It doesn't matter, though. Samantha's Jaguar is with Stephanie's body."

Chapter 57

∼

Dalton tired of the dark road and clicked on the sedan's high beams. Staring at the empty ribbon ahead, he forced his mind to retrace the last few hours.

After President Franklin called for help and Dalton hung up on her, he had become troubled almost immediately. The woman's voice he'd heard sounded so much like his president—and it had been an anxious voice that reached out to him over the line. His uneasiness turned to suspicion when Tony galloped off to find Samantha, without wanting the Secret Service involved.

Dalton had sent Stanley and Stein to guard him, but Tony left them standing in the parking lot while he and Macy supposedly had a tryst inside his Lincoln. Before the agents realized it, the lovers had driven out the gate.

After the red-faced agents called Dalton in the control room, he sent teams in all directions to find the couple. Even Dalton had driven up and down the streets near the Capitol.

By a stroke of luck, Dalton had spotted Tony driving Samantha's Jaguar on Independence Avenue. Dalton's curiosity peaked as he watched Tony's mistress trailing him in the Lincoln.

Dalton shadowed Macy at a distance as they left Washington and drove into West Virginia. He didn't want his black sedan noticed on the sparsely traveled road, so he had pulled back on WV-55. No problem. He knew they were heading to Wardensville and the GPS showed no intersecting roads for twenty miles.

Now he decided to catch up. He pressed the pedal and the speedometer flew upwards. As Dalton crested the hill, the Lincoln pulled out from Reed's Diner, spraying gravel behind the tires.

Seeing the limp form laying in the dirt near the Jaguar, Dalton slammed on his brakes, skidding to a stop. He exited his car on the run, going directly to the female and kneeling beside her.

It was the president's sister. Dalton wouldn't have recognized her if the Jag hadn't been there. Her face and scalp were streaked with blood. Her hair looked as if someone had chopped it off.

He pressed his fingers to her throat, and finding a weak pulse, called for an ambulance. He made an effort to revive her, rubbing her limp wrists, patting her cheeks.

"Samantha? Can you hear me?" He removed his jacket and pressed it against the bleeding head wound. "Samantha?"

At last, she moved her head slightly, nodding, but she was not yet fully conscious.

"You'll be all right," he assured her. "I'm here, Samantha."

Moaning, she opened her eyes with difficulty, only for a brief moment, but time enough to tell him that Tony had shot her. "I'm the president," she said, barely audible. "Sam is pretending to be me. She tried to kill me."

For a second he had doubted the switch, until he searched both of her hands and found no scar.

"Are Tony, Macy, and Samantha in this together?" Dalton asked.

The president had passed out.

When the ambulance arrived only minutes later, Stephanie was still unconscious. With the blood on her face, no one seemed to recognize her.

"She's lost a lot of blood and may have a concussion," the medic said, as he and his partner lifted Stephanie onto a gurney. "Head wounds bleed profusely, so they often look more serious than they are."

Dalton telephoned Dr. Pierce.

Chapter 58

∽

The road climbing uphill through the canyon was twisty and narrow, barely wide enough for two vehicles to pass each other. The headlights of the Lincoln provided the only visibility. Tony planned to take another interstate highway south at the next town and get back to Washington before Samantha's flight.

Macy unbuckled her seat belt and snuggled next to him. "It's just the two of us at last."

Tony chuckled. "I still can't believe we got away with it."

"What if we don't get back in time to tell Samantha what happened?"

"She already thinks Stephanie is dead, so we don't need to tell her anything." He draped his arm around her. "Look in my inside pocket."

She reached into his coat and pulled out Samantha's check. A squeal of joy rose in her throat. "Five million!"

"I'll put it in the bank as soon as we get back."

"That's the first thing I would have done. What if flaky Samantha changes her mind and stops payment?"

"I had no time. Stephanie called the White House and I had to find you fast." He returned the check to his pocket, and gripped the wheel with both hands to make the curve ahead.

The radio was tuned to a news station, so Macy leaned over and scanned for music stations. She found "Winner," sung by Jaime Foxx and Justin Timberlake.

"Let's make this our song," she giggled.

Tony tapped a finger on the wheel in beat with the music, while Macy sang along.

You know you lookin' at a winner, winner, winner
I can't miss, can't lose, can't miss,
You know you lookin' at a winner, winner, winner
Cause I'm a winner, yeah I'm a winner.

They were happy.

"We belong together," Tony said. "We know how to reach out and grab the things we want. We are winners."

A van came up from behind, going fast on the way up the hill.

"Where'd he come from?" Tony muttered, slowing to make sure there was enough room for the van to go by. He edged slightly to the right, but he was cautious because the road dropped off sharply in spite of guardrails.

After the van passed, another car came up behind them in the darkness. The vehicle had its bright lights on, and its glare, reflecting in the rearview mirror, blinded him. The road was too twisty here, so Tony considered pulling over after the curve. The headlights edged closer now, seemingly pressing against the back bumper, too close for safety.

When they made the curve, the blue van swerved across both lanes and blocked the road a hundred yards ahead. Tony braked desperately, trying to avoid a collision. The high headlights behind them still pressed him to drive faster. He braked again, and the other vehicle plowed into his bumper, pushing him, going faster.

Macy screamed. "There's not enough room!" She stared out at the mountainous terrain on the edge of the road.

Tony slowed again, staying away from the edge. Suddenly a white Bronco moved abreast of him. It slammed its full body against the side of the Lincoln. Tony glanced over at the hostile driver, and what he saw was the malicious grin of Willy Wurtzel.

In that one fleeting second, Tony knew he was dead. He fought the steering wheel, straining to hold his course, but another slam against his sedan forced it and its two passengers over the edge. The car rolled over and over and landed upside down at the bottom of the deep ravine.

* * *

Willy stepped out of the Bronco and peered over the edge. It had worked out well. Admittedly, it had been touch-and-go for a while. He had followed the Lincoln when it left Washington, lost it once, and backtracked to I-81. About the same time, his hired men had discovered the lid of the trunk opened and the body missing, so they telephoned his cell. Both cars had sped towards Reed's Diner, coming from two directions, retracing their steps. The blue van had pulled up just as Willy slowed down.

Surprised to see Dalton standing over a body near Samantha's Jaguar, Willy had kept driving with the van following. Half a mile down the road he pulled over and waved the other driver to park beside him. "I've got a contract on a man driving a Lincoln," he had said. "I need your help."

"What about the missing corpse?" asked the man with black teeth. "Your boss said for us to cremate it."

Willy's bushy eyebrows shot up. "How do you do that? The body is gone."

He stuffed his hands in his pocket. He had the needy, approval-seeking expression of a little boy.

"Was there any evidence of someone breaking into your van?" Willy asked.

"No."

"Did you lock it?"

"Yes."

"Then it had to be opened from inside." Willy was irritated with himself for not checking the president's pulse. Then he remembered what he had seen. "Your lost body was back there at the diner."

"How do you know?"

"She's wearing the same dress she had on when I stuffed her in the trunk."

"We need to go back for her," the Latino said.

"She wasn't dead, but now she is?" the tall one asked.

"We don't have time for this!" Willy growled, more at himself than the others. "I need to kill a guy before he gets away. Just do what I say if you want to be paid."

Quickly he gave his cronies their orders. In minutes the van had pulled out, leaving rubber, speeding on the dark road, with the Bronco close behind.

Now Willy and the men from the van stood staring over the edge at the wrecked car below. "Satisfied?" the Latino asked Willy.

Willy dashed to his truck and pulled out the rifle he had used to kill the vice chairman. He aimed carefully and fired. The tank blew, and leaping orange flames danced over the car, consuming it.

"Now I'm satisfied," he beamed. "Let's go home."

Chapter 59

Willy parked on the quiet farm road. He had only two hours of darkness left. He had killed two people tonight and still had one job to do. He was ready to go after the old lady.

Stepping out of the Bronco, he anchored his arms through the straps of a black backpack stuffed with dynamite. His eyes surveyed the countryside, and when he was certain that no one else was around, he tramped through the fence where he had already severed the wire.

You could never be too careful. If Lowe hadn't offered him twice the usual fee, Willy would have waited a few weeks to eliminate Catherine Taylor. He had never been comfortable with the light of the full moon caressing the darkness—that could be dangerous for a hit man who didn't want to be identified. *You get careless and you get killed*, he reminded himself.

He trudged over the wooded terrain of the property adjoining the Taylor estate, until he came to the next opening in the fence, cut days before on one of his scouting expeditions. Under a dead oak on the property line, he searched for the hidden detonators that he had buried previously. Dusting them off, he thrust them in his jacket and hiked on, slowing now that he was nearing the house.

As he reached the clearing, Willy had uneasy thoughts. His military experiences had taught him the importance of surveillance before taking down a target. Although he had scrutinized the estate for weeks, he didn't feel ready. Getting to a member of a president's family was as hard as breaking into Fort Knox.

Since the beginning of March, he had taken the semblance of a worn path to the grassy slope behind the enormous house, trying to find the best way to get to the president's aunt. Unfortunately the elderly matriarch was somewhat of a recluse. When she did leave the house, the Secret Service shielded her with their bodies as if she were the president herself. Willy had also found it impossible to enter the locked garage and place a bomb in her limo. The only way he would get to her was in the house when she was alone. That meant in her bed or her bath.

Because of her crippling arthritis, Willy had guessed that her bedroom was downstairs. Lights in the hours after midnight flickered on and off on the first floor, leaving him to wonder if the old dame slept at all.

One evening, using binoculars to spy on the downstairs, he spotted Catherine Taylor in a bedroom on the east side of the mansion. He also discovered that her bodyguards were wandering around, switching lights off and on after she retired for the evening.

That night Willy decided the safest thing for him to do was blow up part of the edifice. Now he crawled through the vegetation with the explosives to do it.

The unexpected happened. An ambulance came up the drive, its bright lights shining up on the ridge. It stopped in front of the steps just as a SUV driven by the president's physician pulled up behind. Dr. Pierce raced up the steps. Almost immediately, Dalton arrived and a four-man security team materialized from the darkness. They carried the patient on a stretcher into the house.

Willy lay on his stomach and pondered whether to come back another time. In a few minutes, things were quiet again, as if everyone had settled in for the night. No one returned outside. Whoever the patient was, she was a diversion, and that would work to his advantage. If he got lucky, he'd blow up the doctor and aunt when they were together. That would complete Lowe's hit list.

From the weeds on the slope, Willy made another survey of the area. A blue-jacketed night watchman appeared, right on schedule. He ambled along, coming from the back of the house, moving toward the parking garage. He yawned, looking to neither right nor left, as he made sure the garage was locked. He hesitated, as if feeling Willy's eyes, scanned the hill, and then resumed his circuit to the front of the mansion.

No problem, Willy assured himself. *None whatsoever.* He knew that the guard returned to this area every thirty minutes. There was still time.

Slowly, crawling on his hands and knees, he slipped through shrubbery, bushes, and trees, hunting for a perfect spot to plant the explosives. In less than ten minutes, he had crawled closer than he had ever been, past the huge trunk of a leafy oak several yards from the targeted window. There, next to the house, he began digging a natural depression in the earth.

He heard a sudden clomping over twigs and fallen acorns. His heart skipped a beat. He turned to stare at a shadowy figure beneath the oak tree. The man's dark skin made him nearly invisible, except for his white shirt.

Willy struggled to his feet, clutching for the pistol in his jacket, but hampered by the detonators.

"Don't move," Nat Bobbitt said, stepping out into the moonlight.

Willy fled, fast. He wasn't caught yet, he told himself, dashing towards the woods. He fumbled for the revolver as he ran, pulling it out to fire at Bobbitt.

A second figure appeared, a female agent with her gun drawn. A third agent emerged from the front of the house, shouting for the officer on patrol.

Willy cursed and tried to decide who to shoot first. In that split second, bullets from three shooters tore deeply into his stomach, cheek, and chest. As he lay beneath the giant oak tree, the earth soaking up his blood, he saw the security camera mounted on the tree trunk. His last thought before dying was that he'd screwed up. Senator Lowe wasn't going to be happy.

* * *

Before the shots were fired, Dalton had been asking questions. He didn't understand why the doctor had brought President Franklin to the Taylor Estate instead of a hospital.

"I've sworn to keep the president's condition secret," Dr. Pierce explained.

That left Dalton with more questions. After some probing, he forced her to reveal the president's leukemia. "She didn't want any other doctors to find out. She doesn't want Americans to know either."

"How bad is the leukemia?" he asked.

"Bad." The doctor's reply was abrupt, possibly because she was checking Stephanie's blood pressure.

They had gathered in the upstairs room where Amanda Taylor had died. Stephanie had been placed gently in the hospital bed that remained there after nearly a year. Dalton and Catherine sat near the medicated Stephanie, watching Dr. Pierce insert an IV and carefully clean away the dried blood from her scalp.

When Dalton explained to Aunt Catherine what Samantha had done, the old woman knitted her eyebrows but refrained from making the obvious comment. All she said was, "Don't say anything about this to anyone. Let's see what Stephanie wants to do when she wakes up."

She stuck out her hand and Dalton took it, nodding. "I've grown to love you, Catherine, like a mother. I'd do anything for you."

"I care for you too."

"Doing things in secret is hard for me. When you asked me to bring your niece to the estate, I did. I flashed my Secret Service ID and directed the ambulance driver to deliver Jane Doe here. I told the agents downstairs she was Samantha. But I can't keep piling lie upon lie. Please don't ask me to."

Catherine cleared her throat. "I'm only asking you to do what you've sworn to do— protect your president. You've done nothing wrong."

"Her head's taken quite a pounding," the doctor interrupted, stitching up the president's head wound. "There are two injuries here. I think a bullet grazed her scalp."

"She looks terrible," Catherine said. "Her face is swollen—her nose too. Is it broken?"

Before Dr. Pierce could answer, they heard the shots fired outside. Dalton bolted for the door, gun drawn, but stopped. He had second thoughts about security in the house and returned to guard the president.

He positioned himself at the window and peered out. After a few minutes, he spotted Karen Kelsey running around the side of the house. She toted a backpack. He relaxed, but headed for the staircase with his gun still drawn.

Karen entered the foyer and called up to him. "The intruder is dead. He was carrying dynamite."

"Any ID?"

She shook her head. "He'll be hard to identify. Part of his face was blow away."

Dalton returned his pistol to his shoulder holster. "Call the medical examiner and have him pick up the body. Check the fingerprints."

"Shall I call more agents out here? Looks like someone's real serious about killing the president's sister."

Dalton swallowed hard. He honored his promise to Catherine. "Call in Stanley and Burnside," he answered, turning back to the patient's room.

Bobbitt entered the foyer and started climbing the stairs, but Dalton stopped him with a raised palm. "Get helicopters with lights out here to scan the woods," he told him.

"I want to see Doctor Pierce," Bobbitt demanded. "I've been thinking all of this might have to do with her lawsuit."

"This isn't the time for speculation. I need you guarding outside."

Bobbitt stalled on the fourth step.

"Leave her alone, Bobbitt. Debra doesn't want to see you anymore. I promised the president you'd keep your distance."

He crossed his arms, a scowl flickering on his face. "And if I don't?"

"Is a few minutes with her worth your job?"

A frown of defeat cracked Bobbitt's face. Without another word he retreated outdoors. Dalton stood at the head of the stairs until the door shut, and then returned to the sick room.

All night Dalton and the doctor sat in vigil at Stephanie's bedside, while Catherine sat in an upstairs bedroom and prayed. Dalton dozed off at dawn. It wasn't until he awoke at ten a.m. that he and Dr. Pierce realized Air Force One would have left for Wakembezi with Samantha on board.

Chapter 60

∼

When the president's helicopter arrived at the airport, Samantha still believed she had killed Stephanie. She climbed the steps of Air Force One, waving at the throng of reporters and television cameras. She felt exhilarated. This must be the way Stephanie felt the first time she flew on her private plane.

Sitting in a padded leather chair by a window in her quarters, she fastened her seatbelt and waited for the departure. A wicked smile curled her lips, one that spoke a volume of words that she had tucked secretly inside. She was the president of the United States! Americans always talked about achieving the American Dream, but few had ever experienced anything like this. She had risen from the bowels of prostitution to the most powerful position in the world. The thought both amazed and amused her.

From the window she spotted Adam running to the plane. He wasn't just a good-looking hunk. He was the kind of man who loved passionately and completely. Maybe she had a chance with him now that Stephanie was gone.

He arrived breathless at her stateroom. "Steph, something's happened." He paused, searching for the words. "Tony's been in a car wreck. He's dead, Steph."

"Oh. What happened?" Samantha made an effort to sound concerned.

"He was with Macy Youngblood. They ran off the road in the mountains."

She stared at the floor, wondering what to do. "I think I still have to go, Adam."

"I knew you'd say that. But you had to know."

She sat quietly, trying to cry like a grieving widow, but after decades of repressing her emotions, found it impossible. She settled for a sad expression.

Adam broke the silence. "I've prepared a statement that you're still going to Wakembezi to prevent a war, because you believe a president puts her duty to her people above her grief."

"Of course. That's what I must do." She breathed a whimper. Then she told him to circulate the press release, and he headed to the communications room.

In a few minutes, Air Force One taxied down the runway to begin its journey to Wakembezi.

Adam returned with two cups of coffee. "There is a lot of grumbling going on. The onboard Secret Service and the press have found out they can't leave the plane with you."

She blinked, confused.

Adam handed her the coffee. "Doctor Pierce's assistant made it on board at the last minute."

"I don't need a doctor."

"At no time does the president of the United States travel without a doctor, you know that. We're required to have one with us in case of an emergency."

Samantha shrugged.

"I was also told your friend Ruddy will be there to meet us."

A puzzled Samantha wondered what other surprises were ahead.

* * *

Adam left Samantha alone, believing Stephanie needed privacy to grieve for her dead husband, just as she did when Howard died.

After several hours, he noticed she had left her stateroom. Now she stood in the hall outside the galley, sipping coffee from a Styrofoam cup and chatting with the steward. Eagerly Adam approached the woman he believed to be his closest friend.

He was amazed how refreshed she looked. The color was back in her cheeks and she was beaming, like a schoolgirl going to her first prom.

He followed her down the narrow corridor, past the Secret Service camped on a bench against the wall. He spoke as they entered her quarters. "I want to be the one who goes with you to see Sibaba."

"Sure. I want you with me."

"Security won't like it. They're already drawing lots to see who gets off the plane."

Her smiling face shifted into a perplexed frown. "What's going on?"

Adam chalked up her failing memory to nervousness and grief. "Sibaba said only one person besides the president will be allowed off the plane. He cited security concerns. He doesn't want to be assassinated too."

Her eyes fluttered, but she said nothing.

"He says any gun brought into Wakembezi will be an act of war."

She floated to her desk. "That's stupid. There's already been an act of war."

For the first time Adam noticed her scarred hand. "Samantha!"

Her eyes taunted him. "Yes, darling. Here we are again."

"What are you trying to pull? Where's Steph?"

"She's too ill to make the trip."

"I don't believe you."

"Don't worry. I can do this. I've been told what to say."

"You can't possibly. This isn't a game, Samantha."

"I'm the only one who can pull this off, Adam. Steph knows that."

Adam grabbed the phone off the desk and asked for a connection to the White House. Identifying himself, he asked to talk to the president.

He glanced at Samantha, who smugly sipped her coffee.

The president's secretary told him Stephanie was on Air Force One.

The plane began bucking in the sky. "Oh, hold on." Adam put the phone down and sat, strapping himself in, and then seized it again. "Look, Dawn, I know I sound rattled. Just humor me a minute. Can you remember the last time you saw the president's sister?"

Samantha's smirk widened into a full smile.

The answer was clear, in spite of the air-to-ground connection. "That was days ago," Dawn answered. "Did you hear she was shot?"

"What? Shot! When?" His eyes turned into hot embers. He slammed down the receiver and grabbed Samantha's arm. "What have you done?"

Hearing the outburst, Burnside rose from his seat in the hallway and hustled to the stateroom. He peered inside, only to have Samantha wave him away and shut the door.

She kept her tone low. "Sit down, Adam. Try to be calm. I'll tell you, but I don't want anyone else to hear."

Adam sat, his angry stare fixed on her face.

"Stephanie died this morning. She asked me to fill in for her."

"Liar."

"It was her last request. Sibaba mustn't know."

"She would have told me."

"I think you exaggerate your importance to her, Adam."

"No. No, I don't." He reached for a handkerchief to dab his eyes. "What's this about her sister being shot?"

"It must be a story Steph invented so Samantha would cease to exist."

His brow wrinkled in question. "I still don't get it."

She gripped her nails into the fabric of his sleeve. "Look, Adam. No one planned the leukemia. No one planned for her to die last night. But she did—and there was no time. She had to tell me what to do. She said no one was to know I'm not the president or there might still be a war."

He knew that was true.

Samantha became assertive. "You will help me, Adam. You will because Steph wanted you to, and you don't want to see America blown to pieces."

He nodded his compliance.

A knock interrupted them. Stein entered, followed by a ruddy-faced Marine with a silver briefcase handcuffed to his wrist.

"I'm the one going with you when you leave the plane," Stein said.

"But I've already told Adam he could go."

"No!" Stein roared. "You need Secret Service with you."

Adam felt his worth in question. "I know the Africans and some of their language. You don't."

Stein stepped closer. "You have to be protected, Madam President."

Adam's nostrils flared. "What can one agent without a gun do?"

"A lot more than you can!"

In the silence they glared at each other.

Stein thought a minute, then returned his gaze to Stephanie. "Madam President, I object to this. It's not protocol."

Samantha breathed deeply, her eyes locked on Adam's face. He knew she didn't dare cross him. She turned to Stein. "Just the other day you told me you'd carry out any command I give you. Do you remember that?"

Stein's eyes boggled. "Yes, ma'am."

"Throw protocol away," she ordered in a brisk tone. "Sibaba says that any weapon brought into his country will be considered an act of war. We have to take him seriously."

"Yes, ma'am."

"If we want peace, we have no choice but to do things his way."

Stein ducked his head, hiding his disappointment.

The Marine stepped forward. "What about the Football?" He patted the side of the case. "You're supposed to have it near you at all times—for the launch codes. I should go with you."

Samantha appeared stumped, so Adam answered for her. "In case of war, the vice president has a case of his own." He slid his chair closer to her. "I don't think it would be wise to let Sibaba get his hands on this, do you? I think it should stay behind."

Adam knew what he said made sense. Samantha nodded, visibly grateful for his input. *She's crazy to think she'll fool Sibaba,* he thought. *Not without me.*

Stephanie began adlibbing. "Look, I'm going to have a face-to-face with an old friend. There's nothing to worry about. I'll get him to allow you guys off the plane."

Stein nodded, but his teeth clenched.

When she stood, as a signal for the others to leave, Adam breathed easier. After the door shut behind them, she whirled to face him. "Anything else I should know about?"

He couldn't think of anything, so he shrugged.

She flashed him a wide smile. "I'm going to look though my file on Wakembezi. You will help me with any questions I have, won't you? I'm going to do a little homework for a few hours."

Not waiting for a reply, she headed towards the president's office. Adam studied her at a distance, and then remembered. He raised his voice to stop her. "What do you want me to do with the three letters?"

"Whatever Stephanie told you to do with them," she answered, disinterested. She opened the door and disappeared inside.

Adam sat quietly, trying to control all the feelings churning inside. He had lost the love of his life. The nation was in trouble. He had been forced into complicity with a woman he despised. But through it all, the grief took hold; it stifled the other emotions and buried them beneath unbearable sorrow.

He retreated to the staff office and opened his briefcase. On the outside of one envelope, in Stephanie's familiar handwriting, she had written, "To Adam, upon my death." The words sent daggers into his brain. Still, with every fiber of his being he wanted to read her last words to him.

He tore open the envelope and stared in shock at the message. His lips moved, the words too soft to escape his dry throat.

"*Oh, no.*"

Chapter 61

～

During the long flight, Adam barely saw Samantha. She hibernated in her office, and after a few hours went into her bedroom to sleep. In the morning a steward, doubling as her chef, had taken her breakfast and later lunch while she was alone in the Executive Suite. Now she had emerged from her cocoon, showered and changed, wearing a purple suit with the presidential pin on the lapel.

During the night Adam had moved into an empty section of the plane. What he had read in the letter had shaken him to the core. It was impossible to sleep. He spent hours trying to decide what to do. Now, through the open door, he spotted Samantha strolling in the hallway, the Marine with the Football a few paces behind her.

When Adam finally journeyed to the dining room, he found Samantha sitting at the table. Agent Stein handed her a glass of wine.

Adam frowned. "How many have you had?"

She answered with a toast. "You look like you need a highball." She gazed up at Stein. "Get Adam a drink."

Adam refused with a gesture of his hand. "We'll be landing in a few minutes. I'd like to talk to the president alone."

Without hesitation, Stein joined the other agents in the corridor.

"Ready?" Adam asked the new president.

Samantha seemed very confident. "A direct approach. A peaceful, apologetic attitude. Nothing could be simpler."

"I don't want you drunk."

"I'm not." She pulled a mirrored compact out of her purse and checked her lipstick. "Will President Sibaba meet us?"

"I don't know. Since Ruddy is coming, I doubt it. When Stephanie and I lived there, he often sent his nephew in his place." Adam inhaled deeply to calm his rapid heartbeat. "Whoever greets you, the proper greeting is *habari*, which means *hello*. After that, insist that no one speak anything but English. Do it immediately."

"Sure, I know that."

The pilot's voice resonated throughout the aircraft. "Madam President, we're ready to land now. Buckle up. We want to deliver you safely."

They scurried to the president's office to see Wakembezi from the air. Adam sat in his usual chair and stared out the window at the modern terminal with intricate roofs and domed metal structures. Even after six years, everything still looked the same.

He buckled his seat belt. "You'd better pull this off, Sam."

At last the plane touched down and the scenery outside the window took off in fast motion. As they slowed, Samantha jumped to her feet, not waiting for the craft to come to a standstill. Adam sat a moment, then struggled to his feet and lumbered up the aisle to the exit.

She waited for an agent to push open the door. At the top of the stairs, she offered an eager wave, but few people had turned out to greet her.

She swung around to Adam, who stood several feet behind her. "Where is everyone?"

"You've brought them the body of a dead leader. They're in mourning."

Before he could say anything else, Samantha hurried down the steps and approached a general with a chest full of metals. "Habari." She shook his hand. Beside him was the young man who translated for Vice Chairman Wasswa at the White House party.

Adam descended the steps and stood beside Samantha.

"Speak English to me," she said to the general. "My Swahili is rusty."

"He doesn't speak English," Ruddy replied. "I'm the only one here who does."

Samantha smiled. "It's good to see you again."

He nodded, barely looking at her. He pointed her to the waiting limo, its doors already opened.

As she slid inside, Samantha appeared eager and in high spirits. She glanced back at Adam, who was speaking with Ruddy behind the car. "Come on, guys. Let's go. Sibaba is waiting."

They moved inside the limo and sat across from her.

For a moment, staring at Samantha's broad smile, Adam was almost taken in. She looked so much like her twin, she might fool everyone.

The limo pulled away. Adam shifted his gaze to Air Force One where several agents had planted themselves on the stairs. Discontent lined their tense faces.

Samantha followed his line of vision out the back window. "Separation anxiety," she chuckled. "They don't know what to do without me."

A black hearse passed them going fast. The belly of the plane opened and the vice chairman's shrouded coffin was rolled into the arms of pallbearers.

Samantha turned back to watch the road ahead. For a while she stared out at the landscape. When she decided to speak, her voice was full of admiration. "What a beautiful country this is. I've missed living here."

Adam exchanged glances with Ruddy.

The limo screeched to a stop and picked up two more passengers. Samantha found herself sandwiched between two black men as big as NFL blockers. Her eyes widened. "Adam, what's going on?"

"We're playing out the scene, just like Stephanie planned it. I thought you wanted to do that."

The car sped away again, following the fence.

"We know you killed her," Ruddy said quietly.

Fear crawled into her eyes. "You're wrong. I didn't hurt her. She was my sister."

Ruddy ignored her. "I had a disagreement with my uncle," he told Adam. "He thinks he's punishing me by sending me on this mission."

"Then I won't see Sibaba?" she asked.

"No."

The limo came to an abrupt halt again, this time in front of a small building with flaking paint and rusting walls. Adam stepped out and waited for the others.

"Get out of the car," Ruddy ordered.

Samantha hesitated. "Why are we here? I thought we were going to a funeral."

Adam's stomach clenched but his gaze didn't waver. "You're going to be the president now. Isn't that what you promised Stephanie?"

The heavyweights jerked her out of the limo and dragged her into the shed.

Samantha gasped in horror. She had come face to face with her coffin. "Adam! Adam—" The fear had closed her throat.

The general pulled out a pistol.

Ruddy spoke clearly, precisely. "One leader for one leader. One death for one death. That's the price of peace. That's the way Miss Stephanie planned it."

Samantha tried to pull away, kicking and squirming, but her captors held her tighter. "I'm not Stephanie!"

"None of these men know that," Ruddy said. "The world won't know it."

Adam turned and left the shed. *There were so many lives at stake,* he told himself. *I had no choice. It was something that had to be done.*

A single shot rang out as he slid into the limo.

Chapter 62

Only moments after the media announced President Franklin's death, Kenneth Chang was sworn in by his brother-in-law, a justice of the peace in Oahu, Hawaii. While he was in flight back to Washington, his staff arranged a second swearing in—a more ceremonial one with the chief justice of the Supreme Court delivering the oath of office. It would be witnessed on television by the world.

In flight, Kenneth Chang had telephoned Dalton Mercer and summoned him to the vice president's home at Number One Observatory Circle. Located on the grounds of the United States Naval Observatory, the house was a three-story, Victorian-style home with 9,150 square feet of floor space and 21-foot ceilings.

Dalton hadn't been there in a decade. While he waited, he wandered the first floor for over an hour. He found little had changed, except most areas were filled with white furniture (a dangerous choice, he decided, when you have small children) and enough paintings on the walls to be a museum. For a while, he talked with the servants who were laying out a buffet on the dining room table. One of them reminded him that the 19th century house was originally built for the superintendent of the United States Naval Observatory, but Congress took it over in 1974.

"Walter Mondale was the first vice president to move into this house," said a white-haired Latina who was wrapping silverware in the linen napkins. "I think I liked him best. I had a baby in those days and no money for a sitter. He let me bring her with me to work. He even put a playpen in the kitchen."

"You've worked in this house a long time," Dalton said, more of a realization than a question.

"Yes, sir."

"How do you like working for the Changs?"

"I do. They're polite to the workers."

At that moment the new commander-in-chief arrived. He ushered Dalton into his library, away from reporters and TV camera operators who had camped out in the reception hall to record his oath of office.

Closing the door, Chang signaled for Dalton to sit on an elegant sofa, while he settled into a nearby chair.

"I want you to continue as head of security."

"Thank you, sir."

Chang shifted in his seat, glancing at his watch. "I wanted you here for the ceremony because we're going to be working closely together. Now tell me what you know."

"Not much—just what the media says. Given enough time, we'll get all the facts."

"I'm sure that's true. Right now, tell me about the attempt to kill Stephanie's sister. I'm told you saved her life."

Dalton nodded, unsure of what to say.

"Did Samantha tell you Tony Franklin shot her?"

"Yes, sir."

Chang's eyes narrowed into intense slits. "Stephanie's husband was killed, and I'm told the wreck couldn't have caused the explosion. There was another attempt to kill her aunt—"

"Unless that was a second attempt to kill Debra Pierce," Dalton interrupted. "She was at the Taylor home too."

Chang couldn't hide his surprise. "The doctor too? Who's behind all this, Dalton?"

"I can't prove it, but I think it was Senator Lowe."

Surprise turned into shock. "Why would he do that?"

That was the question Dalton had been asking himself for hours, ever since his trip to the morgue earlier in the day. "I haven't figured that out, sir. I know that the assassin at the Taylor home was Senator Lowe's driver. Even with his cheek blown away, I recognized him."

Chang rubbed his temple. "His name is Willy—I don't remember his last name."

"Wurtzel. We identified his fingerprints. He was a trained killer in Special Forces. He'd been in prison."

"You think Lowe knew that?"

"Sure. You check out your employees, don't you?"

Chang breathed deeply. "Did you know Philip Lowe is a friend of mine?"

"Yes, sir. But you needed to know the truth."

"That's correct. I never want you to keep things from me."

As Dalton contemplated his reply, the doorbell chimed. "That will be the chief justice," Chang said, standing. He lingered for another moment. "I don't like this, Dalton. This is not the way I want to begin my tenure in office. I don't want to be connected with anyone who is a criminal."

The door opened. The new first lady had come to escort her husband to the reception hall.

"I need you to keep this between us until we can talk again." Chang hurried to the ceremony without waiting for a reply.

Dalton joined the solemn witnesses who had lined the walls for the occasion. Thirty-six hours after Stephanie Franklin (Samantha) was declared dead, Kenneth Chang stepped into her shoes. With an estimated seventy million viewers watching, the chief justice requested that Chang place his hand on a Bible. His wife Lily stood at his elbow, the epitome of a devoted wife, smiling with pride. Beside her stood their oldest son, 19, who had cut classes at Harvard to be present at the swearing in ceremony. The youngest son held his mother's hand as his father repeated the oath of office. His little sister sat on the floor, more interested in petting the family dog than in the proceedings.

"I do solemnly swear that I will faithfully execute the office of President of the United States…" Chang repeated the words, phrase by phrase, as the chief justice stoically delivered the oath. In less than a minute, Chang became the leader of the Free World. He beamed, but only for a second, before his expression lapsed into the sad manifestation expected by Americans on this solemn occasion.

After the ceremony, Dalton watched everyone shaking hands with the new president. His mind floundered about, juggling good and bad thoughts about the state of the nation. Stephanie Franklin was unable to serve as president at this time. However, she was still alive in a hospital bed in her family home. It was good that she was alive, and that Dalton had saved her—but wasn't it wrong to allow Chang to take the oath when she was still alive?

In spite of his promise to Catherine, Dalton felt deceit clinging to him like an attack dog he couldn't shake off. This wasn't the way Dalton wanted to start Chang's tenure either.

Chapter 63

Adam stepped out of the sedan that had brought him to the Taylor mansion. His face felt stubby, his mind dull; he regretted that he hadn't shaved before coming, but he'd had no time. Looking down at his wrinkled shirt, he pulled on his suit coat, in an attempt to hide the clothes he had slept in on the plane. He climbed the front steps to the white columns on the porch, oblivious to the security team that had come with him from Air Force One.

Inside his escort scattered. A teary Karen Kelsey sat on the lower steps of the staircase with her nose in her iPod. As Adam trudged across the marble entry, she rose and stood as if at attention.

"Were you there when the president was shot?" Karen asked as he passed.

Adam ignored her. He put Samantha out of his mind as he climbed the stairs to the second floor. On the landing his eyes settled on a photograph of Stephanie and Samantha in an ornate silver frame. Dressed alike for their birthday party, they bore excited smiles, their arms tightly entwined around each other as if nothing in the world could tear them apart. He paused a moment, trying to discern which one was Stephanie.

He heard his name called and wheeled around. It was Dr. Pierce.

"I'm glad you're back."

"Dalton told me Stephanie is alive. Can I see her?"

"She's sleeping. But she's supposed to be Samantha," she whispered.

Adam nodded.

"Why don't you come sit with her a while? Maybe she'll wake up."

They strolled together towards the first bedroom.

When Adam saw Stephanie, he froze in the doorway, his mind unable to buffer the shock. She lay in a hospital bed, wan and pale, her head wrapped up in a turban of bandages. Her nose was swollen and discolored. Dark patches of bruises festooned her arms.

Adam wanted to stick his fist into a wall. He was not prepared for this. Every injury, every bruise on her battered body cried out to him for vengeance.

Talking was hard. He pushed out the words. "Who did this?"

"Tony shot her. Samantha and Macy attacked her physically."

"How do you know?"

"Stephanie told Dalton."

Adam spit out his anger. "It's a good thing they're already dead—"

She patted his arm. "Bruises heal, Adam. It's what you can't see that's harming her."

He frowned, trying to comprehend.

"The leukemia is getting worse."

His stomach clinched into a tight ball.

"Come in and sit a while. Try to think positive thoughts. Maybe they'll reach Stephanie."

He hurried to the bed and buried one of her hands between his palms. "I'm here, Steph. I'm not going anywhere." He pulled up a chair and sat quietly, his mind wading through the chaos of the last twenty-four hours.

On the long flight home, he had been on an emotional rollercoaster. Begrudgingly he had come to terms with Samantha's news that his beloved Stephanie was dead. He had to endure the absurd charade by Samantha, all the while knowing her tragic fate. His complicity in her death had left him visibly shaken and burdened with the conflicting feelings of guilt and patriotism that lingered even now.

During the journey home, with Samantha's coffin in the belly of the aircraft, Adam allowed the tears to flow. Depression gripped him. Then Dalton telephoned to tell him a secret: Stephanie was still alive and asking for him. The joyful news was like spring water reviving his deadened heart.

Now, as he sat by her bedside in the Taylor mansion, he feared that Stephanie might not recover. She looked so wilted as she slept.

He prayed. He ate little and left her side only to use the toilet.

The next morning Doctor Pierce moaned while she checked Stephanie's vital signs. "She's losing the battle."

Adam clung to hope. "What about the transplant?"

"She's too weak now. We should have taken the stem cells from Samantha sooner." The doctor's fingers curled around Stephanie's wrist as she checked her pulse.

"It doesn't seem right that she die—not after surviving all those attempts on her life." Adam's voice reflected his panic. "Can't you do anything, Doctor?"

Dr. Pierce gazed directly into his eyes and reemphasized what she had already said. "By the time she arrived here, Stephanie was very weak. She'd lost a great deal of blood. Her body is exhausted; it has endured so much physical abuse it's giving up the fight."

Determined not to cry, Adam peered out the second-floor window. "She made an agreement with Sibaba. She decided to die, even when she knew the stem cells might save her."

Emotion flooded her voice. "Yes, I know." She left the room in tears.

Outside Adam watched a female cardinal building a nest in anticipation of spring. She had picked a shrub, ten feet above ground, as a safe place to rear her nestlings away from predators. A brilliantly colored male landed beside her on the limb, having brought an offering of dried leaves for the open bowl. Then he flew away again, in search of weed stems and twigs or a thick tangle of vines.

Spring is the season of new life, Adam thought. *Stephanie can't die now.*

As the male cardinal made another quick landing, Adam remembered reading that some species of birds mate for life. Were these two birds building a life together? He focused on the male, and spoke his thoughts. "What happens, ol' man, if your mate dies? Do you find another one?"

"That's what you need to do." Stephanie was awake.

Adam rushed to the bed and kissed her hand. She smiled up at him, her eyelids drowsy. "Life's pulled a lousy trick on us. I realized too late that I love you. Things would have been so different."

He tried to remain positive. "They will be. You're going to be okay, Steph."

"No, I'm not." She swallowed with difficulty. "I want you to find someone to love. You love with such steadfastness, with such a commitment—"

He shook his head and the tears came. "You can't die."

"This is the way it has to be, Adam. It's God's plan."

Tired, she closed her eyes.

Aunt Catherine and Dalton sauntered into the room. They hovered beside the bed, waiting patiently and reverently.

At last Stephanie opened her eyes and gave them that ever-familiar Stephanie smile. "I'm praying for peace in the world to continue— and for Samantha's soul. Jesus said we need to forgive, you know."

Adam's eyes were troubled. "Can you forgive me for letting Samantha die?"

"I didn't give you any choice, did I?" she answered, still clinging to his hand.

"Everything went as you planned," he said. "But why didn't you tell me?"

"You would have stopped me."

"Yes."

"It was the only way, Adam. It was supposed to be me. I didn't plan for Sam to die."

Aunt Catherine inched closer. "There was nothing you could do, Adam. Try not to worry yourself over it."

Stephanie released Adam's hand and reached limply for her aunt. "I'm sorry, but I have to leave you. While I was asleep I saw Jesus and heaven. I've seen mother. I want to go back."

Tearing again, Adam remembered a Stephanie who had once found happiness simply dreaming about Africa.

Stephanie turned to Dalton. "No one can know I died here, or the bomb treaty won't be valid." She waited for the agent to nod his promise, then breathed deeply. "What do the American people know?"

"That you were assassinated in Wakembezi. Your twin was shot by Tony and his girlfriend. You're supposed to be Samantha."

Dalton helped Catherine lower herself into a chair on the opposite side of the bed.

Stephanie was tiring, and battling sleep, but her eyes stayed glued on Adam's face. "Tell the world I never feared death, because I knew that I was saved." Her voice was now only a whisper.

Adam wanted to be alone with her. He wanted to comfort her, to hold her, to grieve with her. But she was unconscious again.

After a few minutes, Catherine spoke to him in a soft voice. "I'm glad you're here. I never told you that I approved of you and Stephanie."

Surprise covered his face. "You knew?"

"There was always this chemistry between you. I could see the love in your eyes every time you looked at her."

"Stephanie was easy to love." Trying to control the tears crawling into his throat, he reached into his inside coat pocket and handed Catherine an envelope. "Steph asked me to give you this when she died. At the time I thought she meant from leukemia, but now I know it was because she planned to die in Wakembezi."

"She's not gone yet."

"I've read mine. Go ahead."

Catherine read silently, her cloudy eyes embracing every word. "Thank you," she said at last. "She says that I was like a mother to her. That I never failed her." She swallowed, skimming again the handwritten message.

"Did she explain that Sibaba demanded an *eye for an eye*—literally?"

"Yes. He called it *proper retribution*. To him that meant assassinating our vice president, to pay for the death of his vice chairman. Stephanie wouldn't do that. She offered up herself instead." Catherine dabbed her teary eyes. "She always put others first, so I guess what she did doesn't surprise me."

"She knew I'd try to stop her. That's why I wasn't supposed to read my letter on the airplane, but after—." He choked on the words. "It's easier knowing that Stephanie got what she wanted in the end, in spite of everything getting so twisted up."

Catherine leaned on her cane to stand. "I'll be downstairs. Call me if there's a change."

The hours and the days passed and Stephanie remained comatose. Two days later Dr. Pierce took her off life support.

Adam was at Stephanie's side during the long vigil. He sat with her, clutching her hand while Dr. Pierce removed the breathing tube, and he was still holding it an hour later when the doctor returned.

She touched his shoulder. "Stephanie isn't going to wake up, Adam."

"I know."

"Are you okay?"

"No, but I will be." He rose and walked into the hallway, feeling dead himself. Without comment, he pushed through the pack of agents on the first floor and trudged to the road where he squatted alone in the grass and released the tears.

Without Stephanie Franklin, how could he go on? It didn't matter that America had lost a president. His grief was all too real as he mourned the woman he knew and loved before America knew her. On that day he finally realized all that happened had to take place for Stephanie to secure her positive place in history. That was the way it should be, but losing her hurt just the same.

Adam knew that time would heal, for God knows how to comfort that kind of grief. Even now, he felt the touch and heard the voice of the One who would walk the path of sorrow with him and restore his aching soul.

Chapter 64

Stephanie Franklin was the nation's twelfth president honored with a state funeral. She had planned the event in detail before she knew about her illness, because all presidents are required to have funeral plans in place upon becoming president.

For her ceremonial funeral procession, President Franklin selected a caisson, a military horse-drawn vehicle to carry her coffin to the funeral. Pulled by six bay horses, with three riders and a section chief mounted on a separate horse, the flatbed wagon traveled from the White House down Pennsylvania Avenue.

Dalton Mercer and Timothy Burnside stood together on the south lawn of the White House and watched the soldiers turning the corner. Near the end of the line was a hearse that supposedly carried the remains of Samantha.

"I heard Miss Taylor wants the twins buried side by side," Burnside said.

Dalton nodded. "Samantha's funeral was earlier. After the president's memorial service, the hearse will take Samantha to the Taylor estate. She'll be buried first."

The procession disappeared. The agents turned back and ambled slowly across the green lawn. In the silence Dalton could almost feel Burnside's thoughts, his mind churning with unrest. "Something about this stinks. It's just too coincidental."

"The husband and twin dying about the same time as President Franklin? Is that what you're thinking?"

Burnside nodded.

"I doubt if Sibaba had anything to do with Tony's wreck." Dalton chose his words with care. "We know Tony went to find Samantha. She told me he shot her. That's clear cut—so what's bothering you?"

Burnside shrugged. "What was Tony doing with his mistress if he'd gone to pick up Samantha? And why was Samantha's driver's license in his burned car?"

"That is puzzling."

Burnside stuck a piece of gum in his mouth. "And what was Samantha doing in West Virginia? She was supposed to be in Mexico."

"I guess we'll never know all the answers."

The truth was that Dalton knew everything. The fact that the twins had been switched and Samantha was in the president's coffin would remain unknown to almost everyone.

* * *

The funeral procession ended at the Washington National Cathedral, where the president's casket lay in state for the national memorial funeral service. It was televised worldwide. Viewers saw Catherine Taylor and family friends, members of Congress, various foreign dignitaries, royalty, and government officials attending a solemn religious ceremony.

Before the memorial service, Catherine went to the president's flag-draped coffin and touched it with her cheek. Overwhelmed by tears, she allowed her attorney Dennis Hargrove to help her to her seat.

Adam placed a rose on the coffin, before moving to the nearby wall, where he lingered, awaiting his part in the service.

The minister prayed and shared scriptures. When time came for Adam's eulogy, he went steadily to the pulpit. He talked about the Stephanie he had known for nearly two decades. "President Franklin loved this country. She loved it more than her life," he said. "She believed in love and brotherhood and that God wants peace. She sought to replace the walls between peoples with bridges of friendship and respect."

His eyes swelled with tears. He removed a letter from his pocket that was addressed to the American People. "I have here a letter that Stephanie Franklin wrote to all of you shortly before her death. Tomorrow it will be on the front pages of our newspapers. Today I want to share it with you."

> *I would like to believe that my life, as well as my death, had a purpose. I had no intention of breaking my promise to you. There will be no war. I would have done anything to assure peace. Try to understand that I was not executed by an enemy nation. My death was my choice.*
>
> *Millions have died with the hope that peace would someday exist. Many brave soldiers have fought to assure American freedoms. I could do no less. I, too, chose to die for my country. In my last moments I am encouraged by the words of Christ in John15:13. Before his death Christ said, 'Greater love hath no man than this, that a man lay down his life for his friends.' Always remember I loved you that much.*
>
> *Pray for my soul. Most of all, pray for your new president and honor him. Kenneth Chang will be an excellent commander-in-chief.*
>
> *God bless America.*

Silence cloaked the assembly. Tears fell from once stoic faces as Adam stepped out of the podium. Walking slowly, hunting a seat, he was surprised to spot a tearful Cheri Eastley in the fourth row.

Adam remembered an Eastley article that accused Stephanie of being unable to make a decision. *This proves her wrong,* Adam thought.

Armed Forces pallbearers gave the deceased president a traditional twenty-one gun salute. Afterwards the coffin (containing Samantha's body) lay in state for public viewing in the Rotunda of the U.S. Capitol. The vigil continued through the night. An honor guard representing each of the armed services maintained watch until the hearse arrived to transport the president's body to the Taylor cemetery.

Chapter 65

The next day, outside the White House, a crowd still stood vigil for Stephanie Franklin. Unable to attend the burial, they had lit candles, prayed, sang, and left flowers and notes well into the night. Some of them remained as the sun settled overhead.

Kenneth Chang watched them from a second floor window in the vice president's office in the West Wing. Behind him, two secretaries packed his files and possessions into boxes for the move to his new office. Beside him stood a silent Dalton, his mind heavy with memories and positive thoughts about Stephanie.

The president spoke. "Stephanie was a special person. We were blessed to have known her."

"Yes, sir. Do you think you could have done what she did?"

"I don't know. She showed incredible bravery."

Without a further exchange, they left Chang's secretaries to box up his belongings. In silence they made their trek to the Oval Office. Stepping off the elevator, they found Philip Lowe waiting in the reception area with a new bodyguard.

"You need to stay here," Chang ordered Lowe's employee. He beckoned Lowe to his office, but in the doorway turned, perhaps as an afterthought, and motioned Dalton to come inside too.

"Well, here we are at last," Lowe said with a smug grin.

Chang leaned against the edge of his desk. "Yes, here we are. Now what?"

Lowe eased his heavy body into the closest chair. He eyed Dalton, obviously hesitant to speak his mind.

"You can talk in front of Dalton. He's loyal to me." Chang motioned for Dalton to sit. "What's next?" he asked Lowe again.

"You pick a vice president. The primaries are only months away."

"I guess that means *you*."

Lowe's smile turned into a self-satisfied grin. "As Minority Leader, I'll get the party approval easily."

"Then what? You'll have me killed?"

Lowe's eye ridges twitched. He looked shocked.

Dalton leaned forward. He understood why the president wanted him present.

"I never knew how far you'd go," Chang continued, his tone now frigid. "Stephanie sure pegged you right."

The new president's bluntness left the seasoned senator speechless.

Chang straightened his back and paced the room. "I know you're behind this madness, Philip. I don't know how—but I want you as far away from me as possible."

Lowe squirmed in the chair. "I thought we had an understanding."

"Do you expect me to believe that the deaths of Samantha, Macy and Stephanie's husband are all coincidental?"

Dalton watched the senator's face go through a series of subtle changes as the reality of the situation began to form in his mind. "What are you accusing me of?"

"You once told me that I'd be president at any cost. What exactly did that mean?"

"You're wrong about me, Ken."

"How are you going to explain the fact that your driver tried to blow up the Taylor house with Stephanie's doctor and aunt inside?"

"Why would I want to kill an old woman and a doctor? There is no motive."

Chang stalked to the door and admitted two men that Dalton recognized as FBI. "You need to explain that to these agents."

Nervously Lowe struggled for answers. "Sure, I knew Willy had been in prison, but I believe in rehabilitation. What's wrong with that?"

Chang studied Lowe for one short moment. "Stop it. Stop your lies. I'm certainly not going to be impeached because of my association with a murdering scoundrel like you."

Lowe paused, stunned. "I didn't murder President Franklin."

"That's not what I'm talking about and you know it! I think you caused this whole stink with Wakembezi."

"Why would I do that?"

"You told me you wanted to sever Stephanie's and Sibaba's relationship. If I find that you were behind Wasswa's death, I'm going to serve you up on a silver platter to Sibaba!"

Lowe's face flushed pink. He raised his voice a couple of octaves. "How dare you talk to me like that! You're president because of me."

"If you've got any sense, you'll resign and help the party save face. Get out of politics, Philip. Get out of Washington."

The set of his mouth flattened into a stubborn pout. "No one can prove anything."

Chang tilted his head towards the FBI agents. "You tell it to these gentlemen. I want nothing more to do with you. I don't see how you're going to stay out of jail for the rest of your life."

The new president, assertive and determined, marched out the door and left Lowe sitting in the Oval Office. When Dalton left the room, Lowe was stammering, trying to convince the FBI agents not to take him downtown for questioning.

In the outer office, they passed two other Secret Service agents and kept walking. "This is going to be a difficult period for all of us," Chang said to Dalton. "I wanted to be president. But not like this."

They continued a leisurely pace past the secretaries and towards the conference room where the Cabinet waited.

"We're going to dig and dig deep, without reservation. You understand me, Dalton? The American people will expect justice. I'm going to give it to them."

Dalton nodded, looking deeply into Chang's dark, sincere eyes. He decided he liked this president.

Epilogue

This was a special morning. Stephanie was getting out of the hospital.

The chauffeur parked the limo on the curb outside Maryland General Hospital in Baltimore. First to step out was Dalton, holding a large box wrapped in white, shiny paper with a huge white bow. He tucked the present under his arm and offered his free hand to help Catherine out of the car.

At the same moment Adam pulled his sedan into a nearby parking spot. He touted his horn and they shared a wave. "Let's wait for him," Catherine said, leaning on her cane.

"Good morning!" Adam flashed them a high-wattage smile. "Thanks for coming." He greeted Catherine with a bear hug, and shook Dalton's hand. "Did you have any trouble getting off work?"

"No. I'm still the boss." Dalton eyed him with a probing gaze. "Nervous?"

"Heck no. Just eager."

They strolled through opening doors into a brightly lit corridor and quickened their pace toward Stephanie's room.

Catherine couldn't stop smiling. "Does Stephanie know we're coming with you?"

He shook his head. "That's part of her surprise. But I know she wants to say goodbye to everyone." As Adam took Catherine's elbow to lead her to the elevator, he whispered. "Don't forget to call her Ann."

"How long will it be before I see the two of you again?" Catherine asked.

"About a year—unless you want to come see us."

She chuckled. "On your honeymoon? Why would you want me tagging along?"

"Things have changed since you found Stephanie's passport for me. We're not going on a cruise now. Stephanie has to stay close to doctors for at least a year."

An orderly with a wheelchair interrupted them. "Good to see you, Miss Taylor," he said with a toothy grin. "Your cousin asked me to meet you. She's eager to see you."

"Catherine blinked twice. "I can't wait to see her either."

They wheeled her down a long hall, with Adam pushing the chair. The orderly disappeared into a connecting wing.

"I can't get use to the deceit," Catherine said, twisting to see Adam over her shoulder.

"Shush. Be careful," Adam whispered as they passed the hub with computers. The nurses, whose noses were deep in their paperwork, seemed not to have heard.

The group moved on, completing their trek in silence. At the end of the hall, they gazed through glass walls at the five separate suites for the bone marrow patients.

For two months, Stephanie had been recovering from the stem cell transplant. Even without her hair, she feared that she might be recognized, so any likeness to the president had been explained away as family resemblance. She registered under her middle name, Ann, and everyone believed she was a cousin of the twins. The story circulated to the media reported that Ann Taylor needed a transplant, so Stephanie had donated her bone marrow before flying to Wakembezi.

As they waited for admittance to the restricted area, Catherine thought about Samantha. How ironic it was that Samantha had saved her twin's life after trying to kill her.

Inside a cheerful nurse scurried from behind the counter and pushed a button. The door swished opened. "Everyone ready for the big day?" she chirped.

"I don't have to wear one of those dreadful masks today, do I?" Catherine grumbled.

The nurse's eyes took on a baffled cast. "Not any longer. It was necessary to protect Ann from potential infections. The masks were part of our precautions."

Catherine knew that. She frowned, a little embarrassed. "Sorry. I just found them hot and bothersome."

The nurse nodded and motioned for the group to follow her. As she pushed open the door to Stephanie's suite, the first thing Catherine saw was a smiling Stephanie. She sat on the side of the bed, while Doctor Pierce monitored her blood pressure.

"Surprise!" Catherine announced their visit.

An amazed smile covered Stephanie's face. "Hello, everyone!"

While Catherine gave her an eager hug, she took a closer look. Stephanie had applied makeup today and stuffed her sparse hair beneath a red wig.

"What do you think of my new look?" Stephanie asked, putting on some dark-rimmed spectacles.

"With your light coloring, red hair looks good on you." Catherine peered closer. "You've got brown eyes again."

Stephanie nodded, and said nothing more until the nurse left. "Do I look like a different person?"

"Yes," they all agreed.

Stephanie gazed at herself in a hand-held mirror. "If anyone guesses the truth, Sibaba could find out. Then Samantha's death would have been for nothing."

"You really don't look the same," Dalton assured her. "Your nose is different."

"Macy broke it, so it's a little crooked." She smoothed back a stray strand from her wig. "I'm going to dye my hair this color when it grows out some more."

Dr. Pierce interrupted in a cheerful voice. "Are you ready to get out of here?"

Stephanie beamed. "Yes."

"You've been the perfect patient for eight weeks. Your blood tests show good kidney and liver function, and you no longer need blood and platelet transfusions. I only have one concern." There was a dramatic pause. "How fast can you get dressed and leave?"

Overjoyed, Stephanie started to slide off the bed.

"Hey, Steph—I mean Ann. Hold on." Adam took her arm. "Catherine's bought you something special to wear."

Dalton handed Stephanie the box. Eyes glistening with excitement, she tore at the wrapping paper. Opening the lid, she stared down at a white suit with lacy trim. "It looks like a wedding dress."

Adam embraced her. "You still want to marry me, don't you?"

She nodded, her eyes getting larger.

"Everything's arranged," Adam said, taking her hand. "We're going down to the chapel and a hospital chaplain will marry us."

"Now?"

"I can't think of a reason to wait, can you?"

She felt her lips curl into a grin, but caution whispered in her brain. "Will this be legal if I use a different name?"

"For an ID I used your passport from Africa, which reads Stephanie Ann Taylor." Adam pulled the marriage certificate out of an inside coat pocket and handed it to her. "When the clerk didn't notice your name, it occurred to me that everyone knows you as Stephanie Franklin. So with your maiden name and your disguise, nobody will know it's you."

Adam put a muscular arm around her shoulder. "The only people who know the truth are in this room. They have made it possible for us to start our new life together, so I wanted them here."

"I do too. All of you are special." Her eyes shifted back to the box. As she lifted the dress and shook out the wrinkles, she spotted a check hidden beneath the garment. "What's this? A wedding present?"

Catherine stepped closer for a hug. "It's rightfully yours, Stephanie. I inherited your money and Samantha's too, so I'm returning what should be yours. I thought you might need some cash for your honeymoon cruise."

Dr. Pierce frowned. "The honeymoon will have to wait. I need to monitor Ann for at least a year."

"Why don't you just go with them?" Catherine suggested.

Stephanie dangled her legs against the bed. "Debra has accepted a position at a hospital in Denver, so Adam rented us a home two miles away." With hands gesticulating, Stephanie was more excited than Catherine had ever seen her. "Adam's got a job writing for the *Denver Post*."

"That sounds wonderful." Catherine reached for the Kleenex box beside the bed.

Stephanie's eyes flickered in surprise. "Auntie, are you crying?"

"I'm so happy for you. When I think about how close you came to dying—and we thought you were dead."

Stephanie sat speechless for a few seconds, remembering. "I opened my eyes and asked Debra to do the transplant."

The doctor chuckled. "I was shocked when that heart monitor kicked on. I almost had a coronary, but I managed to get you here for the transplant. Catherine signed you in as Ann and Dalton told the Secret Service that Samantha was dead."

Stephanie beamed at Debra. "I owe you my life."

"Don't give me credit," Debra insisted. "I still don't understand your sudden recovery. It could only have been…God."

They all shared nods.

Adam was not ready to exhaust the subject. "I never understood why I wasn't told until after the funeral."

Stephanie smiled up at her groom. "It was important that Sibaba believe I was dead. I needed you to be convincing."

"You gave up a lot," Dalton said to Stephanie.

"Our country is better off with President Chang. I was ready to let go."

Adam leaned over and gave Stephanie a prolonged, soft kiss. "You need to give me time to dress," Stephanie giggled, shooing him and their friends from the room. "I'll meet you in the chapel."

Only Debra remained behind to help the bride dress.

The wedding party left the room, a tight little group with tight lips, excited that Ann and Adam Thorsten were starting their new lives.

As they moseyed along, the wheelchair pushed by Dalton, Catherine thanked a sublime God for raising Stephanie from near death. *Stephanie and Adam really do make a nice looking couple,* she thought, smiling. They had journeyed a bumpy road together to get to this day. She prayed for the Lord to give them an easy, straight road from now on.

Discussion Questions For Book Clubs

- How did you feel about Stephanie? Is this the story of an incompetent president or a competent one? What makes you say that?

- How many times did Stephanie "die"? Did the author surprise you repeatedly?

- The author reports that the epilogue was not in the original draft. Examine the novel with it missing. Which makes the better book? Are you the kind of reader who needs a happy ending?

- What happened in the beginning of the novel that fueled the plots to kill the president?

- Describe the main characters—personality traits, motivations, inner qualities. Why do the characters do what they do? (Lowe, Adam, Stephanie, Samantha, Cheri).

- Several characters change or evolve throughout the course of the story. Which one was your favorite? What events trigger the changes?

- Did certain parts of the book make you uncomfortable? If so, why did you feel that way?

- Discuss the book's structure. Does the author use any narrative devices like flashbacks or multiple voices in telling the story?

- What made you want to read this book? Did it live up to your expectations? Why or why not?

Theological Reflection

- Did the author lead you to a new understanding or awareness of God's role in your life?

- Do you believe in the healing power of God? Even if there is no healing miracle, where have you seen God at work during an illness?

- Do you think illness makes people closer to God or causes them to distance themselves from Him? What has been the pattern in your life?

- Were you satisfied with Stephanie's answers to Debra about God and her sinfulness? (See Chapter 46.) What else would you have told the doctor? Have you seen God working through human beings to accomplish His plan? When?

- How do you feel about having a Christian president? Do you agree with Ken Chang's statement that a leader's faith is unimportant? (Chapter 26) Why do you feel that way?

- What are the Christian themes that thread the plot? What does the storyline reveal about love and war?

- Do you believe that a Christian should be willing to sacrifice for others? Do you think sacrificing your life is only done by physical death?

- How effectively does the author portray the presence of spirituality in the characters' lives? Does the author succeed in presenting prayer in a way that feels relevant? Are there specific characters whose beliefs resonate with yours?

- What do you see as the major message of the novel? Would you recommend it to a friend?